Owen Lipke is looking for adventure. When he hears about a ranch in the Muskokas catering to kinky men who don't want to settle for backroom amateurs, he signs up in a second.

At the Braided Crop Ranch, Owen finds what he's looking for: A sex-positive space with safety protocols and Doms (trainers) who know their business. And a stable full of well-behaved ponyboys to prove it.

Owen thinks his trainer, Kamal, is hot as hell but finds being a ponyboy isn't as intuitive as he expected. As he struggles to learn the basics of equine pet play under the firm hand of his trainer, he finds himself falling for the experienced older man.

And perhaps Kamal is developing a thing for the young, adventurous newcomer. But there are rules about fraternizing with staff at the ranch. And Owen wonders if it's wise to fall in love with the pragmatic trainer who unravels him layer by layer to expose his deepest needs and most secret proclivities.

But perhaps wisdom is overrated. And maybe the rewards of adventure are only achieved when you abandon caution and take a huge leap of faith.

PONYBOY

The Braided Crop Ranch, Book Two

AE Lister

A NineStar Press Publication

www.ninestarpress.com

Ponyboy

Printed in the USA

ISBN: 978-1-64890-250-5

First Edition, April, 2021

Also available in eBook, ISBN: 978-1-64890-249-9

CONTENT WARNING:

This book contains sexually explicit content, which may only be suitable for mature readers.

This book is dedicated to those who have the courage to take a big chance on love.

Chapter One

Shadows and dim lighting made the inside of the club appear deceptively edgy. The Stocks boasted a selection of the most overrated brews and clientele in the city, in my opinion. But this particular club was one of the few places I could go to try to find the kind of man I was looking for.

"Hey, Lipke, what are you doing here again?" Sandro smiled, clapping a hand on my shoulder and taking the stool next to me. "I thought you had the real deal? You know, a nice cozy apartment with your man."

"We broke up," I said, staring at the bar and trying not to let the fact I didn't feel much disappointment about the end of my relationship bother me.

"Ah, shit, that's too bad," Sandro replied, but I saw a glimmer of satisfaction in his eyes as he motioned to the bartender. "Hey, a drink for my buddy here, Paulo." He turned back. "What are you having, Owen?"

I shook my head and tossed the dark hair out of my eyes. It was getting way too long in front. I'd been meaning to get it cut, but I was so unmotivated to do anything these days. "Thanks, but I'm hoping for some action tonight."

I never trolled for Doms with alcohol in my system. I'd learned that lesson a long time ago.

"How about a Coke, then?"

"Okay, sure. Thanks."

He was trying to butter me up because he wanted to hook up. He'd tried with me before, but I had been in a relationship that didn't allow for "extras" so I'd had an excuse to turn him down.

"A Coke for Owen, please. And a ginger ale for me," he said, throwing a tenner on the bar.

"Thanks," I said again, looking Sandro over and wondering if he could give me what I wanted.

He wasn't a bad-looking guy; a little heavier in the gut, but it worked for him. He had a decent "Daddy" vibe going on and appeared to be pushing forty. Maybe he had the experience to give me something...more. Something solid and demanding and ruthless.

The Stocks was an underground fetish bar, where I'd come innumerable times to find the type of hook-up I was after. But anyone I'd ever gone home or played downstairs with, had disappointed. It wasn't operating on the down-low. The club was literally underground, which made it even darker and dingier inside than most places—almost claustrophobic.

Everyone played games. That was often the point with fetish and BDSM, and a lot of guys were perfectly happy with that. But I was tired and bored with it all.

I'd had a connection with Simon, my ex, but even he couldn't give me what I wanted in the end. I couldn't define that particular desire but I knew I hadn't fulfilled it—ever.

At night I'd dream about a Master who took total control, put me in my place easily and perfunctorily, without a thought to my comfort, yet took care of my needs like they were his own. This mystery man became a shadowy, elusive presence in my waking world. I'd never encountered an actual human being who could measure up to the Dom in my dreams. Maybe no one ever would.

Maybe I should make the most of what I could get, here and now.

Sandro handed me the Coke and winked. "So, you're a free agent tonight," he said.

I grinned. "Yep. Trolling for Doms."

He laughed, looked away, and then back. "Wanna come home with me? We could have some fun."

I picked up my glass and sipped the cold, sugary-sweet syrup, considering his offer. "You live close?"

Sandro nodded. "Down the street. Walking distance. You can leave your car here, and pick it up later, or in the morning if you decide to stay over."

It was thoughtful of him to offer me the whole night. Such an invitation was rare in this environment, where most people simply wanted a quick fuck or a fun kink session and didn't give a shit what you did with yourself after.

"Yeah, okay."

"Really?"

I found his excitement flattering, if misplaced. I didn't feel like anything special these days, but I was up for a quick screw.

"Sure. But let's enjoy our drinks first. We've got all night."

Sandro had fair-to-good conversation skills. He was intelligent, perceptive, and witty. I warmed to my decision over the time it took to finish our drinks. Maybe the evening wouldn't be a washout after all.

Sandro sighed. "I wish there were more kink places in this city. I mean, this place is fine but it gets boring after a while."

I agreed with his observation completely. There were several options across the river from Ottawa in Quebec that offered more hard-core entertainment, but in terms of convenience, this place was closest. And even when I had ventured as far as Gatineau or Montreal, I'd been largely disappointed.

"I hear Toronto is the place to be for this kind of scene," I said. "Maybe I should move to the Big Smoke."

"Maybe. I thought about it a couple of times. But my family is here, and my job."

"I don't know if I could sacrifice the green space," I said.

The easy access to nature was one of the things I loved about Ottawa. There were a multitude of parks and treed spaces; bike paths, beaches, and water everywhere. And the Gatineau hills were right across the Ottawa River. I enjoyed hiking and camping more than almost anything else. Spending regular time in nature was essential to my being. I doubted I'd be happy in a concrete city like Toronto.

Then again, was I happy here?

"I heard about this place in the Muskokas," Sandro was saying. "It's a ranch, but not the kind of ranch you'd expect in that touristy area."

"Huh?" I asked. A ranch? I had absolutely no interest in horses.

Sandro nodded. "It's set up like a real ranch, but instead of horses, they get men to dress like ponies."

If I had been a pony, my ears would have swung toward him. "What? No way." Something in me thrilled to the thought of it.

He laughed. "Yeah, they put them in harnesses and bridles and make them do stuff. It's all set up to make the experience as realistic as possible. At least that's what I heard."

I pretended not to be as interested as I was. "Hmm. Weird."

"Yeah, well, I guess some guys get off on that stuff. Not me. I'm happy with the regular kink experience myself, although it would be nice to have a few more bars to go to."

Men in harnesses and wearing bridles? A ranch for pony fetishists? Why hadn't I heard about this before? My balls ached at the thought of it. I'd never explored animal role-play, but the thought of being a pony at a fetish ranch rang every one of my bells. Maybe a fetish ranch was the kind of immersive experience I needed. Sure, it was still a game, but maybe they did it so well you forgot it was a game and became fully invested in submission and objectification.

I drained the rest of my glass. "Ready to go?"

Sandro beamed as his gaze raked over me. "Absolutely."

*

The next morning, I snuck out of Sandro's bed and gathered my clothes so I could get dressed on the main floor of his townhome without disturbing him.

The experience had been interesting. Not the domination I was looking for, but Sandro was a decent guy and had a big dick, so the evening wasn't a total loss. He pretended to dominate me for a little while until he lost interest and only wanted to worship my body. He'd gotten me off a couple of times, but it was all too "nice."

I'd had "nice" and my experience in my relationship with Simon had been less than fantastic. To all outward appearances, Simon Defalco had been a decent, upstanding, sweet man. He was good-looking too. For the first few months of our relationship, I'd thought I'd found Mr. Right. Not that I was looking for marriage or anything permanent, but I'd thought I'd found the right guy for me—laid-back and confident with modern attitudes about sex and relationships until we'd lived together.

I was becoming more and more interested in kink and Dom/sub dynamics, and he seemed to move the other way, wanting a predictable intimacy with practiced moves and conventional guidelines. I hadn't realized how conservative he was at heart until it was too late, and I had developed strong feelings, and we'd started making a life together.

My friends had warned me not to move in with the guy after only a few weeks, but had I listened? Nope.

The situation had been tolerable for a little while. But much too soon my passion had dwindled and died and I'd posited the idea of expanding our romantic relationship to include the occasional casual hookup or a visit to a kink club. And he'd gotten angry and acted like I was a deviant for not wanting a standard vanilla partnership with one person—him.

I didn't want nice. I didn't want sweet. I wanted rough and hard and relentless. I wanted someone to control me, to place me the way they wanted me, to *use* me. But in a sexual way.

Otherwise, I wanted to be free. I'd gotten out of a confining relationship, and I wasn't looking for something permanent. For fuck's sake, I was only twenty-seven.

The guys I went home with invariably turned out to be one extreme or the other. Either they were too careful, like Sandro, or they were complete assholes who didn't understand that domination was an art, not a function. There were a lot of people in the scene who didn't seem to comprehend the finer points of consent-based and risk-aware kink. They were pricks who wanted to hurt someone for kicks, without any of the subtle gradations of domination I dreamed of.

I'd gotten into sketchy situations with overzealous Doms and I was wary of hooking up with guys obsessed with power and control. I might not be sure what I wanted, but it wasn't that.

I got dressed and found some paper and a pen so I could at least compose a message to explain my departure.

Hey, I had fun. Thanks for the drink and the bone. See you around. Owen.

It wouldn't win any awards for kindness, but it summed up the experience for me.

I let myself out the back door quietly and walked to the club in the predawn stillness. Birdsong filled my ears as the sun peeked over the horizon. The day held promise.

I had my pack of Belmont Edge cigarettes out of my pocket before I even got to the car. Fucking disgusting habit, one I'd gotten into when my relationship with Simon bit the dust. But it was either nicotine or a prescription for antidepressants, and I felt like smoking was a safer option. I had a deep suspicion of all types of brain-altering drugs.

And I limited myself to five of these babies a day. Belmont Edge were slightly smaller than a standard cigarette, but they were damn expensive. They took the edge off, but I felt like I had it under control, and I was only waiting for an excuse to quit. This was a temporary measure while I dealt with the emotions from the break-up.

It wasn't emotional fallout from the relationship that stressed me out, but the fact I didn't have a clue what I was looking for. I knew it wasn't what I'd had with Simon. I'd felt mostly relief during the weeks afterwards. Then I'd been filled with a sense of failure and confusion, as if I should have been able to make it work with him, should have wanted to make it work, but for whatever reason hadn't been satisfied.

I put the butt between my lips and flicked the lighter, inhaling as the cigarette flared and burned, closing my eyes with the familiar taste and sense of relief. Sandro was a decent guy, but nothing about him excited me or even made me want to consider a friendship. I was starting to think there was something wrong with me and that I'd never find a guy who'd make me want to abandon the single life for something more permanent. But that was okay.

I didn't mind being single. In fact, I enjoyed the freedom of being able to live my life the way I wanted. Fuck the guys I wanted to fuck. Suck the guys I wanted to suck. Explore my admittedly unusual sexuality with no strings. I was only twenty-seven.

As I keyed open my car and started the engine, my thoughts returned to the fetish ranch Sandro had mentioned. I couldn't get it out of my head. I needed to find out more.

*

A few hours later, once I'd had a shower and some breakfast, I texted my friends in the scene. Had they heard about this place? Did it really exist or had Sandro made it up to pique my interest and persuade me to come home with him?

Tamara got back to me first.

> TAM: *Hmm. Let me do some digging. If it's out there, I'll find it.*

This was true. If the ranch Sandro had described existed, Tamara would locate it. She was relentless. If she were a gay male Dom, my life would be perfect.

Lawrence replied that he'd never heard of such a thing but to let him know if I found it. And Dig called me a perverted ass, but that was expected. Not sure why I mentioned it to him except to piss him off. He wasn't into the kink scene.

I waited on tenterhooks for Tamara's reply. In the meantime, I got out my sketch book and played around with a pencil. It wasn't until I was half done that I realized I was sketching a man in a harness and bridle. Fuck, I was a perverted ass. But I needed—desperately wanted—someone to stick a pony tail in my ass and lead me around on a set of reins, something I'd never thought about until Sandro had mentioned it the night before.

I'd heard about pony play and puppy play, of course, but I'd never explored anything similar. The puppy thing didn't appeal to me; the idea seemed silly, to be honest. But for some reason, maybe because horses were bigger, more intrinsically dignified animals, the idea of a pony play fetish ranch ticked all of my boxes. Domination, objectification, leather, bondage, humiliation.

The concept of immersing oneself in a total kink environment seemed ideal. If the place actually existed.

By the time Tamara got back to me, I'd finished my sketch and applied the finishing touches on the shading. I put down my pencil and picked up my phone.

TAM: *I found it.*

I felt lightheaded. I knew those three words would change my life.

ME: *Tell me more.*

TAM: *I found one for women first, so I thought you were out of luck initially. But then it seems there is one for gay men run by the same organization.*

ME: *Interesting.*

Tam: Yeah, it's pretty fucking interesting. Winky face.

ME: *Tell me more.*

TAM: *So your source was correct. The Braided Crop Ranch is in the Muskokas in Northern Ontario. On Skeleton Lake, near Huntsville.*

The Braided Crop Ranch. Everything about this was ticking my boxes. Thank you, Sandro. Even though I'm not that into you, you did me a solid.

TAM: *I can link you to their website. It's hidden but I found it.*

ME: *Of course you did. You're an angel! And yes, please.*

She sent me the link and asked if I was serious about making enquiries.

ME: *I think so. I want to.*

TAM: *Go for it. I think it's something you might enjoy. You're the kinkiest of all of us!*

ME: *Do I get a trophy?*

TAM: *Sure. A big dildo.*

ME: *I've already got lots of those.*

TAM: *Ba dump dump. Keep me posted, Owen. You know I live for this shit.*

ME: *Lol. I will. Love ya.*

*

Well, well, well.

Sandro's fetish ranch did exist.

The private link Tamara sent took me to a fancy website with a welcome page that showed a group of cheerily painted farm buildings in the middle of an expansive green landscape edged by thick forests and blue skies—a decidedly idealistic setting for a traditional western adventure. Except a warning popped up explaining you had to be eighteen or older to access the site.

I clicked it and the page changed:

Welcome to the Braided Crop Ranch

A fetish farm for pony play enthusiasts

*Please proceed to the following link to access the site for our sister ranch, the Pretty Pony Palace.

I inhaled sharply as I perused the collection of photos under those words. They were of men—attractive, muscular, young men—naked except for leather body harnesses, wide collars, cock cages, boots, and leather armbands that kept their arms pinioned behind. Some of the men had been photographed in a large indoor arena, others outside in fenced paddocks. There were about a dozen photos—some close-up, some from farther away. All of the images intrigued and aroused me.

I looked for a contact section, found it, and clicked.

An electronic form popped up: *If you are interested in our program, please fill out the following questionnaire. An agent will be in touch shortly.*

I blinked, wondering if I should fill out the form now or think on my decision. Except I was placing an inquiry, not signing on for six months. And what was there to think about? This place was a revelation. I'd always wanted to visit the Muskokas. The fetish angle was icing on the fucking cake.

It also meant I'd have to give up these goddamn cigarettes. I'm sure the BCR didn't allow smoking on its premises. More and more, smoking was becoming a forbidden activity, every-fucking-where.

The questionnaire asked for my contact details— name, age, address, email, phone #—the regular stuff. Then it asked why I was interested in the BCR.

I thought for a moment, then typed: *I am very interested in exploring the world of animal role-play in such a professional and comprehensive setting. I am experienced in the world of BDSM and pride myself on being willing to experience new things.*

I had to upload a recent full-body photo so spent about thirty minutes trying to locate one. The men in the photos had been stunningly attractive in their pony gear. The BCR obviously had high standards when it came to physical attractiveness.

I'd certainly never had any complaints. I was in the prime of my life, kept fit and active, and came from good-looking people. My genes were decent, and I felt like I could, *maybe*, compete with the men in the photos if only in a superficial way. I wasn't at all sure how good I would be at playing pony. I figured they'd have to teach me. That was the point, right?

I finished filling out the form and hit Submit.

Then I bookmarked the website and closed my browser, wondering what the hell I'd gotten myself into.

*

Two days later I received the following email:

Dear Mr. Lipke,

Thank you for your interest in the Braided Crop Ranch. Generally, new applicants are put onto a comprehensive waiting list and notified when a spot opens. However, we have had a cancellation for our summer session. If you are available to attend the ranch from June 25 to August 6, we can add you to the session.

I realize this is very short notice but you had indicated your availability to be fairly open. If you can't attend the summer session, we will add you to the waiting list, and you should be able to visit the ranch within the next six months.

Please advise ASAP as to your preference as we will need some paperwork completed posthaste for a June 25 intake. Thank you for your interest.

Sincerely,

Adam Marsland

The Braided Crop Ranch
341 Stellar Private
Muskoka, Ontario

I stared at my computer with wide eyes and an uncomfortable boner for ten minutes. June twenty-fifth was only two weeks away, but if I didn't take this spot it could be months before I'd have a chance to find my inner pony. Could I arrange to go on leave from my job at this late notice?

Yes. Yes, I could. If they didn't let me take the time off, I'd fucking quit. I could get another IT job in a second.

After several moments, I typed:

Mr. Marsland,

Thank you for the offer to attend the summer session at the Braided Crop Ranch. I will book the time off work so I will be able to do so. There won't be any problem, even at this late notice. I appreciate you accommodating me so quickly, and I look forward to completing my intake information.

I am very excited about the opportunity to spend six weeks at your ranch.

Sincerely,

Owen Lipke

I sent the message, and by dinnertime I had the paperwork to fill out. I paid my membership fee, and it was a done deal. In two weeks, I'd embark on the biggest adventure of my life.

*

Later that evening, I texted Tamara.

>ME: *So, I'm going to the ranch in two weeks. They had a cancellation.*

>TAM: *Don't mess with me, Owen.*

>ME: *I'm dead serious. I've filled out the paperwork and everything. It's...pretty comprehensive. I had to check off my hard and soft limits. It asked if I was okay <u>with anal toys and anal play</u>.*

>TAM: *Shocked face emoji. Did you check off All The Toys and All The Play?*

>ME: *Uh, yeah. Of course.*

>TAM: *Wait, what are your hard limits?*

>ME: *Actually, it's stuff they don't do anyway. They had a list of activities, and I had to check off what I was prepared to do and what I wasn't prepared to do. There wasn't anything on that list that I wasn't prepared to do. In fact, now I'm really, really, excited about going.*

>TAM: *Squee!!! I will need daily updates from you. They have cell service, right?*

>ME: *They do but we hand over our phones and they keep them locked at the main house. We theoretically have access whenever, but they encourage us to only use them once a week and we can't take them out of the main building. It's better to disconnect as much as possible from the real world. It's mostly so they can keep us from posting photos, which I understand.*

TAM: *Well then. I'd better get weekly updates, Owen. I'm so excited for you!*

ME: *Good. Because my car finally died yesterday and I'm going to need a ride. It's about four and a half hours away.*

TAM: *ME ME ME ME ME!!!*

Now I'd have a road trip with Tamara to look forward to and a six-week leave of absence from my job to explore my kinky fetishes in a safe and exciting place.

*

It was easy to book the time off work. The job I'd had for five years would be waiting for me when I returned. When asked, I said I was going on an all-inclusive vacation at a resort in Northern Ontario. That was all they were getting, and it was mainly true. I didn't go into the details of exactly *what* was included and nobody asked, likely assuming they were the standard things: meals, drinks and accommodation.

Once my payment cleared and my intake papers were accepted, Mr. Marsland emailed me:

> *Mr. Lipke,*
>
> *Welcome aboard! We look forward to seeing you on June 25. When you arrive, buzz in at the gate and come on through. We provide free parking on-site for the duration of your stay. My office is in the main house and that is where you need to report when you arrive. I'll take things from there.*
>
> *Cheers,*
> *Adam Marsland*

I thanked my lucky stars and the universe for hooking up with Sandro that night, because if I hadn't, I'd never have found out about this place. For the first time in years, I felt excited about something.

Chapter Two

"Where do you sleep? In the stables?" Tamara asked when she came over to help me pack the day before I was due at the BCR.

"Nope." I took a hit off my smoke and spoke around the cigarette. "There's a bunkhouse."

She whistled. "Like, with cowboys?" she said, peering at me from beneath her purple bangs.

"No cowboys." I frowned, considering, as I inhaled again. "At least I don't think so. Just me and the other ponyboys."

Tamara stopped what she was doing and stared at me. "Ponyboys?"

"Yeah. That's what we are." I inhaled the nicotine, savoring my last cigarette before heading to the ranch.

She stood and crossed her arms. She was wearing the cutest pair of dark-denim overalls with a rainbow flag patch on the front pocket. Tamara was one of the most aggressively bisexual people I knew. She had so many casual fuck buddies, of both sexes, I'd stopped keeping track. And it wasn't like she was stunningly attractive, although she *thought* she was, which made all the difference. And she was cute as fuck, with her big boobs and thick thighs, kissable lips and overbearing attitude. If I wasn't thoroughly gay, I'd have fallen under her charms by now. "So, it's essentially one long perverted camping trip? Oh fuck, Owen, that sounds insane. And amazing."

"Do you think you could check on my apartment every few days? Feel free to hang out or have friends over. But don't mess it up too much."

"For sure. Only fifty of my closest friends."

"Har har." I stared at the cigarette in my hands and sighed. "I guess that's that then." I took a final drag and stubbed it out on the ashtray.

"It's about time you tossed that habit," Tamara said. "So gross."

"Yeah, I know."

*

The journey from Ottawa to the Braided Crop Ranch in Tamara's silver Mazda was enjoyable enough, although I became bored looking at nothing but trees. As we got close to the ranch, we had to exit the main highway onto some quieter roads. Luckily, Mr. Marsland had sent a detailed map with directions for the off-highway driving. Without it, we'd have been doomed.

"Rattlers Revenge?" Tamara commented. "We're really in the Old West now."

"Whoa, this is pretty remote. I hope the photos on the website were accurate."

"I can't remember anything except skin and harnesses and cock cages on pretty boys."

"Men, Tamara, not boys. Jeez, we're all consenting adults."

"Yeah but you have to agree that ponyboy has a nice ring to it."

I grinned, nodding. "Yes. Yes, it does."

After about twenty minutes, the trees thinned, and an expanse of blue sky became visible in the distance. We rolled up to an imposing set of iron gates with BCR in large iron letters on its front.

Tamara pressed the intercom buzzer.

"BCR. Connor speaking."

"Hiya, Connor. I'm delivering a pony for you."

"Oh. Fantastic. What is this pony's name, please?"

Tamara waved a fly away from her open window. "Fuck, it's hot out there."

I leaned over her. "Hi, I'm Owen Lipke. My driver is a little insane.

"Hi, Owen. Ask your driver to come on through."

Tamara pulled into the small dirt parking lot and slotted the Mazda against the fence. She turned off the engine.

"I need to use the bathroom. Do you think they'll let me?"

"Fuck, I'd kill for a cigarette," I muttered, craving the familiarity of it more than the hit of the drug. I was a bundle of nerves.

"Something tells me you'll be so busy and overwhelmed for the first couple of days you won't even remember you used to smoke," Tamara said.

I sure hoped she was right.

We stepped out of the car into the warmth of the day and took in our surroundings. Tamara craned her neck and shaded her eyes, searching the distant paddocks for half-naked, harnessed men. Her red denim shorts stopped at a frayed edge above her knees and her polka dotted shirt skimmed midthigh and pulled against her cleavage. Her lipstick matched the red of her shorts.

"The new session doesn't officially start until tomorrow, Tamara." I yawned, stretching out my arms and shoulders. "I'm sure the men from the previous session have gone."

"Well, fuck."

The disappointment on her face made me laugh. I grabbed my duffel bag and walked past her, up the porch stairs to the door. I put my hand on the knob and glanced back. "Are you coming?"

She nodded. "Yep. But I better see some ponyboys today, Owen, or this entire trip has been wasted."

I had no idea if either of us would see a ponyboy today.

"It's not a fucking petting zoo, Tamara."

"Ooh. Could you imagine? I wonder if they've given that any thought." She tapped her finger on her chin as she followed me.

The inside of the main building was spotless, smelling of lemon-scented cleaner. Cool air from the vents began to dry the sweat on my neck, much to my immediate relief.

A young man, presumably Connor, waved us over to his reception desk. "Mr. Lipke?"

"Yep. That's me." I gestured to Tamara who smiled and waved. "She's the driver. Tamara's leaving but she needs to use the bathroom if that's okay," I said.

"Sure, of course. There's a bathroom three doors down." He pointed to the right.

"Thanks, Connor. You're a peach." Tamara took off to find the bathroom.

I smiled at Connor. "I think she was hoping to get a look at a ponyboy or two."

Connor laughed. "Yeah, we're kind of between ponyboys right now."

"That's what I told her."

He looked me over. "So, you're Owen, our last-minute substitution. Adam was so glad you could come at such short notice. It's tough when someone cancels last minute and nobody on the list has the availability to fill in. We're lucky you found us."

"I'm the one who feels lucky. I only heard about this place a few weeks ago."

The door at the far end of the corridor opened and a man in washed-out jeans, red T-shirt, and a faded grey cowboy hat strode into the building, heading our way. The back of his brown hair reached almost to his shoulders, and as he came closer, his hazel eyes flashed with intelligence and warmth.

"Fuck me." It came out louder than I'd planned. "I didn't know there would be cowboys!"

Connor laughed and stood, taking some papers from his desk and handing them to the newcomer, who grinned and tipped his hat with a sexy smile.

"Only one," Connor explained. "Owen, meet Jensen. Jensen, this is Owen. Owen's starting with Kamal tomorrow."

Jensen took off his hat and offered his hand. I shook it, trying not to ogle his narrow hips and long legs.

"Jensen Moriarty. Pleased to meet you, Owen." He turned back to Connor. "This is all I need?"

"Yep. That's the paperwork for Miles and Andrei. Kamal has Owen, here, and Sam. The others have been matched with Hiro and Lorraine."

"Is everyone here now or are we still waiting for people?"

Connor checked a piece of paper on his desk. "Now that Owen has arrived, we're just waiting for one more."

"Who's doing the orientation? You?"

Jensen sounded relaxed and laid-back. I got a good vibe.

"I was going to wait for the last one and take him and Owen around together." Connor checked his watch. "Jake Francis should be here in less than twenty minutes."

"I can do it if you like," Jensen said, glancing at me. He smiled. "I don't have anything else going on right now."

"That would be amazing, Jensen. I'm still filing all the forms and catching up on some other administrative stuff. Thank you."

"No worries."

At that moment, Tamara came out of the washroom and started toward us. She saw Jensen from behind and glanced around to give me a thumbs up and an excited facial expression as she gestured toward his ass before he turned.

"Oh, hi," she said smoothly, going all normal in a split second so he didn't suspect anything. "I'm Tamara. Owen told me there wouldn't be any cowboys here. I feel like he was downplaying this whole ranch thing."

Jensen laughed. "I'm the only cowboy, and I only play it up because Adam thinks the ponyboys get off on it."

Connor coughed. "Oh, they get off on it."

"Are you a real cowboy or pretending?" Tamara asked, looking Jensen over like he was a grilled steak on a plate.

"Tam," I said, blushing. She was hilarious, but sometimes her filter malfunctioned.

Jensen didn't seem bothered. He shrugged, replacing his hat. "I'm from Alberta, and before signing on as a stable hand here I worked with real horses. So, you could call me a real cowboy, yeah."

"You're a *stable hand*? Here?" Tamara gaped. "What exactly does that *mean*?"

A red flush had creeped up Jensen's neck to his cheeks. "I'm learning how to be a trainer now."

Tamara gaped at him.

Jensen cleared his throat. "Anyway, I'm sure Owen will fill you in on all the fascinating things we do here," Jensen finished, gesturing to me and seeming out of his depth—a standard situation with Tamara.

"He'd better."

"Okay, bye Tam," I said. "Thanks for the lift."

She tore her gaze from Jensen and threw her chubby arms around me. "Have a fucking wonderful time playing pony. You deserve it. Please call me and let me know how your first week turns out," she said, kissing me on the cheek.

"I will. Are you sure you can come get me when the session's over?"

"Of course. I'll be here." She turned back to Jensen. "Is there a final pony show or something? At the end of a session?"

"Tam!" I was going to murder her.

Jensen laughed. "Well, yeah. But only our paid members are invited."

"Well, that sucks balls. Anyway, nice to meet you all, but I must fly."

She waved and she was gone, the eddies of her departure disrupting the quiet of the room.

"Wow," Connor grinned. "She is awesome."

I lifted my brows. "In small doses, yes. The car ride was...interesting."

"Welcome aboard, Owen," Jensen said. "Do you have any questions? As soon as Jake gets here we'll do a little walkabout and get you oriented."

"Uh, yeah, I have one question," I said. "Connor said I'd been assigned to a trainer named Kamal."

"That's right."

"Is he...good?"

Jensen gave me a queer smile. "Depends on your definition of good, I guess."

At my expression, he laughed. "He's amazing. But he's tough. Not for the weak at heart. If you're coming here for solid, unflinching discipline, he's your man."

My eyes widened. "Fuck me."

"He's not allowed to do that."

I blinked. "I beg your pardon?"

Jensen looked at the ground, then shook his head. "Sorry, I forget sometimes how bizarre this all seems at first. I've worked here long enough to get used to it all."

My head still swam with thoughts of Kamal, the mysterious disciplinarian.

"As your trainer, he's not allowed to fuck you. As much as you might want him to, and you probably will. Kamal is very good at what he does."

"So...so there are restrictions on physical intimacy?" I croaked, mouth dry.

"There are between trainers and ponyboys, and *actual fucking* is the only restriction, depending on your hard limits, of course. Everything else is on the table."

Everything else is on the table. Yeah, okay. *I'm gonna go jerk off now.* Holy fuck. This place was my Shangri-La.

Jensen turned to Connor. "We'll wait for Jake out on the back porch. Send him out after he checks in, please?"

"Will do."

"Is Adam in his office?"

"Nah, he's checking on some things over at the resort at the moment. He should be back in an hour or so."

"Okay." Jensen turned to me. "Put your duffel bag by Connor's desk here. We'll come get it before I take you guys to the bunkhouse. And I'll need you to give your phone to Connor."

The *bunkhouse*. I'd almost forgotten about the bunkhouse. This was all beginning to remind me of my first visit to Disneyland as a kid. So many cool new things, it was overwhelming, and my body hummed with excitement. I didn't know where to look or what to do.

I dug my phone out of my pocket, made sure it was locked, and gave it to Connor.

"This will be in a locker here at the front desk. You can access it at any time but you can't take it out of this building until you go home."

"Okay."

I followed Jensen out the back door of the main building onto a narrow porch that ran the length of it. He pointed to a wooden bench under a window.

"Have a seat. We'll be doing some walking once Jake arrives."

"Thanks." I plopped down onto the bench and stretched my legs. Jensen sat beside me, removed his hat, and wiped his forehead.

"That hat must get hot on warm days."

Jensen smiled. God, he was good-looking. His hair was smooshed from the hat but little tendrils curled around his ears and the ash-brown colour suited him. He had freckles on his nose and the tops of his cheeks.

"I'm used to it. Kind of feel naked without it. And it keeps the sun off my face. You think I have freckles now? I'd have three times as many if I didn't wear this hat."

I laughed. "I like your freckles."

"Thanks. Listen, I'm serious. Ask me anything. I'm sure you're bursting with questions." He rubbed the brim of his hat with his thumb. "I was confused for more than a month when I started working here." His forehead creased, and his thoughts seemed directed inward. If there was more to that story, he wasn't going to tell me now.

I looked into the distance where a large red barn rose into the sky. Behind it and to the side stood another, bigger, red building.

"What's that building?" I asked, gesturing.

"That's the grooming barn. Ponyboys go in one side; stable hands go in the other. It's where you get showered and scrubbed and outfitted for the day."

I remembered something Jensen had said. "You used to be a stable hand."

"Yes. I began as a stable hand; then Kamal decided to mentor me as a trainer. Now we have Carrie here taking over my stable hand position. She worked at the Pony Palace before that, so she knows what she's doing."

"The BCR's sister ranch?"

"You've done your homework," Jensen said, smiling.

He gazed at the imposing buildings. "The big building beyond the grooming barn is the arena. That's where you'll spend a lot of your time as a ponyboy. That and in the paddocks. We have a few of those."

"It looks amazing. Better than the website."

We spoke about random subjects until the back door of the house opened and Connor brought a young man out.

"Hiya," the man said, offering his hand.

I stood quickly and shook it, looking him over. He was a big guy, taller than me and more muscular. His brown hair was cut pretty short and a bit spiky on top. He was cute, in a high school quarterback kind of way, his features soft and boy-next-door attractive. I figured you had to have a certain level of good looks to be a ponyboy here since the resort guests paid for their entertainment. That was one thing I had going for me.

Jensen stood and shook Jake's hand, doffing his hat and replacing it. I watched Jake's gaze track it as he licked his lips.

Yep. Cowboy's rule.

"This is Jake. Jake, this is Jensen and this is Owen. Jensen will take the two of you on an orientation before getting you settled at the bunkhouse."

"Sounds great," Jake said in a soft, eager voice. His brown eyes flashed intelligence and curiosity.

"Okay, then. We should get started," Jensen said, nodding and extending his arm. Jake and I descended the porch steps and onto the gravel path.

The weather was warm but not sweltering, although I imagined it would get hot here over the summer. I wondered if there was a beach. The BCR was on Skeleton Lake, after all.

"Is there somewhere we can swim, when we're not actively 'pony-ing'?" I asked.

Jake laughed as Jensen nodded. "There's a place at the lake where some of the guys go to swim. It's nice. There's a dock and a bit of a beach. It's rocky, but there's a grassy area you can put your towels on.

"Nice."

"We have a bonfire for Canada Day every year too," Jensen said as we trudged to the grooming barn. We approached a door with the word "PONIES" written on it.

"Okay, step inside, boys. This is where your day will begin."

Jake and I went into the building and stopped inside the door, looking around at smooth wood floors, benches, and lockers. It could have been the change room at a gym. In fact, it looked like the change room at a *fancy* gym.

"Wow," I said.

"All the buildings on the property are air-conditioned," Jensen said. "it gets extremely hot during the summer months."

"Are locks provided?" Jake asked. "I didn't bring one."

"No, no. We haven't had any cases of theft. The only people around are the staff and the other ponyboys and any valuables you have will be kept in locked storage at the main house. Only your clothes and shoes go in these lockers, and any accessories like bracelets and neck jewelry. You have to be completely naked when you go around that wall," Jensen said, pointing at the corner of the wall where the lockers were.

Jake and I glanced at each other. This was becoming very real. It was nerve-racking but also exciting and hot. I wouldn't mind getting a look at his unclothed body one little bit. Even though he wasn't really my type, I could appreciate masculine beauty in many forms.

"Follow me," Jensen said, leading us around the wall into the other space.

This room was about three times the size of the locker room. The same wood floor spanned the space except for a tiled section around the wall that held three shower areas with what looked like rubber bondage cuffs attached above each one.

"Holy shit," I couldn't help saying. This was like an elaborate porn setup at the Armory in San Francisco.

"Christ," Jake said, staring at the showers.

"Kink-dot-com anyone?" I muttered.

"This is the grooming barn. At the beginning of each shift, you'll be bound by your wrists in a shower stall and buffed and cleaned to a shine before the stable hands dress you in whatever gear your trainer has put on the chart for that day."

Jensen's smile acknowledged that he knew how bizarre this sounded but that he figured he might as well lay it out for us. Which I appreciated.

"Okay," I said, swallowing thickly.

"Yep," Jake echoed.

We subtly checked each other out, realizing we might be naked or pony-ing together by this time tomorrow.

"See the chart there? That's where the trainers write directions for the stable hands, by date. One day they might want you in only the basic gear; another day they might want to put you in bridle and tails. It varies."

"Fuck me," I said. *Bridle and tails*. This was becoming so damn real and I couldn't wait to get started. This would beat trolling the Ottawa gay bars for halfway decent Doms in a second. I hoped the trainers at the BCR were as impressive as the website and Jensen professed. If I got all dolled up as a play pony and then discovered my trainer was useless, I'd be demanding a fucking refund.

I didn't think that was going to happen. I really hoped the BCR would live up to my high expectations. I needed this adventure more than I'd needed anything in a very long time.

Chapter Three

"This table is used to clean tack and store items of regular use." Jensen touched the weathered surface fondly, with a faraway look in his eyes. "Also for ponyboys to bend over when they're having their tails inserted."

Jensen spoke with practicality and amusement. He'd worked as a stable hand before he'd started learning to be a trainer so must be intimately acquainted with everything that went on in the grooming barn. As I pictured bending over this wood table while Jensen pushed a pony-tail butt plug into my ass my semi became full. I shifted and cursed as my gaze flew to Jensen's.

He gazed back at me with a bemused acknowledgement that the things occurring at the BCR would be some of the kinkiest shit we'd ever seen.

"Well, fuck," I said, because I couldn't think of anything else. Jake breathed heavily beside me.

"You'll find out what it's like tomorrow. I think you're both on the morning shift, from nine to twelve. You'll be morning this week and afternoon next week. You'll need to be naked and standing under one of these shower heads by 7:30 on the dot. You can be a little early but don't be late. The stable hands have a lot to do to get you ready for training each day."

We stared at Jensen silently.

He smiled. "Any questions?"

I raised my hand slowly because I couldn't quite get the words out.

Jensen nodded at me. "Yes, Owen?"

"Um, do they like, uh—" I made squeezing motions with my hand, as if holding an invisible bottle. "—clean us out? Or anything like that? I mean, how—?"

"No. The bunkhouse washroom is stocked with anal douches so you can take care of that yourself before you arrive. There are disposable enema kits as well, but they don't get used too often."

I heard a choking noise beside me as Jake tried to hold his laughter in. His face had turned beet red.

"Thanks," I said, scuffing my boot against the floor. I shrugged at Jake. "Hey, it was a good question."

Jake couldn't hold on. He hunched over as peals of hysterical laughter escaped.

"It was a great question," Jensen agreed, regarding Jake with an amused grin as Jake gulped and shook with laughter.

"What the fuck is your problem?" I said, offended Jake thought my question so ridiculous.

"I'm...sorry. I'm sorry," Jake gasped, holding onto a corner of the table and blinking back tears as he tried to calm himself.

Jensen and I waited for him. Eventually, the hysterics subsided, and he slumped down in the plastic chair near him.

"Oh, God. I...I mean, the reality of this situation just kind of clicked, and I can't help seeing the ridiculousness of it all," Jake murmured. "I'm sorry. I'm glad to be here. I'm into it... It's only I was so nervous driving up and not sure what to expect and...this is all so matter-of-fact and... I don't know."

Jensen grinned. "I mean, it's a lot to take in."

I was relieved to find out Jake was reacting to the absurdity of our situation, which was bizarre, honestly.

"Oh, sorry. I thought you were laughing at me," I said.

Jake shook his head vehemently. "Never. You're pretty awesome for even asking that question."

"Can we see the arena next?" I asked Jensen, wanting to see it all right now. I needed to know what went on here in a big, big way.

"Sure. That's where you'll spend most of your time. And in the paddocks."

The paddocks.

He led us out of the grooming barn and along a wide gravel path to a bigger and more imposing building.

I glanced beside me at Jake and wondered what he'd look like with his pony gear on. Imagining it, brought my erection back with a vengeance. It occurred to me this would likely be a recurring issue.

"Have you role-played like this before?" I asked him.

Jake nodded. "Sure. But only with my ex. I mean, we didn't have a lot of gear or anything. And I've never done it in a setting like this before."

"What made you want to come here?"

"Well...we broke up, and, y'know, it's hard to find other people with the same kinks sometimes. A friend recommended this place, and I decided to try it out. I'm always into learning and experiencing new things."

"Yeah, same," I admitted.

"Of course, I've been on the waiting list for a while and I actually met someone in the meantime, but he doesn't have a problem with me exploring this side of myself at the BCR, and my name came up so..." He flourished his hands along his body. "Here I am."

"Wow. That's great."

"Yeah. Best of both worlds, I guess." He frowned slightly. "Except I miss him already, and I know we're supposed to limit the use of our devices. It's gonna be rough."

"Sure. But you'll have plenty of distractions," I pointed out.

He laughed. "That is true."

My eye caught sight of a tall, dark-haired man with a close-cropped black beard leaning against the outer wall of the arena. He was dressed in a pair of form-fitting navy cotton shorts and a white polo shirt that emphasized his olive skin, and he was holding a stack of papers and reading the top sheet.

Speaking of distractions...

My gaze ran along what looked like trim, muscular thighs beneath his shorts, then over his well-shaped calves to the white trainers on his broad feet, and back to his veined arms and hands as he turned toward us.

"Hey, Kamal," Jensen said and touched the tip of his cowboy hat.

When the man named Kamal grinned, dimples pitted his cheeks, and fine wrinkles appeared beside deep-brown eyes.

"Jensen. They've got you doing orientations now?"

His deep and confident voice sent a warm shiver along my body.

"Well, I offered," Jensen said. "Connor has a busy day ahead of him."

"Aren't you sweet," Kamal said, still grinning.

Kamal looked Jake over briefly before meeting my gaze. "Which one's mine?" he asked. His comment and the objectification it implied, made my dick harder than it had been a moment ago.

"This one," Jensen said, gesturing to me, and I almost died.

Fuck, this was my trainer? This was the guy who would teach me the art of being a human pony?

Goddammit, I was either the luckiest motherfucker on the planet, or I was in way over my head.

"What's your name?" Kamal asked, his authoritative gaze still directed at me. I couldn't decide if I was thrilled or alarmed that he effectively ignored Jake.

"Owen. Owen Lipke," I stated, trying to maintain my composure while the reality of my situation came crashing down.

Kamal extended his hand. "Nice to meet you, Owen."

His fingers enveloped mine in their warm, firm grip. I purposefully kept my hand rigid to let him know I was no pushover. His gaze ran up and down my body with deliberate leisure. I hoped he liked what he saw. He'd be seeing a hell of a lot more of it tomorrow. Perhaps he was thinking the same.

His eyes narrowed as he focused on my cheek. I stood still as he reached out and cupped my chin in his hand, wiping at something on my cheek with his thumb, then releasing me. It was an astonishingly intimate gesture. "How did you get lipstick on your cheek, Owen? Say goodbye to your girlfriend this morning?" It was an honest question, not teasing in any way. But it was personal and I didn't know this man.

Ah, fuck. I was going to murder Tamara and her goddamn fire-engine-red lipstick. She must have applied a fresh coat in the bathroom.

I brought my hand up to my cheek to get rid of any leftover stain and shook my head. "Just a friend. Who drove me. Nice to meet you," I managed, wondering how I could still form words. I cleared my throat, about to attempt something profound, when Kamal turned to Jensen, ending our connection.

"These the last two?"

Jensen nodded. "Yep. When we're done, I'll get them settled in at the bunkhouse. You want to meet for a consultation before supper?"

"Sure. Let's have a drink at the resort, and we can discuss our plans."

He glanced back at me, and I felt like his plans were going to include devising numerous ways to introduce my naive ass to the intricacies of pony play. Another shiver passed through me.

Kamal glanced at Jake and smiled. "Welcome to the Braided Crop Ranch, boys."

When his gaze returned, it raked me up and down again as he licked his lips. I legit wanted to drop to my knees then and there and lick his white Keds all over. What the fuck was wrong with me?

"Thanks," I muttered, put off balance by my reaction to Kamal. Was my insecurity a result of this realistic and kinky environment, or would the man actually prove to be the kind of Dom I'd been looking for all along? What were the fucking odds of that?

While Jensen led us into the arena, I tried to gather my thoughts and get my body under control. My heart beat rapidly and my palms turned clammy. My dick was a fucking baton. I was so screwed.

"This is the arena, where your trainers will teach you everything you need to know about being the best human pony you can be," Jensen was saying, as I tried to wrap my head around the fact I'd be here tomorrow under the competent hands of the man we had just met.

"I need to sit down," I said, feeling like a wimp and a failure already, and we hadn't even started. I leaned against the wood wall and slid down to the polished floor while Jensen came forward and stared at me.

"You okay? Do you need a drink of water?"

"I might need something stronger."

He crouched so we were eye level. "Hey, I get it. It's overwhelming at first. You're not the first man to wonder if he's made a mistake."

"Is that what I'm doing?" I said.

"Probably."

Jake moved closer and bumped my shoe with his foot. "I'm feeling the same way if it makes it any better. I mean, the reality of all this is hitting me full force right now."

I nodded, licking my lips. "So, that guy we met outside...Kamal?"

"Yeah?"

"Is he going to destroy me?"

Jensen stared for a second. "Only if you want him to."

"Oh, shit," I said.

Jensen grinned. "Look, Kamal's amazing. He'll start small; don't worry. He's worked here for years. You're in good hands." Jensen said, trying to reassure me. "He seems scarier than he is. I mean, he won't let you get away with anything, but he'll make your time here worthwhile."

"I'm kind of jealous of you, Owen." Jake said. "That man can tell me to giddy-up *anytime*."

Jensen laughed and stood, offering me a hand. I took it and he helped me stand.

"Now you, Jake, will be with Lorraine, who is as strict as Kamal but with a softer hand."

"Okay. Sure."

"She's almost as devious and creative as Kamal, though."

Jake flushed from his neck to his ears in an instant. "Okay. Jesus."

"Shall we get on with the tour?"

I nodded. "Yeah. I'm fine."

Jensen had it wrong. I didn't think I had made a mistake at all. I already felt like this place was exactly what I needed. I'd had stronger emotions and more visceral reactions here than I'd experienced in ages, and we hadn't even started.

After we toured the arena, Jensen showed us the outside paddocks and rings and where the pony shows were staged during the good weather. I'd forgotten, somehow, about the pony shows. There were layers upon layers of fetishes here—service, exhibitionism, objectification, submission, primalism, humiliation. It was mind-boggling.

"Any questions?"

For once in my life I was without words. I wanted tomorrow morning to come so we could get started. The anticipation was going to kill me.

"Okay. Let's get you to the bunkhouse."

We walked back to the main house and grabbed our bags, then followed Jensen across the field to the edge of the forest.

The bunkhouse was at the end of a narrow path winding through the field—a large building with grey clapboard siding and several large windows all around and the word BUNKHOUSE burnt into a slab of wood on the wall. We heard men's voices as we neared the door, but Jensen didn't knock. He twisted the handle and pushed the door open, stepping inside and beckoning us to follow.

"This is the bunkhouse," he said as we followed him into the building.

Multiple eyes were on us as men looked up and stopped what they were doing.

"Hi, everyone. This is Jake, and this is Owen. They're the last two for this session. Can someone help get them sorted out? I need to get back."

A tall slim man with copper skin and long jet-black hair pulled into a ponytail stepped forward.

"Hi. I'm Biskane." He gestured to three other men in turn who were leaning or sitting on bunks along the windows. "This is Miles, Andrei, and Sam."

"Awesome. Great to meet you all," I said.

"Same," Jake added.

"I'll see all of you at supper," Jensen said before touching the brim of his cowboy hat, nodding, and leaving us.

Sam moaned, falling back on one of the bunks dramatically. "Oh my God, that man is going to be the end of me."

Andrei whistled. "He's super cute; that's for sure."

"Why can't he be my trainer?" Sam moaned. "I'm pretty sure I requested a cowboy."

Biskane laughed and gestured to some beds nearby that didn't have any belongings on them. "Pick a bunk, guys. There's lots."

"Thanks," I said, looking Biskane over quickly. He was stunningly handsome and athletic. His features were soft and warm and he had a beguilingly androgynous look even without the long hair. I tossed my duffel bag on the top of an unoccupied bunk as Jake placed his on the one below.

This place was cool, and it reminded me of summer camp when I was a kid. I turned to grin at the guys still standing around. "So, you all here for the kink or what?"

"I'm here for the kink," Andrei said. He was compact and tanned, with tight muscles and powerful shoulders. Probably the shortest one here. He had wavy brown hair and a scruffy, close-cropped beard.

"The kink," everyone else said.

"Well, I mean, obviously," Miles added. "I don't think any of us are here for romance."

I snorted. "Yeah, not me; that's for sure. I want to ride the fetish train for a few weeks to take me out of my ordinary life. Then it's back to the meaningless grind with a headful of memories.

There was a chorus of agreement before everyone drifted off to their bunks and returned to what they had been doing before we arrived.

Biskane smiled and folded his long arms over his chest. "Toilets and showers are over there," he said, nodding toward a broad green door to the left. "And a kitchenette on the right."

"Thanks," Jake said. "I could use a snack."

"There's cereal and nutri bars and some fruit. Coffee and tea. Bread."

"Cool."

"Anyway, I'll leave you to get settled in. I've been here a few hours, so I'm figuring things out."

"Thanks, man. Appreciate it." I held my hand out to him again, just to feel the warmth of his handshake. I liked him already.

While Jake got a snack, I sorted out my stuff and headed to the washrooms to brush my teeth, all the while thinking about Kamal and what it would be like to be his bitch tomorrow.

Let me rephrase that. *To be his gelding.* That was what a neutered horse was called, right? With that fucking cock cage on I'd probably feel neutered. The thought sent a hot jolt of electricity through me, and I realized I'd made the right decision to come here.

I stared at my reflection in the large mirror over the sinks. I hadn't been this excited about anything in a long time. Or so terrified. But terror was the furthest thing from boredom.

Terror was *invigorating.*

Chapter Four

By suppertime the sky had clouded over, so there was an awning set up over the picnic tables in front of the main house in case of rain. I happened to spy Kamal tying one end of the awning to a post and couldn't help picturing him using a rope in a different context.

A buffet of barbecued steaks and burgers, potato salad, coleslaw, grilled vegetables and rolls had been laid out on a large rectangular table. I was hungry but also nervous about tomorrow so I only filled a small plate. Biskane loaded up with a ton of food, which he probably needed for his tall frame, and the others chose smaller helpings. I wasn't the only one feeling anxious.

Besides Kamal, I recognized Jensen, Hiro and Lorraine, and the four stable hands—Liv, Adrian, Enzo, and Carrie. It was strange shaking hands with people who would be treating me like an animal come morning. Because everyone was so friendly and funny and welcoming, it eased some of my anxiety. The professionalism and affability of everyone reassured me that I had picked the right place to explore this side of myself.

I couldn't eat much. Although the barbecued burgers, steaks, salads and bread looked and smelled delicious, my anxious belly warred with my eager dick to drive me crazy with anticipation, and I didn't have much of an appetite. The craving for a cigarette hit me harder than I'd anticipated. I thought because I'd only smoked for a few months, and not much, it would be a piece of cake to quit the habit. I may have underestimated the difficulty. Still, better to be in completely different surroundings and unable to access a hit to force me to abstain. I was sure after a few days I wouldn't even think about cigarettes.

But I didn't sleep well. The worry and excitement of what the morning would bring, coupled with the strange environment of the bunkhouse, caused restlessness and agitation. Used to having a queen bed to myself, the single bunk and the noises of snoring and mumbling around me kept me awake until my body succumbed to exhaustion, and I fell into a fitful sleep for a few short hours.

A rough shove on my shoulder woke me from a deep sleep before I was ready.

"Hey, wake up, Owen. It's six. We have to get ready."

I opened my eyes to see Jake peering at me from beside the bunk. I wiped my hand over my eyes and propped myself on my elbow. "What time is it?"

"Six."

"Oh, God. That's early."

He grinned. "Well, next week we'll be on the afternoon shift, and we can sleep in."

I groaned. "Thank God."

I dragged myself out of bed and into the bathroom, where I used the supplied products to prepare for the morning. It was weird doing this in essentially a "public" washroom, but since the other guys were doing the same thing as me we dealt with our embarrassment with humour.

"Make sure you put that in the right hole," someone joked. Another guy said, "Why do they want us to use these? Horses shit everywhere, so why can't we?"

"Yeah, I'm not shitting on the floor of the arena. Be my guest, though."

"Are we supposed to shower?" I asked Jake.

"You don't need to shower." A voice came from a closed stall. "But Kamal will expect your face to be clean-shaven."

Jake and I stared as the door opened and Adrian exited. He grinned as he came to the sink and pumped some soap from the dispenser into his hands. "God, you guys are hilarious. If I have to clean shit off the floor, I'm asking for a raise," he said to the guys who had been joking around.

He turned back to us. "Unless you want to make my job way too easy, don't shower, just shave. You will be well looked after by me and Enzo and Carrie this morning, so don't worry. But get your asses to the grooming barn by 7:30. I'm looking forward to getting some fresh ponyboys this week." He clapped his hands together and washed them vigorously, then grinned as a flush of heat travelled from my feet to my forehead.

"Okay, sure, yeah," I said.

Jake remained silent but stared as Adrian left the room and let the door swing shut behind him. We blinked at each other, both of us blushing furiously.

I smiled. "I guess we signed up for this."

Jake chuckled. "I'm starting to wonder if it was actually a good idea."

"I guess we'll find out today."

"I guess so."

*

Stepping out of the air-conditioned bunkhouse into the muggy heat of the morning made me regret not showering. I probably should have had one before I went to bed. At least my face felt clean and soft. I'd bought a different, travel-sized shave gel for the trip, and it smelled good.

As I followed Jake and Biskane along the narrow path to the grooming barn, I wondered what it would mean to stand beneath one of those showerheads and await the care of the stable hands. I suppose I'd find out soon enough.

We stood outside the door labelled "Ponies" for a few moments, exchanging nervous glances before I shrugged and pulled it open, stepping into the small space and moving so they could follow.

The short walk in the humid air had caused sweat to accumulate in all the normal places, and I was equally eager for, and dreading, the showers. On the other side of the wall, the stable hands talked to each other and prepared for their busy morning.

My pulse spiked as I started to strip. I avoided looking at the others and wondered how long it would take me to get used to this strange environment. I wondered if I'd made the right decision to come here and whether the BCR would live up to my expectations or if the entire adventure was a stupid idea.

I shoved my stuff in a locker, glanced at Biskane and Jake, and was the first to walk around the partition.

I kept my gaze on the floor as I found a place under the furthest showerhead and stood there silently, wrists crossed behind my back and head bowed, taking deep, steadying breaths. I heard the others follow and take their positions but I didn't look up from the grey-tiled floor.

When nobody approached, I peeked through my eyelashes to see the three stable hands assembling our gear and talking amongst themselves.

It was comforting to be ignored, and my anxiety began to fade. The knowledge that I couldn't control anything that happened after this moment became an invisible blanket of comfort that settled over me, letting me focus on what good things might await me. I didn't look at Biskane or Jake because I already had a semi from the nervous anticipation and seeing them standing naked beside me would make me fully hard in an instant.

I accidentally let my gaze drift to the wall, focusing on the whiteboard chart where my name stood out as if written in flaming letters.

Owen: harness, collar, cage, arm bands.

My dick became hard as a fucking rock, and I wondered how they were going to get the cage on me. Seeing those words written on an office whiteboard that could have been hanging at some accountant's meeting made my kinky soul take notice.

If there had ever been any doubt I had made the right decision to come to the BCR, as soon as I saw those words on the board referring to me like some dumb animal to be tacked indicated I was right where I should be. My visceral reaction to being objectified told me everything.

I closed my eyes and concentrated on listening to the stable hands discuss random subjects until I felt subtle movement of the air near me and a warm hand landed gently on my cheek.

"Open," a familiar voice said, and I obeyed, opening both my mouth and my eyes as Adrian gently placed a red ball gag between my teeth. "If you need to safeword hold up two fingers, okay?" he said, as he efficiently buckled the strap behind my head.

I nodded, trying to hide how excited and into this I felt. He only had to look down at my full cock to realize my investment.

"Arms up."

I moved my arms from behind my back and lifted them over my head, trying to center myself as Adrian competently buckled the rubber manacles around my wrists.

"Good boy, Owen. You're doing great," Adrian said. "Nice tat, by the way. I like this," he said, tapping the black ink on my right shoulder.

It was a mariner's compass, tilted on my shoulder, with N,S,E, and W at the appropriate intervals. I'd gotten it after university, when I didn't know what direction my life might take. I still didn't. I still felt lost and directionless, even though I'd gotten a good job in IT and was able to afford my own place in Ottawa's pricey rental market.

I blinked at him, wondering how he felt about this, whether it got him worked up or not. He was probably so used to it that it didn't affect him at all. I pulled at the cuffs to test their strength and was not disappointed. This wasn't a game. This was some seriously organized BDSM bullshit, and I loved it.

"I can see you're enjoying this," Adrian commented, running a finger up the underside of my dick, causing me to gasp. "That's good."

I hadn't expected him to touch me. Which was pretty fucking stupid since that was his job. I just didn't think he'd touch me *there*. I didn't know what the rules were.

Except, yeah, I did. And the rules were that the stable hands and the trainers could touch me any way they liked as long as they didn't fuck me. It had taken until this moment to realize those rules gave them a ton of leeway.

When I glanced at Adrian again, he smiled and teased me again.

I groaned and closed my eyes. *Bastard.*

"Don't worry. We'll have this guy under control in a bit," he said, flicking my dick with his finger, causing another gasp. "Might as well enjoy the freedom while you can."

He rubbed his palm over the tip with a laugh and then turned on the showerhead with no further preamble. I struggled to keep control of my dick, which somehow thought it was sixteen instead of twenty-seven and was ready to explode at a feather-light touch.

The warm water poured over me as I sighed with relief. This completely indulgent, sensual thing I could enjoy without worrying about embarrassing myself. The water felt so good on my sweaty skin. I closed my eyes and tipped my head back.

Then Adrian began to rub my back vigorously with something rough, and my cock throbbed because it felt so good. Maybe I would embarrass myself constantly at the ranch. Humiliation might be something to get used to. Maybe that was the point—to let yourself go so you didn't care anymore.

He scrubbed me thoroughly all over but avoided my tender bits with the loofah. Once I got used to it, the rubdown became invigorating. I kept my eyes closed and enjoyed the fruity scent of the body wash. Adrian hummed to himself while he worked and the soft sound soothed my rattled nerves. I heard the other stable hands speaking to their charges. The entire procedure was well-organized and effective.

"Okay, Owen, I'm going to use a cloth on you now," Adrian said. "How are you feeling? Everything okay?"

I opened my eyes to stare into his and nodded. We were approximately the same height, but Adrian was skinnier. I wasn't all that built but at least I had some defined muscle. I was definitely slim, but not skinny. Compared to Kamal, I looked like a pretty princess. I'm sure he could bench-press me. The thought gave me chills—good ones.

I appreciated the check-in. He put the loofah down and picked up a soft terry cloth square. He squirted some body wash onto it and proceeded to rub it into my pubic hair and over my dick and balls. He was gentle and thorough and winked as he dragged the soapy cloth through the crack of my ass, cleaning me in all the necessary places. He got another cloth and followed the same path with water to get the soap off.

"Now, hair."

He proceeded to lather my hair and massage my scalp as I tried not to moan with the sheer indulgent pleasure of it. I'd let the top grow long, and the ends came past the tops of my ears now although I'd had the back trimmed short. Tam said the waves of dark brown made my green eyes pop and told me not to cut it. She also said the way it swooped across my forehead reminded her of the forelock of a horse, especially when I tossed it out of my eyes. I didn't know if she was right but decided to listen. Adrian rinsed the shampoo out, then turned off the shower and toweled my hair. Afterwards, he patted my body dry with a gentleness that surprised and pleased me.

When he grabbed a pair of small shears from the table I made a noise of surprise as Adrian laughed. "I'm not going to cut your hair, silly. At least, not the hair on your head."

I felt relief, then fear again as he threw down a dry towel and knelt before me.

"I need to trim and shave your pubic hair, Owen. Believe me, you don't want any hair down here with a metal cock cage on. Wouldn't be very comfortable."

I nodded and stood still while he trimmed the substantial amount of dark hair growing around my dick, then applied shaving gel to my skin.

As he carefully shaved around my cock and balls with obvious skill and a steady hand, the feeling of being pampered and cherished filled me, even though I knew he was only preparing me for the cage.

I thought back to the photos on the website. I hadn't noticed, but of course, the ponyboys had been shaved there. I only hoped the same didn't apply to my asshole. I shuddered at the thought.

But Adrian finished with my pubic area, dried me off, and then said, "All right. Let's get you into your gear."

He stood and released my wrists from the cuffs. It was a relief to drop my arms and shake them out. I rubbed my wrists as Adrian went to get my gear. While he was doing that I glanced at Jake and Biskane, both in different stages of their grooming procedure.

Enzo, almost as tall as Biskane, was finishing his manscaping, and Carrie already had Jake's body harness and collar on.

"You're way ahead of me, Carrie. Trying to show off?" Adrian laughed.

She smiled, her septum piercing glinting off the overhead lights. "Yep. You got it."

Adrian grinned and Enzo said, "I'm taking my time because…" He gestured at Biskane's glowing skin and tall stature. "I mean, wouldn't you?"

I would have felt insulted but for the obviousness of Biskane's superior beauty.

"I don't know. I've been enjoying this ponyboy of mine very much," Adrian said, voice low. Perhaps he liked caring for me this way as much as I enjoyed his attention.

I glanced over and tried to smile around the gag.

He reached out and gave my cheek a quick pat. "Yeah, you don't need to worry, you pretty thing. Kamal will be very pleased with you once I get you decked out."

I wanted to kiss him because if I had ever needed words of reassurance more than I did at that moment, the memory escaped me. I'd never been so worried about putting my best foot forward with anyone before. I wasn't even sure why doing it today mattered so much. But as Adrian carefully buckled me into the body harness and arm bands, then fastened the broad leather collar around my neck, I began to feel like I might be ready for what was coming. I began to feel more and more at ease in my role of objectified stable beast. Passively letting Adrian clean me and dress me in the standard ponyboy gear felt like the start of a cherished ritual.

"Ooh, can I braid your ponyboy's hair?"

I turned to see Carrie speaking to Enzo and gesturing to Biskane, whose hair, damp from its wash, looked even longer and darker now.

Enzo shrugged and stepped away from Biskane, nodding. "Go on. As long as he don't mind." He nodded toward me and Jake. "Seems like a good idea to ask 'im, in case Biskane feels like we're takin' the piss. But it makes sense, since it'll keep his hair back and out o' th' way."

Carrie walked up to Biskane, looking like a little pixie next to his intimidating presence, with her short, layered hair, perky nose and freckles. "Not to mention it will look amazing," she commented. She ran her fingers through the length of the young man's hair. "Do you mind if I braid your beautiful hair, Biskane?"

The tall, handsome ponyboy smiled around his gag and shook his head.

I watched this exchange, admiring the tight muscles under Biskane's smooth skin. I'd not noticed that Adrian had left my side until he appeared suddenly with the metal contraption I'd been dreading.

While I understood its purpose and appreciated its necessity, I'd never worn one before. I wasn't sure how it would feel.

Would it be painful? Would I like it? Would I hate it?

I gazed at the device in Adrian's hand with trepidation.

"Don't worry. You'll get used to it. Soon it will be an intrinsic part of your training. It will also help avoid any embarrassing accidents in the heat of the moment." He winked, and I blushed.

Yep, I'd need it.

Luckily, my dick had relaxed once the shaving was over and Adrian could fasten the device around my balls and uncircumcised cock. I gazed down and felt decidedly humbled. It didn't look sexy to me at all, only pitiful.

Adrian slapped me on the ass. "Stop mooning over your cock, Owen. You need to put your socks and boots on."

He stood in front of me, holding a worn pair of scuffed Docs and some wool socks. "Size eleven, right?"

I nodded.

"Good. These are sanitized and cleaned between each session and they have your name on them now. They're for your exclusive use for the next six weeks as is the rest of your gear. The leather tack is cleaned between each use, and the tails and cock cages are cleaned and sanitized between each use as well."

He watched while I pulled on the socks then tugged on the used Docs and laced them up. As I stood, he put his hands on his hips and ran his gaze over me, smiling and nodding. "Oh yeah. You look like a pony now, Owen. Want to see?"

I blinked, gathering my courage, and bobbed my head.

He beckoned me past the table to a full-length mirror on the wall. I followed him and stood before it, staring at the startling image of myself in pony gear.

I'd been blessed with good genes and never had trouble picking up. But to see myself decked out in pony-play tack caused a shock to my system. Where I had usually looked sexy enough, now I looked kinky as fuck and hot as hell.

"Wait. Cross your arms behind you," Adrian instructed, and I obeyed. "I won't fasten these because that's for the trainer to do, but look at the way it improves your posture."

Adrian held my wrists together at the small of my back, forcing my shoulders to square and my chest to stick out. My pectoral muscles looked more impressive pushing against the harness and my chin automatically lifted. The minor imperfections on my skin—a random spattering of dark moles here and there on the tanned surface—only emphasized the otherwise smooth expanse. The muscles I'd honed from years of hiking and running were perfect for a lean ponyboy. I looked fucking regal all of a sudden, except for the ball gag and the saliva already coating my chin. I tossed the hair back from my forehead.

"Such a handsome ponyboy," Adrian said. He patted me on the backside and crooned, "So clean and fresh. I think you're ready for your trainer, Owen."

Once the three of us had been prepared properly, Enzo attached leather leads to our collars and took us across the field to the arena. He was a crazy-haired sprite with a British accent and a chronic grin. I liked him already.

"How are you feeling, you lot? Ready for your first day as ponies? Oh, that's right, you can't answer me 'cause you're gagged. What a fucking shame that is," he said, flashing bright white teeth and making me feel like I was in a Monty Python sketch.

Trudging in my boots across the grass dressed like a human pony, I felt vulnerable and strange, although it was nice to have so little on in the summer heat. I kept my eyes on Biskane's long black braid as it hung down his narrow back, swaying slightly with the motion of his walk. As Enzo opened the door wide and led us into the arena I realized I was *not* prepared for what lay ahead. I kept my eyes on Biskane's braid until he and Jake were handed over to their trainers, Lorraine and Hiro. I gazed hard at the floor, terrified to look ahead and determined to be the well-behaved pony my trainer wanted.

I followed Enzo's feet in his flip-flops across the wood floor, expecting to see one pair of black boots, not two.

Drool dripped from my gag down my chin as my gaze followed the first set of boots up to Kamal's grinning face, then slid to the side to see Jensen, in a black T-shirt, jeans, leather wrist bracelets and his cowboy hat. He touched the brim and tipped his chin to me, smiling.

What the fuck? Were they tag teaming me? How come I got two trainers? Did they think I'd be a handful when I was quaking in my fucking boots at what Kamal might demand of me? Was this some kind of a joke?

Kamal full-on laughed at the expression on my face while Jensen offered an explanation. "I'm shadowing Kamal this session. It's part of my training to be a"—he shrugged, likely embarrassed at his word-choice—"trainer."

I blinked.

What the fuck?

I got two trainers for the price of one? Sure, they were both hot as fuck, but that meant two sets of eyes watching every move I made, and Kamal would want to teach Jensen...everything.

Fuck my goddamn ponyboy life.

Chapter Five

I grunted and tossed my head back and forth, feeling like it was the first day of school and I'd been put in the *bad kid class* already.

"Relax, Owen," Kamal said in that rich, sexy voice that could peel my clothes off all on its own if I was wearing any. "It means you get more attention; that's all. Isn't that a good thing?"

Was it? Maybe?

Kamal raked his gaze over me. "Well, don't you look a pretty sight, all decked out in your tack. Turn around slowly, so we can get a good look," he said, raising his hand and spinning his index finger in a tight circle.

I grunted but did as he asked, the heat rising in my cheeks as I became an object to admire. Some of my blood flowed lower, but that only made me uncomfortable seeing as my dick was caged in steel.

"Eh, Jensen? Does he look the part, or what?"

Jensen cleared his throat. "He looks gorgeous. Owen's a very pretty pony."

Jensen's kind words softened the part of me that wanted to bolt for the door. They gave me the confidence I needed, standing here in pony-play tack in front of two handsome men. I took a deep breath and waited for one of them to tell me what to do.

Instead, I felt hands on the buckle behind my head, and the gag went slack, falling wetly to my chest before dragging over my shoulder. I heard a *thunk* as it landed on the table.

"Turn around and face me," Kamal said as I licked my lips and wiped my wet chin on my shoulder.

I did as he asked, gazing at him through my dark bangs before tossing my head, relieved to be able to close my lips. At least he afforded me that dignity.

"I don't use the gag during the first week, because everything is so new, and we are getting to know each other. It's important for you to have a voice," he said, with a sexy smirk. "I'll lay out my expectations so there is no confusion."

I glanced at Jensen, who stood to one side, leaning against the wall, watching intently as Kamal spoke.

"Eyes on me, please. I will probably have Jensen assist me in numerous ways, but your attention should always be on me, unless I tell you to keep your eyes down."

I nodded, licking my lips again and ignoring the soreness in my jaw from having the gag in for that short amount of time.

"You may speak when spoken to, and you are to address me as Sir when in pony gear, do you understand?"

"Yes, Sir."

"If you are consistently well-behaved I will probably leave the gag out most of the time, unless it's part of a specific exercise." He began to walk around me, his eyes exploring my form at every angle, examining me from all sides. I followed his movements with my gaze but didn't budge from my position.

I felt like a sex object under that stare, and I desperately wanted him to be pleased with me. I lifted my chin and stared at Jensen, since I couldn't turn and follow Kamal now he'd gone behind me.

Jensen winked and quirked his lip, eyes flitting down to my cock. He wasn't unaffected by my presence. That gave me the confidence to return a slight smile until I felt broad hands on my shoulders and smelled the clean male scent of Kamal as he moved in close behind me.

I felt Kamal's fingers softly touch my right shoulder and trace my compass tattoo. "Nice ink," he said. "You trying to find your way, Owen?"

"Hopefully, I've found it, Sir," I said.

Kamal laughed. "Hopefully."

My smile wavered as Kamal's hands slid down my biceps, leaving electrified nerve endings in their wake. His fingers brushed over the leather of my long armbands and one hand wrapped gently around my left wrist.

"Bend your elbow," he said softly. "I'm going to cross your arms behind your back and buckle them together."

"Yes, Sir."

I sounded hesitant and lost. I let him manipulate my arms and fasten the buckles on the leather cuffs. There were two buckles—one near my wrist and one closer to my elbow. I was forced to square my shoulders and push my chest out in order for my arms to be positioned in this way, feeling at once more dignified and more debased. This pony-play bullshit was a serious mindfuck.

I had a thing for leather, specifically *leather bondage*. The smell of it, the softness combined with its strength, well, it did something to me. It was doing something to me now, and the steel cage on my dick became painful. I whimpered and shifted my feet as my cock swelled and pushed against the metal. I felt moisture leak out the tip and was unable to do anything about it.

"Hmm, you like that. You like bondage, Owen?"

How could I deny it? And even more relevant, why would I?

"Yes, I do, Sir. I love it."

His bare hand connected with my ass, the loud smack startling me as much as the sudden sting of pain.

"Ow." The word came out before I could stop myself, sounding ridiculous in this setting.

"We can incorporate some interesting bondage into our pony-play sessions," Kamal said; then his eyes narrowed. "Did you say, 'Ow'?"

"Fuck," I said. "Maybe?"

Kamal stared at me until I remembered where I was. "Sorry, Sir."

"I should think so." He sounded stern but I could swear the two of them were trying not to laugh. Jensen had his hand in front of his mouth, ostensibly to swat a bug away but the skin beside his eyes wrinkled briefly.

Those fuckers. Now they were laughing at me.

"Turn around, Owen," Kamal said. "Face the wall."

Oh, crap. Now what had I done?

I turned.

"Closer—so you can press your forehead against the wall without falling over."

I got myself into position, my heart rate increasing. The dark wall with its shiplap beams felt rough against my forehead.

Shit, fuck, shit. Now he was going to do what exactly? Shove a pony tail up my ass? Paddle me with a two-by-four?

My imagination ran wild.

"Relax," Kamal said.

I felt his hand on my back, above where my arms were bound. It was heavy and warm and full of reassurance. I needed it.

"What's your safeword, Owen?"

My brain scrambled for purchase. It was hard to think with everything else going on. "Like, my normal one? That I usually use?"

"Yes."

"Pineapple."

Kamal barked a laugh. "Really?"

"Yes, Sir. It's what I've always used." I felt called-out but wasn't sure why.

Kamal moved behind me and pressed his body against me, causing an unintended groan to leave my mouth. A sizeable erection pressed against me through his jeans. His hand slid around my torso, and his fingers found my nipple, rubbing it, pinching, as I made embarrassingly vulnerable sounds.

"Pineapple is one of my favourite things, Owen. How on earth did you know that about me?" he murmured in my ear, his warm breath tickling the nerve endings while his fingers on my nipple made my eyes roll back.

"Lucky...guess?" I panted, voice low and gravelly with lust. I had begun to understand this pony-play thing. We weren't exactly playing pony as of yet, but the whole objectification and bondage and domination thing was already working for me. Especially because Kamal smelled so good, and sounded so good, and felt so good...

His fingers pinched harder, and I groaned, feeling my cock drip fluid over the metal bar. He held on, the pain jabbing deep inside but becoming pleasure in my gut and then pain in my captured cock.

I gasped.

He let go and backed off.

I stood with my forehead against the wall, shaking and panting.

Holy shit.

He'd barely touched me, and I'd gone to pieces. It had been a long time since I'd subbed for anyone remotely effective.

"Hand me the crop, Jensen."

"Sure."

I didn't dare turn to look.

"We might as well demonstrate where the ranch got its name."

"Great idea," Jensen said. I heard the smile in his voice.

Fucker. Kamal was a goddamn pro.

The cage was starting to bother me. I was so turned on and my cock wanted in on the party. But the pain kept making it retreat, then swell again. It was a vicious, vicious cycle.

The leather tip of the crop traced a line from the small of my back over my ass and down between my thighs as Kamal said, "Spread your legs."

I closed my eyes and moved my boots farther apart, the soles squeaking on the polished wood.

Kamal pushed the tip between my legs, nudging at my balls with enough force that I squeaked in fear. It retreated down my inner thigh and across the back of my knee and up to my ass.

When the crop came down on my right buttock, I was completely unprepared and made a startled sound.

"Owen, I want you to feel free to use your safeword whenever you need to. If something's not right physically, or mentally, or emotionally, feel free to use it. I'll never be upset."

He brought the whip down in the same spot. This time my skin burned and throbbed.

"I need to know how you're feeling, and if you need to take a break. It's important for us to communicate. Understand?"

"Yes, Sir," I said between gritted teeth. I'd never been struck with my arms bound behind me. My helplessness caused a strange, uneasy feeling.

He brought the stick down hard on my other buttock. "How are you feeling right now, for instance?"

"Scared. Amazing. Perfect."

The words were out before I could stop them. They were true. This was what I'd been looking for. A Dom who scared me a little, who wouldn't put up with any shit, who was experienced and not playing games. I blew out a long breath in relief. I'd been right to come here.

"Good. That's good to hear." He brought the crop down again in the same spot. "Are you going to be a good little pony for me, Owen?"

I couldn't help smiling a little and was glad he couldn't see. "Yes, Sir. I'm going to be your perfect little pony." My dick throbbed in its cage, and my ass sang with the sting of Kamal's whip, and I was in heaven.

I doubted I could be anyone's perfect anything, but I was sure as hell going to try. I wanted to do my best to obey Kamal but also to please him.

He began to lash the sensitive backs of my thighs, gently, but enough to get my attention. My forehead had begun to hurt from pressing against the arena wall even though most of my weight was on my legs. The crop stopped coming down, and I felt someone grab my arms where they were bound and pull me up straight.

Kamal spun me around to face Jensen.

"See the pretty pony, Jensen? Look at his cock. It's leaking and trying to break free. That's what we want. Most of the men who come here are looking for straight out domination and objectification, but they also want caring, loving attention. They can get that as pets and service animals, when they're too scared or stunted to ask for it from human lovers back home."

Jensen nodded, eyes fixed on my cock, and then he tracked up my body to lock his gaze on mine. "Sure. That makes sense."

It did make sense. Even I could see that.

"Even though we treat these ponyboys like dumb animals, we make sure they get loving care and affectionate praise as if they were cherished pets."

While Kamal spoke, he pushed his long fingers through my hair, kneading my scalp, sending shivers and electric shocks through my body. "They'll usually do whatever I ask for a chance at an encouraging slap to the rump or even a smile. They want to please you. So, let them and encourage them."

He grabbed a fistful of hair and yanked my head back, running the fingers of his other hand over my collar and exposed throat while my brain exploded and my cock throbbed. "But never let them forget who's the boss either."

"I see," Jensen said. "He likes that."

I couldn't help whimpering as Kamal held me in place. His broad hand flattened over my throat with the hint of a threat, then slid lower, over the chest piece of the body harness, to my heaving belly to play tenderly with the hairs that led into my groin under the pelvic straps. His fist still gripped my hair. The pain in my scalp, the low hum of heat and residual sting from the crop, and the squeezing agony of the cock cage all combined to lift me to a level of intense desire I wasn't sure I'd ever reached before.

This was the real deal. This was what I'd been searching for. I'd finally found it.

"Let's go outside."

Chapter Six

They took me out into the bright summer sun to the grassy paddock. Kamal held my arms and propelled me forward while Jensen led the way. I tried not to look at Jensen's ass in his tight jeans, but it was hopeless. I was surprised the fucking fence posts didn't turn me on right now, the state I was in.

God, if Simon could have seen me now, all geared up and controlled and debased. He would have run screaming to his mommy.

We'd left the others in the arena. I'd had a glimpse of Biskane trotting around the ring that caused a surge of lust inside me, but I'd been largely unaware of anyone but Kamal and Jensen for the past half hour. Or hour. I wasn't sure how much time had passed since I'd entered the large barn. And now we were out in the heat of the morning as the sun climbed higher.

Kamal pushed me forward into the paddock.

"Stand."

One word, but I did as he asked, standing still and trying to calm my breathing. He walked around in front of me and stood there, crossing his arms and gazing at me sternly. "You want to be a good pony?"

I licked my lips, staring back, squinting in the brightness. "Yes, Sir."

"Then you need to learn to trot."

I could do that. How hard could it be?

I started to move, but he held up his hand and barked, "Wait."

I froze, moving my boot back to where it had been.

He smiled, pleased at my recovery. "I have some further instructions."

"Yes, Sir."

"Trotting is done at a jogging pace, and you need to be careful at first because I don't think you're used to running with your arms bound behind your back, are you?"

"No, Sir." *Good point.*

"It will be difficult and feel unnatural at first, so go slow. If you lose your balance and think you're going to fall, curl your shoulder in so you roll when you land. That will distribute the force of the fall. I brought you out here because the ground is softer than the floor. Some trainers don't care. Maybe they want their ponyboys more motivated not to fall."

He reached out to cup my chin and stared into my eyes. "But I think you're pretty motivated to please me, so I'm not concerned about anything but your safety." He dropped his hand and stepped back. "Jensen is going is run beside you, and if he sees you start to lose balance he'll steady you, but only for the first round or two."

"Yes, Sir. Thank you, Sir," I said, glad to be so well-cared-for. It lit a flame inside me that burned in the background of my desire.

He nodded and gestured to Jensen, who moved close.

"Around the ring four times, please." The lines beside his eyes deepened as he smiled, and I clung to that as I set out, Jensen beside me, to learn my first task as a BCR ponyboy.

Trotting. Can't be too difficult.

But it was. Having my forearms pinioned behind my back felt completely unnatural and strange. I stumbled almost immediately, and Jensen steadied me with a hand to my shoulder, murmuring, "Easy now."

I shook him off. I could do this. It was only jogging, and I'd get used to the position soon enough. I heard Kamal's quick laughter in the background, which only spurred me on. I wanted to impress him.

I sped up, trying to keep my centre of gravity, well, *centred*, which was challenging. I'd never jogged with my posture so straight before, but I guess that was the point. I had to learn how to do it and how to perform the motion as easily as possible, so I might as well start now.

"Careful," Jensen said as I stumbled again but quickly recovered myself and kept moving, determined to prove to them both I was a natural. My swelling dick in its metal cage proved a constant distraction, although my focus on the task helped my desire diminish and cleared my head.

I went faster, feeling confident in my technique and hoping I didn't look like a complete idiot. I rounded the corner and was trotting back to Kamal when it happened.

A buzzing insect came at my face and without thinking I tried to swat it away, forgetting my arms were restrained. The sudden action caused me to lose my balance, and I canted away from Jensen and toward the fence. In horror, I realized I was going down and tried to curl my shoulder like Kamal had told me as everything unfolded in slow motion.

"Shit," Jensen swore, reaching out to grab me, wrapping his hand around my bicep but unable to do anything more than steer me away from the fence as I fell onto the grass and dirt, my arm screaming with the pain of impact. I rolled to my chest and scrambled with my knees to get some of the pressure off my arm and instinctively protect my junk, rolling around on the grass like a roped calf. I felt like a fool and panted into the dirt until Kamal's face dropped into view.

"Well, that's one way to get my attention."

I blinked at him, wondering what to do. There was no way I could stand by myself.

"I told you to go slow," he said, amused rather than angry. "Are you hurt?"

I coughed and cleared my throat, not sure I could speak. The impact had knocked the air out of me.

"He landed on his arm," Jensen said, "I tried to grab him but he went down fast."

"Yeah, I saw," Kamal muttered, running his hand along my shoulder and bicep, pressing gently in certain spots. "I think he's okay. Nothing feels broken or dislocated. I'm sure it hurt, though."

I grunted and tried to speak. "I'm...so...stupid," I gasped, still coughing.

"You're not stupid, Owen. You're trying hard for me, and I appreciate that." He was crouching beside me and smiling. "Would you like to stand or do you want to lay there for a minute? You came down pretty hard."

"Stand. But I need help," I said, voice raspy.

"Are you sure you're okay?"

"Yes, Sir. It's probably the cigarettes."

"What?"

I managed to inhale a deep breath finally. After a few of these, the coughing subsided.

"The cigarettes, Sir."

"You're a smoker?" Kamal said, eyebrows raised.

"Not anymore. And I didn't smoke much or for very long. I quit before I came here."

"Oh. Well, that's good."

"Yeah. But maybe my lung capacity isn't the greatest."

Kamal nodded. "No doubt. But it should improve quickly. How long did you smoke?"

I shrugged. "Like, three months?"

"Oh. Well, that's not too bad."

"Only ever five a day. No more than that, Sir."

"How reasonable," Kamal said, hooking a hand under my elbow.

Jensen grabbed my other arm and they helped me up from the ground, brushing grass and dirt off my knees and elbows. I felt a tickle where I shouldn't and looked down to watch Kamal pull a buttercup out of my cock cage.

He held it in front of me with one eyebrow raised. "This is no time to pick flowers, Owen."

I couldn't help fighting a smile at his joke, even though I felt humiliated and sore. Figured I'd make an ass of myself on my first day.

I shoved my bottom lip out and huffed enough air to lift the bangs off my forehead. "Funny."

Kamal dropped the flower and glanced at Jensen before turning back to me. "How's your arm now?"

I gazed at him fiercely. "Fine, Sir."

"Good. I want you to trot around the ring again. This time, go *slow*."

Ah fuck. Fine. "Yes, Sir."

This time I paid attention to what my feet were doing, to my centre of balance, and kept my pace slow until Kamal urged me to step it up. By the end of my first lesson,

I was confident in my ability to trot like a proper ponyboy. It was tricky and required concentration if I wanted to avoid another fall. But I knew I could do it. I did my final few turns around the ring on my own, while my trainers watched and chatted together by the fence.

I felt good. The endorphins from the exercise flooded through me. I felt alive and energized. My dick was more comfortable in the cage because the workout had taken my mind off all of that.

As I stood there sweating and panting, chest rising and falling, legs aching from the workout, arms sore from being restrained, Kamal came up to me and pushed the damp hair off my forehead, so he could look me in the eyes.

"I'm pleased with you. You gave it your best today, Owen."

"Thank you, Sir. I'm glad."

He seemed to be probing me for something, trying to plumb the depths of my soul with that intense gaze. Jensen stood off to the side, his arms folded on the fence railing, staring off into the distance. I wondered for a second what he might be thinking about.

"Do you like to please me, Owen?" Kamal said in a voice that poured through my ears like the trickle of soft sand.

I opened my mouth but nothing came out. I swallowed thickly as my cock filled the cage once more. "Yes, Sir."

Kamal stared hard at me for a moment longer, then smiled. "Good. Then, I think we'll work fine together."

He glanced down at my caged cock and flicked it with his finger. "You were a very good ponyboy today. Would you like to come now?"

I stared at him, not comprehending what he'd said. "Come? Now?"

He laughed, and I saw Jensen had turned back to watch.

"Yes. My ponyboys get rewarded for a good session. And this was a good session."

I looked down at my cock, swelling painfully in the bars of the cage, and thought about everything I'd seen and done since I'd arrived. Images of Kamal and Biskane and Jensen flashed through my brain as I nodded and murmured. "Yes, Sir. Please, Sir."

Kamal reached out, and with a few flicks of his fingers, unfastened the cage and slipped it off my dick. As my cock swelled and lengthened, I groaned with relief.

"Isn't Lipke a Jewish name?" Kamal said unexpectedly, examining my growing cock with confusion.

"Yeah. My dad's a lapsed Jew. My mom's kind of a hippie. She said she didn't even consider it when I was born, and my dad didn't care one way or the other."

"Ah," Kamal said, as he wrapped his hand around my dick and pulled me forward so I was standing up against him, chest to chest. "Well, in my culture they always do it. It's a tragedy, when an uncut cock looks so much better." He began to stroke me slowly. "Works better too."

The pre-come that had gathered at the tip now served as lubrication under my foreskin, so Kamal could jerk me pretty easily without using anything else. I stared wide-eyed at his hand moving the skin of my cock back and forth in a lazy way as the pleasure built and built.

Jensen watched avidly from a distance. I wondered what it must be like working at the BCR every day, watching these sex games all the time. Did you get bored after a while or did it get you hard every time you saw it?

He seemed into watching Kamal jerk me off, and I figured it would keep its appeal. Guys loved to watch other people come, almost as much as they liked to come themselves.

Kamal stopped for a second and reached in his pocket, pulling out a small tube of lubricant. In a moment he had me lubed properly and worked me with gusto, using long hard strokes that had me at the edge in a few moments.

He lifted his chin as I shook the hair out of my eyes again, staring into his deep-brown orbs. He was only slightly taller than me.

"Come for me, pretty pony," he said in a low voice as I spilled over his fingers with a soft cry. He kept stroking until I'd spent myself, then lifted his hand to my lips. "I don't have a towel."

I opened my mouth and sucked his long, muscular fingers inside, cleaning my spunk off with my tongue. Kamal didn't make a sound but watched me intently, then pulled his hand away when I'd finished.

"Excellent job today, Owen," he said. "They'll hose you down in the grooming barn and you've got the afternoon free. I'll see you at supper."

"Yes, Sir."

"Jensen, can you take him? I want to check the fence on the far side. It looks like it might need a repair."

"Sure," Jensen said, picking up my lead rein from the rail and attaching it to my collar. Kamal handed him the empty cock cage.

"See you at one o'clock," he said to Jensen, then quirked his lip. "Learning anything?"

Jensen grinned. "Yes. It's amazing watching you work, Kamal."

"Think you'll enjoy being a trainer?"

"I just might."

"Yeah, I have a feeling you got some practice in with Luke and Noah when they were here. Unofficially."

Jensen blushed and looked at his boots, then glanced at Kamal. "Not telling."

"You don't have to. I can read you like a book." He laughed and saluted us as Jensen turned and led me back to the grooming barn.

*

The hose-down wasn't as pleasant as the complete rub-down, but it served to get the obvious dirt off, and at least the water was warm.

I glanced at Biskane and Jake when they came in looking haggard and exhausted and wondered how long until we'd be in shape for ponyboy life and not wrung out after every session. Then again, it looked like everyone had gotten their cage off so that could also affect a guy's energy. I wondered if that was a standard practice here at the BCR? Perform well—get a hand job? If so, I was definitely in the right place. Seemed like a pretty legit way to motivate a guy.

Sure enough, Enzo gave a little whoop, and we looked over. He held his hand up with all three cages dangling from his fingers. "Looks like you lot were very well behaved today! Good on ya. Let's keep it up this week, yeah? Better to go home happy and leave your trainers satisfied than end up scrubbing floors at the main house in your pony kit," he said with a laugh as he flung the cages into the sterilizer.

I blanched at the idea of that utter humiliation and vowed then and there that I would do everything Kamal asked of me with a smile on my face and a song in my heart. Besides, how hard could it be?

*

Back at the bunkhouse, we headed for the showers to clean up. It had been a stressful, eventful morning and nobody spoke as we washed the sweat and dirt of the day off.

After drying I pulled on a clean pair of boxers and walked to my bunk, searching in my duffel bag for a pair of shorts and a T-shirt. When I was dressed, I wandered to the kitchenette and scarfed down a bagel with cream cheese and an apple, while the others grabbed snacks and drifted to their bunks. We didn't speak as it seemed weird to have gone through what we had together. Presumably, within days it would become a normal part of our existence here at the ranch.

As I walked back, Andrei looked up from where he lay on his bunk reading a book. He raised his eyebrows with a questioning expression.

"So?" he asked quietly. "How did it go?"

I didn't even know how to reply. "Good. Really good. Fucking strange. But really good."

He seemed relieved. "Okay. Good."

I climbed up and lay on the thin mattress, folding my arms over my chest and staring at the ceiling. Memories from the morning flitted through my brain. My muscles were sore and my arm hurt from the fall. I felt tired and well used and better than I'd felt in a very long time.

My experience with Kamal and Jensen had exceeded my expectations. I'd hoped the staff would be competent and capable. I hadn't expected the sheer talent and charisma of the trainers at the BCR.

After a few moments, I sat up and reached for my bag again, searching for my sketchbook and pencils. I found them easily and sat cross-legged on my bunk, flipping to a blank page and beginning to sketch the outlines of a face.

Chapter Seven

By the time the other ponyboys returned from their afternoon sessions, I had recovered from the intense exercise of the morning but still felt thrown by the level of emotion I'd experienced under Kamal's domination. I watched Sam intently as he returned to the bunkhouse, looking shaken and drained. I knew he was Kamal's afternoon charge, and I wondered if he'd had the same experience as me.

"Hey," I said, leaning over the edge of my bunk. "How did it go?"

He seemed to have stars in his eyes as he looked at me. "Amazing. That guy is a fucking pro."

"Did he take you out to the paddock?"

"No. I think it was too hot. He had me trot around the arena though. Thank fuck for air conditioning."

"Did you fall? It's tricky with the armbands, huh?"

"No. I mean, I almost did a couple of times. Did *you* fall?"

Oh, nice going, Owen.

I blushed. "Unfortunately, yes."

"Don't worry. You'll get the hang of it."

My cheeks burned. Why did he have to go and show me up by being the perfect pony for Kamal when I couldn't even jog once around the ring?

Sam was the quintessential American boy next door, albeit Canadian. I think he was from New Brunswick. But he looked like every little schoolgirl's (and gay boy's) dream of the blond quarterback with his "Awe shucks" features and bright-blue eyes, whereas I had way more emo bullshit going on than I wanted. I should have cut my hair really short, so I'd at least look tough.

"Yeah, thanks." I rolled onto my back and stared at the ceiling again. I wondered how awesome Sam must have looked in his pony gear. The thought of Kamal staring at Sam the way he'd looked at me gave me a sour taste. Which was completely stupid and ridiculous.

I couldn't control how Kamal felt about Sam, and I couldn't control how Kamal felt about me. All I could do was try my best to be a good little ponyboy, and I'd get everything I wanted from this experience; namely, expert domination, humiliation, objectification, control, and some sexy playtime now and then as a reward.

I didn't need more than that to be happy.

*

When we headed to supper at the main house, Biskane walked beside me. His hair, out of the braid and now held back from his face in its standard ponytail, revealed his aristocratically sculpted cheekbones and delicate jawline. He was an intensely handsome man. At least Kamal wasn't training Biskane. That would have killed me. There was no way in hell I could compete with that.

"Your hair is epic," I said.

He smiled. "Thanks. I've been growing it since I was twelve."

"Anyway, it's beautiful. I like it in the braid, too, even though that's kind of a stereotype since you're indigenous."

Biskane stopped dead and placed his hand on his heart, looking at me with an affronted expression. "I'm... *what?*"

I swallowed as my heart jumped into my throat. "Oh shit. Aren't you? You look like—" I stopped, feeling like anything I said would dig the hole deeper.

Biskane's mouth broke into a broad smile, and he barked a laugh, making finger guns at me. "Gotcha."

I stared at Biskane. "You fucker. I thought I was in so much trouble."

"Well, you shouldn't make assumptions." He grinned.

I waved my hand at him. "Fine. I guess the braid is a non-issue. Fuck you."

"Yeah, I like it. I braid my hair pretty often. And yes, since you didn't ask, I'm indigenous."

"Cool."

"Yeah, I think so."

"How did it go with Hiro?" I really wanted to get off the topic of Biskane's heritage.

He blushed and cleared his throat. "Fine. I like him."

"That's good."

I wondered what happened if a ponyboy and a trainer didn't click? Did they switch us around? I sure hoped not. Because they'd have to tear me away from Kamal kicking and screaming.

By the time we got to the house I was sweating in the heat and wishing I had a cowboy hat like Jensen, or at least a baseball cap. There was shade under the awning they'd left up from the day before at least. I caught sight of Kamal at the barbecue, turning some of the meat, and my stomach did flip-flops.

Those hands holding the silver tongs had been on me earlier. One of them had jerked me off. The mouth that had given me orders and whispered in my ear curled into a smile as he chatted with a gorgeous woman in white shorts and a pink tank top. I shuddered. Then shook my head from side to side to get rid of those memories.

Those memories didn't matter right now. I was Owen, and he was Kamal. What happened in the arena or in the paddock didn't apply to our relationship in the real world. There was nothing to be embarrassed *or* excited about.

I turned away to clear my head and when I glanced back, my gaze drawn to Kamal, he regarded me with a strange look. But he quickly schooled his features into a generalized greeting as he smiled and saluted me with the tongs.

I felt like a teenage girl whose crush suddenly noticed her existence. Despite the things I'd told myself, my body reacted to his gaze in a visceral way, and now my stomach was in knots, and my dick swelled like it wanted to say hi to Kamal too.

Then the craving for a cigarette hit me so hard I could taste it.

Fuck it. What was wrong with me? The only thing to do was distract myself.

"Hey, Jake," I said, swinging onto the bench of the table where he'd sat down. Biskane slid in beside me.

"Hey," Jake said.

We hadn't spoken since the day before when we'd gone on our walkabout with Jensen.

"I heard through the grapevine you got Jensen *and* Kamal. What the hell was that like? And if you say it was awful I might have to punch you." He looked like he was totally serious until he winked.

I smiled and picked up an apple from the platter in the middle of the table, taking a bite. I chewed and swallowed, then licked my lips and wiped the juice from my chin. "Well, it was interesting. I wasn't prepared for it, to be honest."

"Like you can be prepared for any of this," Biskane muttered, laughing softly. "I've done some pet play before but nothing on this level."

Jake nodded. "No kidding."

"You have the female trainer, right? Laura?" I said.

Jake rolled his eyes. "Lorraine. Yeah. Fuck my life."

I laughed. "That bad, huh?"

He laughed. "No. That good. She is fucking gorgeous and she looks like that sweet girl you knew in high school who shared her lunch with everyone but she is fucking relentless." He scanned the crowd of people in the yard. "That's her, there," he said, nodding toward a group of people where the woman in the white shorts who had been speaking with Kamal was standing with a beer in her hand as she laughed.

"Holy shit," I said. "*That's* your trainer?"

Jake sighed happily. "Yep. She's already got me by the fucking balls and it's been one morning."

"Wow," Biskane murmured, trying to watch Lorraine surreptitiously.

I, on the other hand, stared and took in the beautiful almond-skinned woman who was Jake's trainer.

She was probably only five and a half feet tall and slim as a dancer, with deep-chestnut hair that reached to her waist in a loose ponytail. Her features were delicate and small. A silver stud sparkled in her nose. There was definitely something about her. Even I, a gay man, could appreciate her aesthetic appeal.

She turned and caught me looking. I smiled, so it wouldn't seem creepy, and she smiled back. That was when her true beauty emerged.

"Oh shit, she's coming over," Jake said, glancing around as if he wanted to escape. "Nice going, Owen."

"What? It wasn't my fault."

"No one else was gaping at her."

"I wasn't fucking gaping at her, I was admiring—"

"Why don't you introduce me to your friends, Jake. They seem to want to get to know me." Lorraine gracefully perched herself on the edge of the picnic table by my elbow as the heat rose in my cheeks.

I hadn't done anything wrong, but she immediately made me feel as if I had as she stared right at me.

"Hi," she said, grinning.

Jake cleared his throat. "Hello, Ma'am. This is Owen and this is Biskane."

"Hi. I'm Lorraine," she said, holding out her hand to me and then to Biskane. We shook and she touched me on the shoulder. "How did you like your trainers, Owen? Bet you didn't realize you'd have two, eh?"

I nodded. "It was quite a surprise."

"A nice surprise?"

I smiled. "Sure. Nice." I wasn't going to tell her how terrifying it had been to have two sets of eyes on me and everything I did.

She chuckled and ruffled my hair like I was a kid in her elementary school class. She reminded me of a teacher. That teacher that always smelled amazing and had cool jewelry and a fun home life and made the classes interesting.

"I'm teasing you, Owen. I'm sure it was alarming for a brand new ponyboy." She smiled at me warmly. "I'm sure you pleased them immensely this morning. I saw you in your gear and, whew, my, my, my, so sexy."

Me and the other ponyboys gazed desperately at each other, unsure how to reply until a voice nearby suggested, "Thank Lorraine, and ask her when the food will be ready."

I swiveled my head to look up at Kamal, who had come over without a word and stood there, gazing down at me with something that seemed like understanding.

"Thanks," I murmured, not daring to ask about the food.

"Geeze, Kamal, am I that scary?" Lorraine asked, gazing at us.

Kamal laughed. "Oh, you're terrifying, and you know it."

Lorraine tossed her head, sending her ponytail across her back. "Oh, yes, that's true," she said as if she'd forgotten. "Anyway, Owen said he enjoyed having two trainers this morning."

"Did he?" Kamal asked, sipping his beer. "One not enough?"

"Oh, you're enough for anyone," Lorraine laughed. "But who could object to Jensen, our resident cowboy."

Kamal nudged my shoulder, and I glanced up at him, feeling put on the spot and not relaxed at all. "How are you feeling about this morning?"

"Fine," I said defensively, glancing at the others. "Fine."

"How's your arm?"

The heat rushed to my cheeks. "It's fine. I'm fine." Did everyone need to know about my mishap?

"You fell pretty hard."

"I'm fine," I said again in a firm voice, begging Kamal silently to shut the fuck up. The other ponyboys regarded me with sympathy.

Great.

"Owen," Kamal said sternly, and suddenly I was in the paddock again.

"Yes, Sir?"

"Relax. Nobody cares that you fell. We want to make sure your arm feels all right." Kamal said, staring at me intently and raising the beer bottle to his lips.

He took a lazy sip. I focused on his lips on the bottle, my cock twitching. He let the bottle drop to his side and licked his bottom lip. "Wouldn't want you to miss a session."

God, no. I didn't want to miss a session either.

"No, Sir. Honestly, it feels okay. A little sore but not that bad."

"Good. It may feel worse in the morning. We'll evaluate it then. I can make accommodations if it's bothering you."

"Yes, Sir," I said, wanting this conversation to be over. "Thanks."

"Hey," he said, making me look up at him again. He smiled, a kindness that made my belly relax a bit. "It's your first day. Give yourself a break. You did great."

"Yes, Sir."

"Get some supper, and I'll see you in the arena tomorrow."

"Yes, Sir."

Lorraine stood and gave us a cute little wave. "Bye."

*

Back in the bunkhouse, Biskane approached me. "I think he likes you."

"What?" I said, leaning over the side of the bunk, taking my earbuds out. Biskane was so tall we were at eye level. "Who?"

Biskane laughed and shook his head. "Kamal."

I rolled my eyes. "Well, he likes my ass. Likes to whip it. Probably looking forward to doing a lot of other things to it."

Biskane nodded, looking slightly uncomfortable. "You *do* have a great ass."

I stared at Biskane, enjoying the way his broad mouth moved when he spoke, and the way his soft, dark eyes were looking at me. I assessed him. Was he interested? Because I definitely was.

"Thanks. You too."

He looked down at the ground, shy all of a sudden, but smiling. He cleared his throat and looked around.

The others were nowhere near us at the moment. He crossed his arms on the guard rail of my bunk, glancing at me shyly. "There's nobody in the showers right now."

His statement hung in the air between us. We stared at each other silently. Biskane's red tongue came out and stroked along his upper lip and my cock responded.

"Really?" I said, affecting disinterest. "How about that."

He laughed. "If you come in there with me, I promise it will be worth it."

Well, how could I resist?

I put my crossword puzzle down and swung over the side of my bunk to the ladder as Biskane gave me some room. "I'll go first. You follow in a minute." I grabbed some clean shorts out of my bag like I was simply going to take a shower and walked casually to the washrooms.

It was a large room with benches and stalls, a couple of toilets, a urinal, and showers lining the walls further in. I decided it would be nice to clean the sweat of the evening off as well as possibly get a blow job or more, so I stripped quickly, piling my clothes on a bench, and got under a showerhead, turning the water on. I kept the temperature lukewarm in order to feel some relief from the heat of the day.

Wetting my hair, I closed my eyes and enjoyed the sensual feel of the water on my skin and the anticipation of what was coming.

I heard the door creak open and smiled, keeping my eyes closed, pushing my hand down my chest and belly, over the clean-shaven area around my erect cock, angling so Biskane would get the full view.

I heard his curse and the frantic divesting of clothes as I continued to stroke my body in a deliberately tantalizing way. If Kamal could only see me now. He'd stop worrying about my stupid arm and start thinking about how good I looked wet and naked in the shower. Why I was thinking about Kamal when gorgeous Biskane was heading my way, probably naked, ready to give me something very exciting, seemed ridiculous. I opened my eyes to see the tall, stunning man approaching me.

My eyes raked his slim form, noting the way his thin cock stood at a jaunty angle against his belly and the way his muscles rolled under his almond skin.

I lifted my chin, holding my dick and shaking water out of my eyes. "What exactly do you want to do in here?" I asked, breaths quickening.

He didn't say anything, his eyes running over me. He shrugged, smiling, and reached out to run a hand along my ribcage. "Maybe I can blow you," he said, eyes going to my cock.

I grinned. "Sure. That works."

He splayed both hands over my ribcage, thumbs rubbing my nipples. "You are so fucking cute."

I made a sound and gazed at that broad mouth, imagining it swallowing my cock. "Yeah, well you're *stunning*."

His eyes flew to mine. He seemed surprised. "You really think so?"

I gestured with my free hand to his tall frame. "Uh, yeah. Fuck, Biskane. Don't you know how you look? I mean, you must."

He shrugged, continuing to rub my nipples and eye my mouth. "I've been called everything from *Hiawatha* to *Indian Chief* to *Savage*, so my confidence in my appearance might have suffered a bit."

I frowned. "That's fucking tragic."

He shrugged again, giving me a tired smile. "I'm used to people making fun of me, not complimenting me."

To me, his stature and distinctly indigenous features were a large part of his appeal. I hated feeling guilty for appreciating this. "Well, I think you're beautiful."

"Thanks. I've been called *faggot*, too, which I imagine travels across racial lines."

I smiled sadly. "Yeah, it does. Anyway, you're a fucking gorgeous representation of Canadian masculinity. Hopefully you feel the same about me."

He smiled. "Oh, I do. I definitely do," he said breathily, then dropped to his knees and cupped my ass in his broad hands, looking up at me from below and rubbing his chin along my erection.

My mouth dropped open, and I gasped. "Whoa."

"*Whoa, stop*? Or, *whoa, I'm really into this*?"

I panted, putting my hand on top of his head, touching that smooth black hair. "I'm really into this."

"Good."

He kept rubbing my dick with his cheek, rough as it was even after a smooth shave this morning. Then he wrapped his long fingers around the base and opened his mouth, his pink tongue coming out to lap at my swelling cock.

"Fuck," I swore, trying to stay still while Biskane tortured me with his casual approach. "That feels good."

I hoped nobody else would enter the showers. Although maybe stuff like this happened in the bunkhouse all the time. It wouldn't have surprised me, honestly, to come upon something like this anywhere on the ranch, honestly. It was such a sexually charged place to be for men in the prime of their sexuality. Hopefully, if anyone did come in they'd turn around and go back out and give us ten minutes, which was probably all the time it would take. For me, at least.

"Aw, God, you taste good. You *smell* good," Biskane said, rubbing his nose along the length of me.

I didn't answer, just stared down at his mouth and lips and nose, wanting him to swallow me and make me come, but enjoying how he looked down there, savouring me like I was a gourmet meal.

He gazed at me with his rich brown eyes and licked a line from my taint to the tip of my dick while my chin dropped and I gasped in short bursts. Fuck, he was killing me.

"Holy shit," I panted. "I'm gonna come before you even get my dick in your mouth, B."

He moaned then and his hand squeezed me tighter. "Well, that would be a waste," he said, before he opened his mouth and plunged down on me.

My hand came out and slammed the wall to keep my balance. The force that suddenly worked my cock was a shock, and it only took me a minute or two before I stuttered a warning that he didn't heed and spilled down his throat, trying not to scream by biting my tongue and pressing my fingernails into my palm. What came out instead was a stuttering moan as the orgasm ripped through me and Biskane swallowed everything before slipping off me and licking his lips in triumph.

"Fuck," I said again, staring down at his smug face and beautiful features as the water rained over us. "That was amazing."

"You needed it," Biskane said, pushing off the floor and standing up. His height made me feel small and vulnerable. His dick pointed right at me.

"You want the same thing?" I asked, not one to take without offering to reciprocate.

His slow smile came as his eyes ran up and down my body again. "I'd love it."

I glanced around the washroom area. "Can we at least go into one of those stalls?" I asked. "In case somebody comes in?"

He looked behind him and then back at me. "Sure. We're wasting water."

"True." I shut off the water and grabbed a towel, throwing it to him. After I'd dried myself I wandered over to one of the changing stalls and went in, putting a clean towel on the bench for him and another on the floor for me.

When Biskane joined me, I pointed to the bench. "Your throne, Sir."

He laughed. "Yeah, thanks," he said and sat, his hand stroking his dick, his eyes on my chest, belly, and legs, before moving back to my face. He licked his lips.

I got down on my knees on the towel and placed my hands on his thighs, rubbing them back and forth. His legs were muscular and covered with a layer of soft dark hair. His cock stood from his neatly shaved groin, and he was uncircumcised, like me. I didn't care, one way or the other, except that uncircumcised cocks were sexier somehow. The wet glans peeking out of the foreskin, glistening and protected, but coaxed into the air like a reluctant sea creature.

"Mm, yummy," I muttered, wrapping my hand around him as he sat up straighter.

"God, you're cute," he said, using his hand to push the hair back from where it fell over my eyes. "You even look like a pony when you're not in gear."

I winked at him. "That was the plan. I almost cut my hair and then my friend, Tamara, suggested I leave it for exactly that reason."

He nodded. "Clever. You should grow it long like mine." His lips parted as I pushed his foreskin back and took the head of his cock in my mouth. "Oh, fuck. Oh, God."

All talk of hair length was forgotten as I worked Biskane's cock. He kept his hand on my forehead holding my forelock out of the way as I bobbed up and down, using spit and the motions of my hand to get him to the edge. His other hand clutched the edge of the bench, and his fingers tightened as he muttered, "I'm coming. I'm coming now," in a strained voice, right before his cock shot in my mouth. I let the fluid dribble out, nervous about swallowing, even though he'd swallowed mine, and we'd had to submit testing results to the BCR to get in. Old habits died hard, and I felt bad right afterwards.

"Sorry."

"For what?" he asked, wiping some of his spunk off my chin. "That's fucking hot, right there. So dirty."

I grinned and spat more out onto his belly and he laughed. His right front tooth was chipped which I hadn't noticed before.

"Is that from hockey? Your tooth?"

His expression went from jovial to suspicious in a moment, and I wished I hadn't said anything. "No. Not hockey." He seemed embarrassed. He shifted and I stepped back so he could get up. He used the towel he'd been sitting on to wipe up his belly.

"I'm sorry. I didn't mean anything." God, why did I have to open my big mouth?

"It's fine. Not a big deal," he tried to recover but I could see his eyes had dulled, and I hated to be the cause of that. "Y'know, people don't only throw slurs around."

"Aw, shit man." I didn't know what to say.

He took my chin in his hand, holding me firmly as he used a clean part of the towel to wipe the rest of his spunk off me, turning my head this way and that to make sure he got it all. Then he held me still and stared into my eyes with a fierceness that almost frightened me. Until he leaned forward and placed a chaste kiss on my lips.

"Thanks for the blow job, Owen," he said and let me go.

Chapter Eight

Lying in my bunk that night I thought about what had happened with Biskane in the shower. It had all been good. Until I'd mentioned his tooth. What horrible memory had I dredged up with that offhand comment?

I dug my sketchbook out of my bag and flipped to the drawing I'd completed the day before. Even from the paper, Kamal's serious eyes stared at me as if he wanted to punish me for something. I'd captured their intensity and intelligence and the way his lips pursed in frustration. My dick responded as if the subject of my sketch stood in the room with me.

"Psst, Owen," I heard from across the bunkhouse.

I looked over the rail to see Biskane lying on his bunk, reading a Steven King novel. He raised his eyebrows and nodded at me. "How are you feeling?"

I grinned. "Great. You?"

He smiled widely. "Relaxed and happy. Ready to pony it up tomorrow."

"Same," I replied. "Good night, B."

"G'night, Owen."

I stared at my sketch of Kamal for a few more minutes before I closed the book and shoved it back in my duffel bag.

*

My arm was a little sore in the morning, but not too bad. If anything, it made me more determined to avoid any accidents today.

In the grooming barn, I felt less self-conscious submitting to the routine procedures. I enjoyed the full-body massage and scrubbing Adrian gave me and found it grounding to be dressed in the pony gear and ball gag.

However, when Adrian picked up two items and waved them teasingly at me as we headed for the arena, I balked. My eyes widened and I stopped walking as I stared at what looked like a bridle and a butt plug horse tail.

Adrian winked. "Kamal told me to bring these with you today."

Jake and Biskane stared at the items Adrian held in his hands and glanced at me. I tried to process.

I mean, I knew I'd eventually have to wear them. I didn't think it would be on my second day. And it didn't seem like Jake and Biskane were being introduced to the formal tack so quickly.

Adrian laughed and tugged me forward. "Relax, Owen. It'll be their turn soon enough. Don't worry."

How could I not worry? I'd been put in pony gear for the first time yesterday and today I was getting the whole shebang? I started sweating and internally freaking out.

When Adrian brought me to Kamal he was alone, which gave me a little relief. At least I wouldn't have to worry about Jensen watching me get the bridle and tail treatment. At least not the first time.

Adrian handed the tack to Kamal. "He's freaking out."

Kamal grinned. "I can see that."

He perched himself on the edge of the table and regarded me calmly as Adrian left the arena.

Being the object of Kamal's steady silent gaze became overwhelming in a matter of seconds. He didn't say anything, just watched me carefully as he held the bridle and tail, contemplating.

If he wanted to stop me from freaking out, this wasn't the way to do it.

I made a noise of desperation and discomfort from under the gag.

Kamal stood and set the items he was holding on the table. He came over and unbuckled the gag, removing it.

"Good morning, Owen," he said.

I licked my lips, eyeing the items laying benignly on the table. I wasn't sure I was ready to be a proper pony yet but obviously Kamal thought I was. My eyes flew back to his.

He smiled.

"Jensen is busy this morning. His partners came for a visit. How is your arm?"

What?

"It's fine. A little sore. Uh, his partners, Sir?" I was curious.

What did he mean? Business partners? Did Jensen have some other operation on the side?

"Luke and Noah are here."

Luke and Noah? Who the fuck were Luke and Noah?

He ran a finger along my jaw and over my lips, parting my mouth and pushing his thumb inside. It was a bold and sexual invasion, and my cock strained within its bars as I accommodated him.

"They're his lovers, Owen. Jensen is a very lucky man."

Holy shit. Jensen had *two boyfriends*?

My eyes widened as I sucked and licked at Kamal's broad thumb and watched his eyes darken with reciprocal arousal. He slid his thumb out of my mouth and dragged it over my nipple, teasing me with its wetness and pinching hard.

I gasped. "*Fuck.*"

He let go and turned around, walking to the table, picking up the leather bridle.

Oh shit, fuck, damn.

"Luke used to be my favourite ponyboy here at the ranch," Kamal murmured. "He was a fucking handful, but he responded well to me."

Why was he telling me this?

"He and Noah had a secret relationship. They didn't tell anyone they were involved back home. And they continued to enjoy clandestine meetings here at the ranch when they could swing it."

Clandestine meetings. Meaning, they'd find a spot to fuck each other where the others couldn't see.

"Then Jensen showed up." Kamal grinned, remembering. "And Luke took an interest right away. I honestly thought he was playing with him, and I was worried about Jensen. But it turned out Luke had nobler intentions." Kamal shrugged. "Well, either that, or Jensen got under his skin."

I cleared my throat. "What did Noah think about it, Sir?"

Kamal chuckled. "Well, that was the strange thing. Noah seemed to like Jensen as much as Luke did." He glanced at me. "Then again, can you blame him?"

"No Sir." Jensen was fucking hot. And smart and sweet. At least from what I'd gathered so far.

"Exactly. But Jensen's future is here at the ranch. And Luke and Noah were only here for a session. So, they're together, but not. It's hard for Jensen. Luke and Noah share an apartment, I believe. And they try to visit when they can. And Jensen has a few days leave now and then, so he goes to them."

"That's...pretty awkward."

"It's not ideal; that's for sure. But if you have the chance to meet Luke or Noah, or both, you'll see why Jensen puts up with it. The three of them work really well together."

I stared at Kamal, wondering why he was telling me all this. I suspected it was to get me thinking about something other than what his intentions were with me today. It worked to a point. But I stared at that bridle in his hands, feeling fear and unease in the pit of my stomach.

"Who's your favourite ponyboy now?"

Kamal laughed. "I don't have one," he said, eyeing me up and down. "This session has only started."

I thought about Sam and his pretty-boy looks.

"Probably Sam," I muttered, stating my thoughts out loud.

Kamal regarded me contemplatively. He didn't say anything for a long moment. Then he held my gaze, his hand running lightly over his dick where it pushed against the crotch of his pants. He was hard. He was hard for me already.

"Probably," he said, even though the way he looked at me and the way he fondled himself told me otherwise.

But what did I care anyway? I wasn't here to be anyone's favourite. I was here for an experience. And if Kamal could give it to me, well, that was fine. But I wasn't out to be anyone's favourite. I'd be lucky if I could get through this without embarrassing myself too much.

Speaking of embarrassing...

Kamal came forward with the bridle. He held it in front of me as my pulse skyrocketed with apprehension.

"You're wondering why I had Adrian bring along these items. Why I didn't get him to put them on you."

"Yes, Sir."

He let me see the bridle from all angles. It was constructed of a few broad straps and buckles with a steel metal bit attached to steel rings at the side and with short reins hanging down with triangular handles.

"The bits and tails are sterilized after each use," he said. "We're pretty big on proper sanitation here as you can imagine. That's part of the stable hand's job."

He stepped forward so he stood right in front of me and I had to consciously stop myself from taking a step back. I inhaled the spicy sandalwood of his body wash and underneath it, his distinctive scent that was even more attractive.

"I like to get my ponyboys used to the bridle and tail fairly early. They're very important for what we do here, and it's all a part of the submissive process."

My eyes had gone wide, but I could see the logic of this.

"Yes, Sir."

It wasn't the bridle that scared me but the tail involved a whole other mindset. Having something in my ass wasn't the issue. But a butt plug tail?

I'd never engaged in animal play before so this was new and intriguing, not to mention terrifying. What if I didn't like it?

It didn't matter at this point. I was on a pony-play ranch. I'd have to fucking wear it and pretend to like it. I started to wonder if perhaps I should have thought about this longer before I'd agreed to take the immediate placement. But it was too late now. My cock was in a cage, and Kamal was about to put me in a bridle. I might as well accept it.

"Ready?"

Something about his question struck me as hilarious, and I started to laugh. This was absurd. We were two men standing in a room alone together—the others had already gone outside into the nice weather—and one man was going to dress the other man as a pony. It seemed ludicrous.

Kamal watched me closely as I dissolved into fits of laughter that I couldn't contain. He'd already bound my arms together, so I tried to balance while my body shook with unrestrained glee until tears slid down my cheeks. Finally, after a long time, I calmed and tried to regain my stature, breathing deeply to recover what I could of my dignity. There wasn't much left at this point. But I also knew Kamal was about to take whatever *was* left and stick a butt plug horse tail up it.

Fuck my ponyboy life.

"Are you finished, Owen?" he said, regarding me with a forced patience and the beginning signs of irritation.

Oh shit. I'd pissed him off. Now I was in for it.

"I'm sorry, Sir."

"Do you think this is funny?" he asked.

I didn't immediately reply. I was trying to decide if I should be honest or say something conciliatory.

"Owen," he barked, in a tone that made me jerk to attention. "I asked you a question. Do you think this is funny?"

He wasn't seriously asking me this, was he? Even though this was Kamal standing before me—a sexy, intimidating man who had a lot of power over me at the moment, something in me rebelled.

"Well, yeah? I'm naked and you're dressing me up as your pony? I think it's pretty fucking hilarious."

He remained silent as I reviewed my statement and realized I'd forgotten one important component: "Sir."

He grinned then, and that slow calm smile, accompanied by the determination in his dark-brown eyes, caused my mouth to go dry and my ass to clench in fear. And then he laughed.

A soft "Oh, you have no idea what's coming for you, boy" laugh that immediately made me want to turn and bolt out of the arena.

I started to take a step back, but he reached out and grabbed my chest harness and held me still. Then he jerked me forward so I almost fell, grabbed a fistful of my hair with the hand holding the bridle, and forced me to look at him. His brown eyes held an iron will that I worried he would apply to me with very little restraint in the aftermath of my disrespect.

"I'm glad you're amused, Owen. Because I'm going to tack you and work you so hard today you'll be very glad you had a moment of hilarity before your life took a turn for the worse."

I felt the heat of his breath on my face and the press of his erection from under his jeans against my hip.

Fucker was getting off on this. And, goddammit, so was I.

My cock ached in the cage, trying to swell and being hindered from it by the cruelty of the steel bars. But my heart pounded, and the pit of my stomach was on fire with arousal from his fist in my hair and the look in his eyes. I couldn't deny how I felt.

Kamal spun me around and marched me to the wooden table, folding me over and shoving the side of my face against its hard surface.

"As a professional, I need to remind you that you can safeword at any time, Owen. Do you understand?"

"Yes, Sir," I panted, eyes wide and body throbbing with need and fear. It was fucking exhilarating. There was no way I was safewording now. Things were getting interesting. All hilarity had left me as I was reminded of the seriousness of my predicament.

"Stay still."

He tossed the bridle onto the table. It landed with a thud, right where I'd have to stare at it through this whole procedure. I heard the snap of a glove, and I knew what was coming. When I felt Kamal's gloved fingers rub lube down the crack of my ass, I whimpered in anticipation.

Fuck, fuck, fuck.

"This what you wanted?" he said, fingering me roughly. "Open for me, Owen." I somehow forced myself to relax the sensitive muscle.

I groaned as he breached me, but welcomed that gloved digit like it was the only thing that could keep me grounded and focused. He pushed it deep and withdrew it, then plunged it in again—all the way.

I cried out with pleasure at the scratch and stretch as he pumped me unceremoniously, first with that finger, then two, then three.

"Better?" he said.

"Yes," I hissed, closing my eyes then opening them to focus on the dark leather straps of the bridle beside me. "Yes," I whispered.

Force me to obey. Make me your fucking pony. I couldn't do it willingly; it was too crazy. But this—this was heaven.

When I felt the hard rubber of the plug, I resisted and he slammed me into the table again. "Be still. I don't want to hurt you."

And my heart warmed to this man who manipulated my body so competently, easing in the butt plug with gentle persistence until my body accepted it, and I groaned with satisfaction.

"Now you're a fucking pony, Owen. You're *my* pony, and you're going to do everything I ask of you."

I moaned. "Yes, Sir."

"Good."

I'd pleased him even though he'd had to force me to obey. There was hope for me yet.

"Now let me fluff your pretty black tail," he said, and I felt a resurgence of my earlier hilarity until he pressed his body against me and I felt the seriousness of the erection he was sporting.

Fuck me. Fortunately, Kamal enjoyed a ponyboy who needed some encouragement to fall in line.

The coarse black fronds of real horsehair tickled my buttocks and thighs as he arranged it. I could imagine how it looked, not sure I wanted to see. But the intrinsic shame of having a horse tail plug in me caused my face and chest to flame. I'd signed up for this in a moment of temporary insanity without realizing how I'd feel about submitting to such indignities.

"Relax, Owen," Kamal said with affection in his voice as he slapped me on the ass. "You look wonderful."

His approval rushed into my ears and down to my belly, leaving a soft red glow there. I hated how easily I responded to him.

He grabbed my hair again, pulling me into a standing position, which caused the plug to feel even bigger and the hair of the horse tail to brush the backs of my knees. He splayed the fingers of his left hand across my throat as he held my head bent backward and spoke softly in my ear.

"I'm going to make you wear this tail every day now because you seem to have such a problem with it. I'm sure after two weeks you'll be used to it. Hell, you might even miss it when you don't have it."

Oh fuck. What had I done?

Chapter Nine

"Yes, Sir," I breathed, relaxing in his grip to let him know I would do everything he told me now I knew how seriously he took my submission and his job. I suppose my submission *was* his job.

"That's better. Now, do I have to fasten you to the wall or are you going to let me put this bridle on you without too much of a struggle?"

"No, Sir."

"I *don't* have to fasten you to the wall?"

"No, Sir."

"Good. Because I will not hesitate to do so if I think I need to." He shook his head and clicked his tongue. "You're a fiery thing, but you've got the ass of my dreams, and I want to spank it into next week."

Wait, where do I sign up for that?

He released my hair but kept his hand on my throat. I waited in that position, swallowing to feel my Adam's apple roll against his grip. Being so vulnerable to a man like Kamal was a heady thing. I didn't know what to expect.

I was startled by a kiss on my ear. My eyes fluttered closed from the surprising sweetness of it. Then Kamal slid his hand slowly—so slowly—along my throat and over my breastbone, sliding over the leather harness straps and down across the planes of my diaphragm which moved in and out with my laboured breaths. He continued moving it over the sparse hairs down the centre of my belly, over the pelvic strap to cup my poor captured cock. My mouth opened, and I gasped as the heat from his hand tormented my already tortured appendage.

Jesus fucking Christ. I'd never wanted to come so badly in my life before. And I knew it wasn't going to happen anytime soon.

"That's right, Owen." He murmured, tickling my balls with the tips of his fingers while he held me. "I control this," he said, jiggling the cage roughly, sending jolts of pain and pleasure through me.

"Yes, Sir," I moaned, thoroughly vanquished at this point—beyond anything resembling dignity or determination or rebellion.

"If you're a good pony for me, I may consider taking it off before I send you back to the grooming barn. Although after your display of emotion this morning, that's going to be a pretty hard sell."

"Yes, Sir," I said, trying not to struggle.

It was difficult to deal with the way I reacted to Kamal. I wanted to fight him, but not to get away. I wanted to turn around and rub myself all over him. I fought the urge, knowing he wouldn't let me, and it would simply make things even worse for me than they already were.

I had the strongest urge to kiss him. I imagined forcing his mouth open and shoving my tongue inside to fuck him that way, since he'd had my dick confined in such a cruel and inhumane device. Not a romantic urge—

I wanted to fuck his mouth with my tongue and make him lose control. Somehow, I figured it would take more than a fierce tongue-fucking from an upstart ponyboy to make Kamal lose control.

"Stay still. Eyes on the wall in front of you."

His voice did strange things to my insides. Sometimes it made me want to throw up, like when he said my name with that sharp bark that demanded immediate obedience. But other times, like now, it made me want to be the obedient pony I was sure I was capable of being, if I could only stop looking at it objectively. Kamal's direct manner definitely helped.

I did what he asked, trying to calm my breathing because I knew I would have to do some trotting and I didn't want to be winded before I began. I mean, it was kind of too late for that but, whatever.

The leather straps of the bridle dropped over my head and startled me. I jerked away as Kamal said, "Easy, easy," and settled me while he lifted the hair off my forehead so the broad strap sat against my skin.

"I love this, by the way," he said, flipping my forelock with his fingers. "I'm glad you didn't get it cut before coming here. Makes you look the part of a fiery little colt."

I grunted, opening my mouth as he pressed the steel bit into it and silently thanked Tam for her instruction to leave my hair alone.

"Good boy."

I shifted my feet as he pushed the bit between my teeth and fastened the chin straps. The steel rings where the reins attached felt cold against my cheeks, the metal unforgiving between my lips.

But it wasn't that bad.

In fact, the equine harness on my head, accompanied by the butt plug horse tail, proved a total mindfuck. I grunted, shifting my feet to feel the bulk of the plug in my ass, the horsehair tickling my thighs, and playing with the metal bit in my mouth as I tried to acclimate, not to the strange equipment, but to the fact I liked it. I shuddered from head to foot and whimpered when Kamal's hand slid around and lay flat against my belly.

He leaned forward to speak in my ear, and I felt his hardness against my hip through his jeans.

"Such a pretty pony."

I closed my eyes and whimpered again as fluid pushed from my aching, trapped cock as Kamal's other hand drifted down to find it.

"Oh, yes. Now *that* was the response I was hoping for," he murmured, swiping the wetness from the metal bars and lifting his fingers to my mouth, pushing them in alongside the bit as a part of my debasement.

I thought I might pass out it was so depraved and fucking hot. I tried to suck on Kamal's fingers, tasting the bitterness of myself, but the bit impeded me. Kamal pressed his fingers onto my tongue and played with the corners of my mouth where the bit held, completely objectifying me and showing me what he could do now that I was outfitted properly for my trainer.

"Fuuuuck," I moaned. It came out garbled and perverse because of the bit, as I dropped my head back against Kamal and his fingers slid out of my mouth and down to find my nipple and twist, hard. I cried out at the pain and the jolt of arousal that surged in my trapped cock as more fluid pushed out.

"Enough," Kamal muttered as he released me and stepped back, pushing me gently forward to counterbalance against the absence of his supporting weight.

I wobbled for a moment, eyes flashing open and regaining my balance as Kamal grabbed my arms and spun me around to face the arena door.

"Trot, pony," he said and shoved me forward, propelling me across the floor and shoving the door open when we got there, pushing me out ahead of him into the bright summer day.

The arena door slammed shut behind us as we moved quickly out to the far field, passing two smaller paddocks where Lorraine and Hiro were training their ponyboys.

By the time we got there, I was huffing, winded already—a tight wire of barely restrained desire. My body was a conduit of pain and pleasure as Kamal forced me to trot around the large paddock, yelling to lift my knees higher and stay closer to the fence while my brain tried to process everything that was happening.

He'd wrapped the reins together behind my head so they dangled and slapped against my neck and shoulders as I ran. The plug in my ass burned with its thick presence, and the horsehair tail stroked the back of my thighs, reminding me of what I was and how I would be treated for the rest of the morning.

But nothing dimmed the erotic bliss of being controlled by Kamal, defiled by his wishes to dress me in this gear and treat me like the submissive ponyboy he wanted. For the first time, I felt I could do this. Fate had sent me here to the BCR and Kamal, to discover my true desires and plumb the depths of my need for absolute submission.

"Faster, Owen! You're slowing down. Keep up!" Kamal shouted, and I heard the crack of a whip that sent lightning down my spine. When had he picked up a whip? And, holy fuck, what kind of whip was it? I caught a glimpse of the thing when I turned and realized it was a fucking bullwhip, like Indiana Jones used to wield, in the hands of my trainer.

"Two more rounds," he shouted, cracking the whip again and my legs worked for him, propelling my exhausted and abused body around the paddock two more times.

I fought exhaustion as I neared him and tried to keep from tripping as my tired legs kept me going forward. I pushed myself so far past the point of comfort that I couldn't stop and almost ran right into Kamal, who moved to the side and grabbed my bicep, spinning me around and holding me up as I collapsed, panting and coughing against him.

"Easy, easy," he murmured, keeping me steady and cupping my chin so I could meet his gaze. I could barely focus but the piercing intensity of his brown eyes helped. The breath rasped in my lungs as I tried to get enough, spit and drool running down my chin as Kamal wiped it away with his thumb.

"Easy, Owen, easy. Breathe."

I shook and trembled in front of him, trying to get my equilibrium and calm my frantically beating heart. I'd done the best I could for him and maybe it had been too much.

He led me over to the fence so I could lean on it while he opened a cooler that he must have placed here earlier. He grabbed a water bottle from under the ice. As he straightened, he twisted the cap off and held it out to me.

"Tilt your head back and open your mouth."

I did and Kamal poured cold water into my open mouth. It sloshed over my tongue and the bit and I swallowed what I could while some dripped over my lips and over the corners of my mouth. It was a messy way to get a drink but it cooled me off and soothed the ache in my throat.

When I'd slaked my thirst, Kamal lifted the bottle to his lips and drank. I watched his throat bob and move as he swallowed, feeling it in my cock. When he finished, he wiped his arm across his wet lips and smiled, tossing the empty bottle onto the ground.

"Well, you've compensated for your earlier defiance. Well done," he said, moving behind me and unwrapping the reins. "We're going to do something a little less taxing now. But it will still be a learning curve for you."

Shit. I wasn't sure I could walk, but I'd try to do what he wanted if it killed me.

"I'm holding the reins, Owen. And you're going to walk in front of me and go in the direction I'm guiding you. Got it?"

His request didn't sound so hard. I nodded and grunted.

"Listen to my commands, and do as I say, all right? This is pony training one-oh-one and it's pretty easy. You've already got through the hardest part."

Thank God. At least the trotting had given my dick a break. I'd forgotten about everything except the pains in my legs and lungs. But now, the thickness of the plug tormented me, and I felt the familiar ache in my cock as it fought the cage. Fuck it. I almost wanted to be running again.

The soft leather reins slapped my shoulders as Kamal barked, "Giddy-up!"

I moved forward as Kamal walked behind me holding my reins and pulling to turn me one way and then the other as we went back and forth across the paddock. I had an out-of-body experience as I saw myself being guided by this incredible rock of a man, completely at his mercy, tacked like fucking Black Beauty and loving every goddamn minute of it.

When he figured I'd had enough of a break, Kamal slapped the reins again, twice, repeating the giddy-up command and forcing me faster as he ran behind and guided me back and forth until I started to flag, panting and coughing from the exertion.

"Whoa," he muttered as he pulled back gently on the reins, slowing me to a welcome walk and finally a stop against the fence. I stood for him, wobbly and winded, as he rubbed his hand along the muscles of my arms and down my legs, squeezing and stroking and massaging me as I trembled with the effort of staying upright.

"Good pony," he praised me, and it sounded like fireworks going off to my tired brain. "Very good pony. That cough doesn't sound as bad. It should go away after a couple more weeks. It's good that you quit."

There was wetness on my face. I didn't know if it was sweat or tears, and I didn't really care. Because Kamal was praising me and stroking me and patting my rump with affection, and that was all that mattered.

He turned me toward the fence and pushed me forward so I was braced against it. Then I felt his fingers on the metal cage, fiddling with the clasp until it swung off my cock which swelled and filled like a balloon on a helium tank.

The relief and pleasure of this unexpected freedom almost made me pass out. I leaned against the fence as Kamal's lubed hand wrapped around me and stroked. I took in a shuddering breath as he pressed against me from the side and my hands clasped at empty air as my arms pulled in their bindings.

I gasped as Kamal stroked me slowly and firmly until clear fluid dribbled out my dick, and I teetered right on the edge. Then Kamal grabbed the base of the tail and shoved the plug roughly into me, and I came with a choked cry as semen shot onto the fence and arced to the ground.

"That's it, Owen. Good boy."

When the shudders ceased and I collapsed for real, Kamal pulled me close and held me up, cooing like the most conscientious pet owner to reassure me that I would be all right, that the day's events hadn't shattered my brain and body beyond all repair.

The BCR required a form signed by a medical doctor to attend a pony session and now I understood why. The physical requirements were substantial. My kink-positive doctor had laughed when I'd shown her the form and said, "Pretty please, will you let me go play pony?" She'd signed it with a laugh, and now I wondered if she'd been too hasty because at that moment I wasn't sure I could reassemble all of my preconceptions and beliefs into a comprehensible world outlook. My mind had been effectively blown, and I finally understood where the expression came from.

It didn't take long to realize the wetness on my face was from tears. Then I heard the sounds I was making as my body was wracked with involuntary sobs, and I became frightened I was going insane because I didn't know where the emotion was coming from. I hadn't cried in a very long time.

Kamal held me tight against his warm and muscular body, comforting and reassuring. When my humiliating performance finally subsided, I tried to apologize and became further embarrassed by how ridiculous it sounded over the bit. Another important lesson—speaking with a metal bit in your mouth was not a good look. Best to remain silent in future.

Somehow, he understood, and I was reassured by a soft chuckle and his fingers coming up to wipe my tears away. They smelled of salt and semen even though he'd cleaned himself with a handkerchief from his pocket. He was a professional, after all.

"Do you know how often this happens, Owen? With a ponyboy at some time in the first week?"

I shook my head roughly on his solid chest, feeling the bridle straps scrape against him and hoping it hurt because he'd put me through so much. But he only chuckled and grabbed my arms, forcing me to stand on my own, and stared at my sweat-and tear-streaked face with the most satisfied expression.

"Almost every single time."

I blinked, surprised. He must have seen the question in my gaze. I didn't try to say anything. I'd learned my lesson.

"It's the relief, I think. The feeling that finally they can let go and release this part of themselves that they always knew was there but could never satisfactorily appease before. And that it's a valid thing and not to be ridiculed or dismissed." He cupped my chin and delved deeply into my eyes. "Does that make sense?"

I nodded, because it made perfect sense. That was exactly how I felt. Like somebody understood me for the very first time and could give me what I needed. What I wanted so desperately.

Kamal held up the steel cage that had been on me all morning. "This is fucking soaked, Owen. You're going to need to drink a ton of water to replenish all the fluid you lost this morning in precome, sweat and the massive load of spunk you left on the fence." But he grinned, like that was the best outcome he could have expected from putting me in full tack on my second day. "Well done, my fiery little colt. Let's get you inside and get you something to drink."

He took the reins in hand and led me back into the arena, standing me by the table and disappearing into a back room. He came back with a bowl of water that he held up for me.

I'd expected him to take the bridle off and hand me another bottle of water, but this was better. While I dipped my chin into the cold water and slurped it up over the metal bit, he smoothed the damp hair from my forehead and told me how good I was, how well I'd behaved for him after he'd tacked me. I could have melted right there into a puddle of exhausted goo and kissed his dusty black boots.

Chapter Ten

In the grooming barn I barely had the strength to stand while Adrian removed the bridle and gently pulled out the butt plug tail, whistling to himself. "I keep forgetting how hardcore Kamal is. I can't believe he put you in full tack on your second day. Usually they work up to that."

He removed the rest of my gear and attached my wrists to the strap in the shower, hosing off all the sweat and dirt and fluid while the other two ponyboys were brought in with only the basic tack on, looking much less worse for wear than me.

Perhaps they had put up less resistance? Maybe it was easier for them to slide into pony play than someone who had never experienced anything like it before. Or their trainers simply had different techniques.

I couldn't deal with their curious looks, so I closed my eyes and let Adrian do his job, then dressed quietly and walked back to the bunkhouse alone. I needed to collect my thoughts after such a tumultuous morning.

My ass was sore from the stretch of the plug. Adrian had given me a tube of something to settle the irritation. I was grateful because I'd never had to run with a plug in my ass and it took some getting used to. My poor hole was complaining. And the sides of my mouth hurt from where the bit had stretched it. My arm was still sore from my accident in the paddock.

But despite the exhaustion and the emotional toll of the morning, I felt pretty fucking great. My head spun with everything I'd experienced and flashes of Kamal's deep-brown eyes haunted me. My dick was already coming back to life, and if it could have walked back to him, it would have.

I pulled open the door to the bunkhouse and stepped inside. A man I didn't recognize stood in the middle of the room, gazing about him as if he were a real estate agent assessing a property.

"Hi," I said, clearing my throat. I'd hoped I could slink in and climb into my bunk for a rest and process everything that had happened with Kamal.

The tall man with the skater-boy hairstyle turned and pinned me with narrowed blue eyes. "What's your name, ponyboy?"

I looked at him like a startled animal on the highway. "Owen."

He smiled, nodding. "Kamal's training you."

"Um, yeah," I managed, my thoughts scrambled and confused.

"That's why you look like you had your brain sucked out your dick. Trust me. I know."

Now it was my turn. I narrowed my eyes at him. "Okay."

He stepped forward and held out his hand. "I'm Luke."

Luke? Oh shit, *Luke*.

Kamal's favourite. Jensen's lover. One of Jensen's lovers, at least.

"Hey," I said, grinning and holding out my hand. "Kamal mentioned you."

"He did, did he?" Luke licked his lips and eyed me up and down. "Kamal and I go way back."

I scratched at my chin awkwardly, wondering how long before the others would arrive. They had to be close behind me.

"Yeah." Luke gazed around at the room. "I just came to look at this place. A lot of good shit happened here last summer."

"Oh yeah?"

Luke laughed. "Yeah."

"Kamal told me you met Jensen last summer."

Luke's soft mouth twisted into a mischievous smile. "I *fucked* Jensen. In the shower. On his second day."

My mouth went dry. "Wow."

Luke nodded. "Yeah, I *owned* that cowboy. And he's still mine. And Noah's. They're back at the house," he said, the light of affection in his eyes. He looked me over. "What do you think of Kamal?"

I swallowed and my dick jumped in my pants to say exactly what *it* thought of Kamal. "He's demanding."

Luke laughed. "Oh, he's demanding all right."

He stepped close and held my gaze for a long, tense moment. "But, you *please* Kamal? You do your best to make that man *happy*?"

I raised my eyebrows, waiting.

"He'll fucking *worship* you. It'll be a strange kind of worship, involving crops and bondage and maybe some weird fruit-printed underwear, but he will devote himself to stripping you of every conventional thought you've ever had."

We stared at each other with ferocity, as if we wanted to physically fight over Kamal but realized it would be ridiculous and stupid and pointless. So, we simply talked.

"Are you up to that, Owen? Do you think you can be a good ponyboy and give Kamal the obedience he craves? The obedience he needs?"

Fuck, yeah, I could. But I only shrugged.

"Do you understand what I mean? That man will devote himself to you if you show him true submission. *Can* you show him true submission?"

"What's it to you?" I was annoyed now, by this interloper who had claims on Kamal's affection, even though he had two devoted lovers.

Luke smiled. He looked me up and down, assessing. "You've got some fire in you. That's good. Kamal likes a ponyboy with fire. With *attitude.*"

I didn't say anything. But I crossed my arms in front of my chest and stood tall, squaring myself against Luke.

Luke's gaze travelled over me with barely concealed interest. "He needs your submission as much as you need his dominance. Never forget that."

I inclined my head but didn't say anything.

"Anyway, I've got to get back to my boys. Jensen's room at the house is almost as nice as Adam's, and we're doing some...catching up." He winked at me, opened the door, and took off just as Jake and Biskane came along the path.

"Hey, Owen," Biskane said as he stepped into the bunkhouse, Jake on his heels. "You okay?"

I nodded, rubbing my face with my hand, feeling the exhaustion rise again. "Yeah. Rough morning."

"Kamal work you hard?"

"Fuck, yeah. I feel like I need to sleep for a week. And I'm sore everywhere."

Jake raised his eyebrows. "Everywhere?"

I gave him a look and walked to my bunk, climbing up and tossing myself over the edge to collapse on my back. "Every-fucking-where."

"Who was that guy talking to you?"

I shrugged. "Just some guy that was here last summer."

"He's hot."

"I guess."

"I saw Adrian carrying that gear to give Kamal. Did he actually put it on you?" Jake said, peering over the edge of the top bunk. "Did he make you wear the fucking tail?"

"Yep."

"Holy shit. How was it?"

"Fine. Good, I guess. Weird. But good." I stared at the ceiling, then glanced at him. "Made me feel like a real pony; that's for fucking sure."

Jake whistled and stepped down. Biskane asked if I was going to shower.

"Not yet. In a bit. I need to recoup some of my brain cells first."

He chuckled. "Okay."

I wondered if he would wait for me. Maybe he wanted more of what we'd done yesterday. I was into it, but I needed to rest first. Being Kamal's ponyboy was a blessing and a curse because I'd probably end up like this most mornings. Somehow, that thought didn't bother me one fucking bit.

*

Biskane and I sucked each other off in the showers again. It was hot and fun, but it didn't come close to what I'd experienced that morning with Kamal.

That afternoon I added two more sketches to my collection. I drew Biskane's elegant profile and the top half of Luke's face, or at least my impression of it from the short amount of time I'd seen it. His eyes were the arresting feature, and his skater-boy hair. I was pleased with my drawing of Biskane, but I wasn't confident I'd rendered Luke's forehead, hair, and eyes with any accuracy.

We walked to the main house for supper without talking much. We'd compared notes at the bunkhouse, and we were all a little unnerved by things we'd learned about the reality of pony play and the secrets of the ranch and its operations.

Jake had found Lorraine to be a strict mistress but he had developed a real affection for her. She used persuasion and temptations of rewards more than outright domination, but had high expectations. And Biskane was acclimating well to Hiro's more gentle approach of coaxing and encouragement. They'd matched us well.

When we got to the main house I scanned the yard for Jensen, Luke, and the other man, Noah, although I didn't have a clue what he looked like. Lorraine and Kamal were deep in conversation again, this time sitting together at one of the picnic tables.

Even seeing Kamal's dark profile, his short beard neatly trimmed and his eyelashes long as he blinked and smiled, made my heart rate quicken and my cock take an interest. When he felt the energy of my gaze and glanced over, our eyes locked and something important passed between us. Lorraine glanced my way to see what had Kamal's focus and smiled. She said something to him. He nodded and beckoned me over.

"Excuse me," I said to Biskane who had asked if I wanted a hot dog or a hamburger as he held a plate out toward me. I walked across the dry grass to the picnic table where my trainer and his associate sat.

"Hi, Owen," Lorraine said as I approached, my gaze still locked on Kamal's. He licked his lips and took a slow bite of his hot dog as my cock plumped. "Kamal tells me you were the perfect pony for him this morning."

I blushed. That wasn't completely true, but it was nice of him to say. "Well, I tried my best, Ma'am."

"Ooh, so polite. What a difference to yesterday."

Had I been rude at supper the day before? I thought back to my interactions with Lorraine and Kamal at the house and supposed it might be true. I was in a completely different headspace now. I didn't know what to say. Kamal rescued me.

"He's a quick learner."

"You're a good teacher," I said quickly, before I realized I was going to say anything.

Lorraine stopped chewing, looked at me, looked at Kamal. "Wow, Kamal. You've got yourself a disciple."

His slow smile did weird things to my insides and my cock pushed harder at the front of my jeans. My dick knew who its master was.

"Kneel," Kamal said, staring at the table.

I stared at Kamal, hardly believing what he was asking me to do. Get down on my knees beside him in the middle of everyone? At the main house? At supper? Was he fucking kidding me?

He didn't say anything else, just sat there, waiting. His calmness and his confidence in me made my breath catch.

I went to my knees, face flushing with embarrassment, multiple cells in my brain firing, cock a hard rod in my pants, and stared at the ground. The sound of my heart pounding filled my ears as I waited for Kamal to do something or say something. I heard the sounds of conversation around me before everything became eerily quiet.

Oh shit. Fucking shit and hell and why are you doing this to me?

I felt everybody looking at me and my face got hotter. I burned with humiliation and self-consciousness. I silently begged Kamal to say something, or do something, anything, to release me from my debasement. At the same time, my level of arousal had gone from a four to a *ten plus* in a matter of moments, and that part of me didn't give a goddamn that everyone on the lawn of the main house was looking at me.

Kamal's loud voice pierced the silence.

"A little demo for my friend, Lorraine, here. Nothing to look at, folks," he said, effectively telling them to mind their own fucking business. I breathed with relief and blinked at the grass, waiting for him to tell me to do...something.

But he didn't speak to me right away. He stood and moved directly in front of me before he said, "Stand."

My breath left my throat in a ragged gasp as I pushed up from my knees and stood face to face with my trainer. He was taller than me but only by an inch or two. I tossed the hair off my forehead. He looked at me, eyes drilling into mine, then clasped me behind my neck and pulled me toward him, lowering his lips to mine in a soft, unexpected kiss.

I froze, but my lips opened under the gentle pressure, only to be abandoned as he pulled back quickly. He seemed as surprised as I was. He turned to Lorraine, who simply gaped at the both of us, then wiped his hand across his mouth and stepped back, sitting on the bench quickly and acting like I wasn't there.

I stared at him for a long moment as he ignored me and began to eat, not looking at Lorraine or me, acting as if his meal was his only focus.

"Go get some supper, Owen," Lorraine said gently, and I made myself turn and walk toward the food laid out for us. I didn't know what to think, but that kiss was still sending shock waves to my soul.

He regretted it. I could see he regretted doing it in front of everyone. But he had done it. And it had come from somewhere.

I was glad to be alone at the buffet table because my emotions were in turmoil. The softness of that kiss had gone right through me. I grabbed a plate, a multitude of emotions rising as I took a burger and some fries and salad. Focusing on the food helped, and I tried not to contemplate what Kamal's sudden retreat might mean.

He was my trainer but there was something explosive between us. And something gentle and emotional too. But what the fuck did I know? I could barely think straight after the day's events.

As I turned, holding my plate and wondering where to find Biskane and Jake, or even Sam, I saw Jensen come down the porch steps, followed by Luke and another man, as if in a slow-motion movie montage. Jensen put his cowboy hat on as they walked and Luke's bleached hair glistened in the summer sun. The other, slighter man, who had wavy brown hair and looked barely twenty, held back as if nervous in the face of so many people.

Luke stopped and held out his hand to the smaller man, who must be Noah. They proceeded down the steps together and approached Kamal beside Jensen.

"Well, colour me surprised," Kamal said loudly, standing and walking forward to meet them. "The three musketeers have taken a break from sword fighting practice to join us for supper?"

Luke grinned and pulled Noah forward. "Look Noah, it's Kamal. The man who strapped me to the boardroom table and whipped the shit out of me in front of you and Jensen. That was fun." He laughed. "Actually, it *was* fun."

I stood there, holding my plate and gaping as Kamal jested and kibitzed with them. When I realized how stupid I must look, I tore my eyes away and finally found Jake and Biskane.

They regarded me with a strange sense of caution as if they thought I'd defected to the other side or something. I had to nip *that* in the bud. It had been a moment of indiscretion, that was all, and it was Kamal's fault.

"What?" I said, throwing my plate on the wooden table and plunking my ass on the bench.

Jake was the first to speak.

"Nothing," he said as he made room beside him and frowned at Biskane, who gave me a weird look. "Who are the guys with Jensen? Do you know?"

I grinned, covering my fries with red glop. "Blond one's Luke. Dark one's Noah. They're with Jensen."

Jake stared at me like I'd lost my mind. "I know they're with Jensen, I just asked who they are."

Biskane, who had been watching the three men closely, nudged Jake. "I think he means they're *with* Jensen."

I nodded.

Jake blinked. "*Both* of them?"

I chewed on my french fry, glancing at the three men and Kamal, who continued to joke with them. Luke made a lewd gesture and glanced my way, then winked and turned back to Kamal.

"From what I understand," I said.

"That bleach blond with the shaved sides is hot. Looks like a skater boy," Biskane said in his deep baritone.

We watched as Luke grabbed Jensen's shirt and pulled him in for a full tongue kiss, knocking his hat onto the ground in the process and laughing against his lips. Noah looked on fondly, their hands still entwined.

"Luke had Kamal as a trainer last summer," I muttered.

Biskane's eyes widened. "Oh, wow."

"Yeah. He was Kamal's favourite or something." I shook my head.

Jake whistled. "Well, the wind has shifted. Looks like *you're* his favourite now."

"What? I doubt it. I think he was putting me on."

Jake nudged my elbow and I looked up. He nodded toward where Kamal stood with Jensen and the others. But Kamal wasn't looking at them anymore. He was staring at me.

When Kamal noticed me, he smiled and winked, and I knew there had been something real in that kiss. Whether it was a friendly *You're pleasing me so much* or a *Wow, I really like you kiss*, at least I knew there was honesty behind it. He hadn't been playing me, even if he'd regretted doing it in public.

I returned his smile and then concentrated on my supper, shoveling salad into my mouth so I wouldn't have to answer any questions.

The others took pity on me and left me alone until we got back to the bunkhouse.

"Holy shit, that guy is totally into you!" Jake said.

"No, he's not. He likes an obedient ponyboy, that's all."

"Yeah, I don't think so. The way he was looking at you? The way he kissed you?"

Biskane cleared his throat, and when I looked his way, raised his eyebrows in a question and glanced toward the showers. His face looked flushed, and I knew what he wanted. But I was too tired and too wound up by what had happened at the main house.

I shook my head and turned to Jake. "Anyway, it doesn't matter. I don't think trainers are allowed to have relationships with ponyboys. I mean, except superficial, physically dominant ones."

Jake shrugged. "I'm sure there are loopholes."

"Maybe," I muttered, climbing into my bunk and grabbing my book. I watched out of the corner of my eye as Biskane bent to whisper in Jake's ear before they shared a laugh.

Fuckers. Anyway, they could laugh all they wanted. I was the one going back to the best trainer at the BCR come morning.

Chapter Eleven

I was surprised to encounter Jensen with Kamal for my session the next morning. I'd figured Luke and Noah would stay for more than a night and that Jensen would take some more time off.

"I managed to tear Jensen away from his fan club for the morning," Kamal explained, eyeing me up and down and taking the bridle and tail from Adrian.

"How long are they here for?" Adrian asked.

"Till the end of the weekend," Jensen replied. "I can keep up with my responsibilities and still have time for—" He cleared his throat. "—other things." The blush and sweet smile he couldn't suppress showed how much he was enjoying their visit.

"Nice! Well, have fun," Adrian said with a wink and left us.

Jensen stepped close to Kamal. "You're putting him in bridle and tail? Already?"

Kamal kept his gaze on me, rubbing the leather straps of the bridle between his thumb and fingers, and shrugged. "Sometimes you realize you need to fast-track a particular pony because his brain won't let him enter the headspace he needs to be in." He glanced at Jensen, smiled. "Worked like a charm yesterday."

"Oh, I see." He folded his arms and looked me up and down. "I hear he knelt for you at supper yesterday. In the middle of everything."

Listening to them talk about me as if I were a dumb animal and couldn't understand felt mildly insulting and embarrassing—unless I let myself get into the mindset that I was the pony here and my comprehension of anything but my trainers' orders didn't matter. All that mattered was that I did what I was told.

Kamal stepped forward and cupped my chin, forcing me to look at him. "Yes, he did. I think he was more surprised than I was. Barely."

I kept quiet, submitting easily to the intense energy from Kamal's deep-brown eyes as he pushed the flop of hair off my forehead and ran his long fingers through my thick strands. My cock throbbed in its cage.

"You want your tail, ponyboy?"

I whimpered and my eyes closed at this intimate question, only to open again as Kamal withdrew his hand from my hair and slapped me gently on my cheek. "Admit it. You love your tail, Owen. Almost as much as you love your bridle."

He held my chin in a firm grip, turning my head to one side then the other as my eyes tracked him. "Fuck, you've got a nice face, ponyboy. Eh, Jensen? He's a handsome little fucker."

Jensen smiled. "He's like a cross between Noah and Luke, honestly. He's dark and slight like Noah, and cute, but he's got that fiery Luke energy."

Kamal released me as he glanced at Jensen, then turned back to regard me contemplatively. "You know, you're right. I didn't see it before but I do now. No wonder I like him so much."

My heart warmed at that admission, and I almost said something but then thought better of it.

"What? You can speak, Owen."

Kamal didn't miss anything.

"I like you too, Sir."

"Yeah, I gathered that. When you fell to your knees at the main house. That was beautiful by the way."

"Beautiful, Sir?" Seemed like a strange way to put it.

But he nodded and picked up the butt-plug tail, holding it for me to see. "Your submission is beautiful, Owen."

He turned to Jensen and handed the tail to him. "I'm going to let you tack him this morning."

"Okay," Jensen said, sounding pleased.

I had no objections. At least Kamal would be watching.

"Have you given him a pony name yet?" Jensen asked.

"I haven't. But he'll need one for the show on Saturday." Kamal shook his head. "I'm still getting used to having shows every weekend instead of once a month. I understand why Adam made the change, and it's a good experience for them. But the first show is always a bit of a rigmarole with such inexperienced stock."

"True. But the closing shows with guest ponies on the final weekend run much smoother now. And I love naming new ponies," Jensen said, looking first at me and then Kamal. "What do you think?"

Kamal looked me up and down, swinging the bridle in his hand, assessing me. Then his frown became a grin. "Blaze."

"Nice," Jensen said.

"Well, he's such a fiery little specimen."

This time I couldn't help saying something. "Little? Why do you keep calling me little, Sir?"

"Oh, there's that temper. Because you're so cute. Don't worry, it's not in reference to your dick, which is pretty substantial as I recall from yesterday, especially when it's about to explode all over the fence."

Fuck. With one sentence, he delivered an electric jolt from my ears to my cock as I remembered the events of the previous day.

"On the fence?" Jensen said, taking a glove from the box and putting it on, then lubing the butt-plug tail in preparation.

Sweat began to bead on my neck as I prepared myself for the humiliation of being plugged and bridled, this time by Jensen.

"Oh yeah. A quart at least." Kamal smiled, remembering.

Jensen laughed. "I bet. After a morning in full tack? With you? Of course, it was."

They regarded each other fondly, and I wondered if Kamal and Jensen had ever fooled around. I didn't think so. Jensen seemed decidedly *with* Luke and Noah. But Kamal had apparently disciplined Luke over a boardroom table with Jensen present, so their relationship wasn't entirely non-sexual.

"Don't worry. You'll only be Blaze in the show ring. Here, you're Owen. And you're mine." Kamal turned back to Jensen and shrugged. "He responded very well to the full tack yesterday, and I want to maintain that momentum. He's got to be ready for his first pony show on Saturday."

"True," Jensen said. "But usually they don't wear full tack for that."

"Blaze will be in full tack. You can count on that."

"You're the boss," Jensen said.

As my mind reeled at the thought of being presented in full tack at the pony show when my compatriots would be in minimal gear, Kamal led me to the table. He used my bound arms to turn me around so I was bending forward with my chest supported on the polished wood.

I tried to get comfortable as Kamal's hand moved from my arm to the back of my neck and held me down, effectively restraining me. "Be still."

My cock throbbed and my synapses fired as Jensen's gloved hand started to prepare me for my tail. Kamal's strong hand on the back of my neck, pressing me into the table, keeping me still for Jensen to probe and prepare, caused excitement and pleasure to roll through me. My cock throbbed with pain and pleasure as fluid pushed out the tip and dripped onto the floor.

"Did you see that?" Jensen murmured, continuing to prepare me. "He's already leaking."

"That's my boy. Told you he liked his tack."

"Have you ever put a new ponyboy in full tack so early?" Jensen asked curiously.

"Nope. Never," Kamal said, relaxing his hand on the back of my neck only slightly as I complied with Jensen's treatment. "But that's a perfect example when I say that each one is unique, and it's important to focus on his needs, even if you have what you think is a perfect routine for initiating a new ponyboy. What may be perfect for one ponyboy, won't be perfect for another. And while you don't want to necessarily make it easy for them, we do want them to be able to engage in the pony play fully as soon as possible. Most of the guys who come here have previous fetish and pet-play experience, so even without a lot of gear they can get into the headspace. But Owen doesn't have any pet-play experience. It's all new to him, and I'm not sure he was invested at first."

I groaned as Jensen pumped his gloved fingers in and out of my ass.

"Pretty sure he's invested now," Kamal said, stroking the nape of my neck with his thumb, sending shivers through me.

Oh, I was fucking invested. I was buying fucking shares in this goddamn ranch.

I wondered if I *could* buy shares in the ranch? That thought dissolved as I felt the press of rubber against my hole, and Jensen told me to relax.

Kamal tightened his grip on the back of my neck as Jensen inserted the girthy plug. I almost passed out from the psychological and physical objectification of this procedure. If what I'd wanted was total domination and complete submission, I'd come to the right fucking place.

The coarse hair of the tail tickled the backs of my thighs as Jensen arranged it, then snapped the glove off his hand and cleared his throat. "Holy shit. That ass is perfect for a pony tail."

Kamal laughed and released his grip on my neck. "I know, right? That ass has been begging for a tail since it walked onto this ranch."

Now I knew how it altered my headspace, I couldn't argue.

"Up," Kamal said, pulling my arms with one hand and pressing his other hand against my chest as I stood and glared moodily at him. I wanted to retain some dignity. Mainly so he'd be forced to train it out of me.

He raised his eyebrows, and I tossed my forelock. Jensen grinned and Kamal licked his lips.

"Fucking upstart. He's as bad as Luke," Kamal said, picking up the bridle.

"Yeah, I don't think so," Jensen said. "Not by half."

"Okay, that's valid. But why do I always fall for the ones that give me attitude?"

"Because they're more interesting."

Was Kamal falling for me? And what did that mean? Did that mean I was his favourite now? But what about Sam? Sam had a pretty spectacular ass from what I'd seen. And muscular shoulders *and* a six pack.

I didn't have a six-pack. I barely had a one-pack.

My thoughts were interrupted when Kamal handed Jensen the bridle and told him to finish before leaning back against the table and folding his arms over his chest.

"Are you going to be a good pony, Blaze? Are you going to let me put this bridle on you?" Jensen asked. He came close to me and whispered, "Or are you going to be difficult because you want Kamal to think he's the only one who can handle you?" He winked at me, like it was a hint.

It was a good hint.

I backed up a step and Jensen told me to be still. I stared at him and hoped he could see that I understood what he was suggesting. I decided I could play the naughty pony all day.

Jensen tried to put the bridle over my head but I ducked and sidestepped, so he missed. He sighed with frustration and turned to Kamal.

"You've got to learn how to deal with this sort of thing, Jensen," he said. "Don't let him get away with that."

Jensen turned back to me, lifting the bridle again and telling me to be still.

And I stayed still. Until he tried to put the bridle over my head again. I tossed my head and snorted, glaring at Kamal over Jensen's shoulder.

If he wanted an angry, obstinate pony, I could be an angry, obstinate pony. It seemed that was what Jensen had been suggesting. Because maybe I'd given in too easily the day before. Sure, I'd pleased Kamal and he'd rewarded me handsomely. But I didn't want him to be bored with me after only a week.

This was one dirty game I had an interest in. Could I keep the hot-as-fuck pony trainer interested in teaching me how to be a well-behaved pony? I didn't want to make it easy for him.

"Owen!" Kamal barked. He uncrossed his arms and strode forward, taking the bridle from Jensen. "You want me to put this on you? Is that it? You can't stand for Jensen but you'll stand for me?"

He rounded behind me and wrapped his arm around my neck, holding me in a headlock and bending me back into his body as he forced the bridle over my head and pushed the bit into my mouth with little ceremony. I knew I was vanquished and didn't put up a fight. I moaned and played with the bit in my mouth as Kamal shoved his fingers over my tongue to make sure I knew my place.

"You are a very bad pony, Blaze," he murmured in my ear, sliding his arm off me but splaying his hand over my throat. He knew I liked it.

I fucking loved it. I swallowed, my heart going a mile a minute, cock throbbing, and I moaned, sounding so fucking pitiful.

"Jensen, come here," Kamal said, nodding toward Jensen, who stepped forward and eyed me sternly.

"Grab his nipples," Kamal said as my eyes flew open.

Jensen did as instructed, his fingers finding my nipples and pinching them, making me gasp.

"Now squeeze. Hard."

Jensen squeezed and twisted my nipples as I struggled with Kamal's broad hand at my throat. I cried out and panted, squealing like a baby, as the sudden agony made my cock swell and surge. Jensen looked on calmly, his fingers like steel vices while I whimpered and struggled in Kamal's grasp.

"Okay," Kamal said, and Jensen released me, licking his lips and glancing at my cock which was trying so hard to lengthen it moved the cage up and down.

Kamal tightened his hand on my throat and moved his lips to my ear. "I know you're putting up a fight because you think I like it," he breathed. "Well, good job, ponyboy. Because I do. I like it very, very much."

He slid his hand down to cup my dick in its cage and jerked it back and forth, sending jolts of pain and throbs of perverse pleasure along my nerves.

Then he released me and buckled the bridle on properly while I stood staring at Jensen with raw need and a barely restrained desperation.

"This pony needs to run," Kamal said, leading me across the floor and out the arena door with Jensen following close behind.

"What about the cart?"

Kamal laughed. "We'll let him practice his trotting first. Then we can try the cart. Maybe."

Oh, holy shit. What had I got myself into?

Four turns of the large paddock later, I felt better. The trotting came easier, even with the plug in my ass and the horsehair slapping against my legs. I liked showing off for Jensen and Kamal, and I think my form was improving, if their shared nods and thumbs up were anything to go by.

"Good boy, Owen," Kamal said as he motioned for me to pull up in front of him. My chest rose and fell with laboured breaths, but my belly glowed with his praise, and I had to force myself not to smile. I couldn't let him see how much I enjoyed this.

I glimpsed the other ponyboys in nearby paddocks, practicing their gaits, but Kamal drew my gaze back to him with a snap of his fingers.

"Look at me, not them. I should be your focus at all times."

I tipped my chin, returning my eyes to Kamal, remembering not to try to speak with the bit in my mouth. I liked the pressure of the steel on my tongue. It had warmed to the temperature of my mouth and only pulled slightly at the edges when Kamal tugged at the reins. It had been designed for a human mouth, I could tell. At least that was something to be thankful for.

"Jensen, get the cart."

My eyes opened wide and I took a step back. *What the fuck did that mean?* Everything Kamal made me do took me one step deeper into the life of a real pony, and I wasn't sure I wanted it.

"Easy, easy," Kamal said, stepping around me and untying the reins from where he'd wrapped them behind my head. "We're going to do the walking again, with me behind, guiding you. Remember?"

I nodded. At least that was familiar.

He gathered the reins in his hands and walked me around the ring, talking the whole time, trying to put me at ease.

"Do you know how good you look from behind, Owen? With that black pony tail draping down over your thighs and those black boots?"

I didn't, because how could I? But his words made me feel like a prize stallion and I held my head higher and lifted my legs better, because he watched and admired me.

"You are a very pretty pony, Owen, and I bet you never thought you would be. I bet you came here looking for one thing and found something else. Am I right? Or you found what you were looking for, but it was still entirely unexpected."

I heard his breathing and footsteps behind me. I felt his firm hold of the reins, his gentle guidance as he directed me this way and that.

"You came here on a whim, at the last minute. You filled that empty slot, just slid right in where you were needed and hoped for the best; didn't you? But you must have been pretty desperate for something to take that big of a leap, right Owen? You must have wanted something pretty damn badly to sign up for this without so much as a week's consideration. I'd love to hear how you found out about us. It's pretty obvious you took a giant leap of faith, and I hope it's working out for you."

Fuck, how did he know all this? Had I put that in my form? I couldn't remember. But then, he knew I hadn't spent any time on the wait list. I was a ringer, and even though I had no advantages in this game, I felt like a fraud.

I wasn't as prepared as the others. I'd thought I could put on a pony harness with the ease of a different T-shirt, when every step of the process turned out to be more difficult than I'd anticipated. But it was also turning out to be everything I'd wanted. Everything I'd needed.

"Then again, I'm not so concerned with how it's working out for you. I just need an obedient pony that can learn new tricks and master proper form. If you can do that for me, Owen, we'll get along fine."

He tugged on the left rein and I turned, sharply so that we went in a tight circle until we faced the other direction. "Good. Very good."

He walked me for a bit, then did the same thing to turn us back. He slapped the reins on my shoulders and told me "Giddy-up." I moved into a trot as he kept pace behind me.

Then I saw Jensen dragging a small black pony cart into the paddock, and I stopped dead as Kamal slammed into me from behind, knocking me into the dirt and falling on top of me before gracefully rolling off and cursing my name.

"Jesus, Owen. *Fucking hell.*"

The wind had been knocked out of me, and I lay there with my mouth open as I tried to inhale. Kamal grabbed my arm and pulled me up, holding me steady and telling me to breathe as I struggled to stand.

Finally, a tearing breath ripped through my sore chest, and I focused on Kamal's reassuring nearness as oxygen flooded my brain and body in a much-needed rush.

"Are you okay? That was quite a fall."

I bobbed my head, licking my lips and wondering if I had grass stains on my chest. I stared wide-eyed at the black pony cart as Jensen abandoned it and walked over to us.

"Is he all right? What the hell happened?"

Kamal came around in front of me and ran his strong hands over my legs and arms and then held my waist in his firm grip and searched my eyes. "Are you sure you're okay?"

I tossed my forelock and nodded again, trying not to think about the feel of his body as it had landed on top of me and how that might feel in less sudden circumstances. I shuddered.

"What happened?" Jensen asked again.

"He saw the pony cart and balked. Doesn't like the idea, I'd guess."

"Hmm. Do you think he's ready? He seems to be doing pretty well with the bridle and his form is fantastic."

"I know. But it would be stupid to bring it out here and not try it." He squeezed my waist and forced my gaze to his. "What's the matter? Are you scared?"

I stared at him, not wanting to admit that I was scared to pull the cart, but not for the reasons he might think.

"It's not that hard to pull an empty pony cart, Owen. It will give you a feel for it before we have someone sitting in it."

Oh, holy fuck. I hadn't thought of that. It was the cart itself freaking me out, but now that I knew I'd have to pull it with someone in it...

I started to hyperventilate.

"Hey," Kamal said, grabbing my chin in one hand while the other stayed at my waist to anchor me. He raised his voice: "Hey!"

I struggled to control my breathing, to focus on Kamal's steadying gaze, his strong grip on my waist and chin.

"It's only a fucking pony cart, Owen. And you're going to pull it. For me."

Chapter Twelve

For Kamal. I could do this for Kamal. He wanted me to do it, and I could do it.

I wasn't scared of the cart itself. I was terrified of how I'd feel when I was harnessed into it. I was worried that once I did this thing, once I submitted to pulling a *fucking pony cart*, I would be fully committed to this journey, and I wouldn't be able to turn back. Not only because Kamal wouldn't let me but because I would have finally found the place I truly wanted to be.

And the idea that *this* was where my need for submission and a truly dominant master had led, in such a short amount of time, made me weak with fear.

What if I wanted to be a pony all the time? What if it was *so good* (and it already was) I'd be willing to be a pony for Kamal whenever he wanted me to be one? What if it turned out to be my favourite thing in the whole fucking world? How would I be able to go back to my normal life in the city, hanging out at lame fetish clubs, waiting for someone I'd never find. Because that guy was here at the BCR, training another ponyboy to do the things *I* loved.

"Owen, if you need to safeword, turn your head from side to side." His voice was calm, steady and soothing. "I won't be upset."

He was giving me a way out. A way to postpone this one necessary humiliation that would simply come tomorrow or the next day or the next if I refused it today. I might as well do it. Kamal wanted me to do it. And, really, that was all that mattered. That and the fact I already trusted him more than I'd ever trusted anyone.

I wished I could tell him what scared me—that I was falling deeper and deeper under his thrall and the exhilarating feeling of leaving myself behind and becoming his fiery little pony scared the fuck out of me. But I wouldn't try to talk with the bit in my mouth because that would make this even more humiliating. So I tried to convey my vulnerability and fear in the look I gave him.

"What are you so afraid of?" he said softly, and I wished I could tell him, although I was afraid to say it aloud, even without the hindrance of the metal bit. I tossed my head and snorted, unashamed to exhibit the sound of a real horse because at that moment, I felt like one. I was Kamal's pretty pony, and I was terrified that was all I ever needed to be.

He smiled then—a genuine, emotional, happy smile that lit him up from inside. His hand on my waist tightened as he held my chin, gazing into my frightened eyes.

"I can tell you right now you're going to love it. Because I can see in you the perfect aptitude for this, and I know you see it too. Stop denying it. Stop pretending it's all a crazy game and not the answer to something deep inside you." He leaned in close and whispered against my cheek. "Because I know it is."

I whimpered at the sheer vulnerability I felt, knowing he could see into my soul just like I'd suspected. He knew me. He saw me. And he wouldn't let me deny myself. I felt moisture collect in the corners of my eyes as he brushed his lips over my stubbled cheek to find my mouth.

As he pressed his lips to mine I felt the reassurance I needed to continue. I pushed all the thoughts about what this might mean for my future out of my head and concentrated on Kamal and our connection and this moment.

My mouth opened, and he kissed me harder, hands coming up to clasp the bridle against my cheeks and touch the bit with his tongue as he explored my mouth with a tentative and restrained need. I let him plunder me, my eyes closed, feeling fear and uncertainty recede as a steady, sure, passion rose.

I heard a throat clear.

Kamal pulled back and released me instantly. He turned to Jensen and they stared at one another, something private passing between them. Kamal shook his head ever so slightly, and Jensen nodded, his gaze serious, as if to say he'd keep our kiss a secret.

I knew my trainer wasn't permitted to fuck me. Maybe he wasn't supposed to kiss me either. His kisses confused me, but they also made my heart sing. They didn't mean I was special, but they helped me get into the headspace of devotion for the man requiring me to debase myself.

In any case, Adam could fuck right off. Because if Kamal couldn't even kiss me, then what was the point of all this anyway?

It was an irrational position, but I stood by it. I'd be his fucking pony. I'd do what he wanted of me. But dammit, I wasn't going to regret a kiss here and there. What was the harm in it? And Jensen didn't seem to have a problem with it.

Kamal removed the pieces of the body harness that attached the chest piece to the pelvic belt. "You need a sturdier harness to pull the cart," he said, as he handed the straps he'd removed to Jensen who passed him a hefty-looking leather belt. It was thick and padded on the inside and sat comfortably around my waist, resting on my hips above the pelvic piece of the body harness.

Kamal fastened the buckles, making sure it fit snug but not too tight. He stepped back to admire his work and grunted, licking his lips.

"I like you in the regular harness, Owen, but this looks pretty fucking good on you too."

I gazed at him and tossed my head, but the hair on my forehead was damp with sweat and didn't move. Kamal pushed it out of my eyes with his fingers and smiled.

"Saucy boy." He stroked the bit of hair he'd pushed to the side and raised an eyebrow. "Maybe I'll have them braid that piece for the show."

I blinked, not sure I liked that idea. I'd have nowhere to hide.

He and Jensen hitched the arms of the black sulky to the rings in the broad leather belt, and I felt the slight weight as the cart balanced against me. It was barely noticeable. The wheels carried the weight of the cart and the weight of the potential person in it so the pony could focus on pulling and steering it.

Kamal flipped the reins over my head and held them loosely in his hands. "Jensen will lead you today, since you've never done this before. Normally, one of us will ride in the cart, guiding with the reins and giving you a little tap on the behind to go faster." He turned to face me and put his hands on my shoulders. "Now look. Watch your step, and no sudden stops. At least the cart has a rigid frame and won't tumble onto you if you fall." Kamal moved close and said in my ear, "I hope I didn't hurt you."

I shook my head and puffed a breath out.

"Good. But keep steady and try not to fall again. Your form and balance have come a long way so you'll do great with this. If you need to slow down or stop, shake your head from side to side."

I nodded. I was hitched and ready so I might as well pull the goddamn cart.

Kamal gave the reins to Jensen and stepped back, folding his arms across his broad chest.

Jensen smiled at me. "Ready, Blaze?"

I swallowed. *Ready as I'd ever be.*

He clicked his tongue and urged me forward with a gentle tap to my rump with the ends of the reins. "Giddy-up."

I stepped forward carefully, feeling the adjustment and hearing the creak of the cart behind me as it started moving.

"Good job," Kamal said as I pulled the cart along, moving away from him. "You're doing great!"

The gentle jostle of the cart behind me, Jensen walking at my side with my reins in his hands, and Kamal urging me on, all conspired to give me a sense of purpose and satisfaction as I concentrated on this bizarre task. The strangest thing about it was that it didn't seem strange. It was merely another thing I needed to learn and master in order to please Kamal, which had become my prime directive.

Huh. Weird how that happened.

I made it around the paddock twice without any problem. Jensen had me trot a few times, which seemed ambitious but I carried it off well. By the time he led me back to Kamal and handed the reins over, I was winded, sweaty, and exhausted but proud of my accomplishment. The physical accomplishment, sure, but also the mental task of accommodating another indignity at Kamal's hands.

"My brave little ponyboy," Kamal said, pushing the damp hair out of my eyes while I rolled the bit on my tongue. It felt good and gave me something to do while I processed the intensity of Kamal's gaze. Kamal cleared his throat. "Jensen."

"Yes, Kamal?"

"Can you grab a bottle of water from the cooler, please?" he asked, not breaking our connection. "This pony's parched."

"Of course," Jensen replied.

My breath caught as Kamal stepped forward and clasped my face the way he had earlier. "You exceed my expectations every time we're together, Owen."

His warm breath feathered against my lips as he spoke. I jiggled the bit harder in my mouth as he leaned close. This time, his mouth on mine became a conflagration in a split second. He kissed me hard, clutching the rings of the bit as I opened to him, helpless against his obvious desire. The bit impeded my ability to return his passion, but I closed my eyes and became an open vessel for his pleasure, my tongue meeting his when possible and my mouth open and vulnerable. I turned my face to better accommodate his welcome attack.

Much too soon, he pulled back, breathless and undone, and stared at me with astonishment.

"Fuck it. Why did we have to meet like *this*?" he muttered, running his fingers through his hair in frustration. "Why did this have to *happen*?"

Jensen had returned with the water. "Kamal, it was bound to happen. It's not his fault."

"It *is* his fault. Why does he have to be so fucking *irresistible*?"

Jensen laughed. "Oh, how the mighty have fallen."

"Fuck you," Kamal said to Jensen, who shrugged and twisted the cap off the bottle of water, holding it out to Kamal.

Kamal took the water bottle from Jensen and tipped it to his lips, swallowing several gulps of cold water before holding it above me. "Open," he said. He poured the cold, fresh water into my mouth, letting it spill out the sides as I tried to drink what I could, and he smiled with some mild cruelty.

"I'm sorry, Owen. None of this is your fault," he said. "I'm trying not to do anything I'm not supposed to. And you're making it very hard." He chuckled and glanced down at the bulge in his jeans. "Yeah. Really hard. But that's only half of it." He turned to Jensen. "Come on, let's get him out of this gear."

After I was detached from the pony cart and the harness removed, Kamal beckoned Jensen. "I'll hold him, and you can jerk him off. I don't trust myself to do it right now."

"Okay," Jensen said, glancing at me.

I was disappointed because I desperately wanted Kamal's hand around my cock. But when his arm circled my throat, and he held me firmly against his chest, while Jensen removed the cage from my dick, disappointment turned into a desperate desire.

Kamal clasped me so tight I couldn't move. His solid arm kept my head tilted up as I felt my cock able to fill and swell, the sudden pleasure igniting a conflagration of need. When Jensen wrapped his gloved fingers around it and started stroking, I struggled in Kamal's vice-like grip, whimpering.

I couldn't get away and I didn't want to. Struggling under that solid grasp while Jensen jerked me off, feeling Kamal's hot breath on my neck, his arm against my throat, was the biggest turn-on I could imagine. His rock-like bicep pressed hard enough to make me struggle for a breath. In the space of a minute I came, cursing and spitting against Kamal's restraint but thrilled to be treated in such a way. I collapsed against him and quieted, his hold becoming an embrace as my breathing levelled out.

"Good boy, Owen," he whispered in my ear as his arm lowered to grasp me across the chest. He placed a soft, sweet kiss against my cheek before he released me and told Jensen to take me back to the grooming barn.

*

In the grooming barn, I stood in my usual daze of emotion and brain fog while Adrian hosed me down. I'd been correct in assuming this would be the way my sessions would end.

Back at the bunkhouse I sketched furiously—drawings of the pony bridles, tails and harnesses, and the pony cart. Getting it all on paper gave me a sense of control. And the drawings were good. They were vivid and accurate and done from memory. Perhaps not incredibly detailed, since I didn't have the objects in front of me, but the way I felt about each item informed the sketch itself, so the bridle was lovingly rendered, the tail a thing of beauty and grace, and the cart a much more angular and fleeting thing.

Biskane and Jake grabbed something to eat and showered while I lay in my bunk staring at the ceiling and wondering how long it would take me to get used to the BCR and the kind of soul-searching it provoked in me.

Chapter Thirteen

The morning of the first pony show, I woke with a nervous energy and apprehension. The other ponyboys seemed anxious, too, which reassured me I wasn't the only one freaking out a little.

Only Biskane expressed an unreserved excitement, with no fear of appearing as a pony before a crowd of eager onlookers.

"They're all here to see *us*," he pointed out. "They're as kinky as we are. Maybe more so."

He had a point. Still, the audience got to keep their clothes on. They didn't have to prance around the ring with cock cages on and horse tails up their asses.

As it turned out, the only one expected to perform in full tack was me.

In the grooming barn, Jake and Biskane, who were to join me in the morning show, were outfitted with the standard tack of boots, body harness, wide collar, cock cage and arm bands. They stood patiently while Adrian led me to the table.

"Bend over, Owen."

I couldn't protest verbally due to the ball gag but I hesitated.

"Kamal wants you in full tack," Adrian explained.

Of course he fucking does. I glanced at the others and returned my gaze to Adrian with my eyebrows raised.

"They've never been in full tack. Usually ponies aren't in full tack for the first pony show," Adrian explained. He held up my tail and nodded at the bridle that lay on the table beside him. "You're very special."

Special. That was one way of putting it. At this moment, knowing there was an audience gathering at the large paddock, I wanted to be normal. I wanted to blend into the crowd, not stand out.

"Hey, it'll be fine. You're used to having this stuff on by now. You won't even feel different."

We stared at each other for a long moment. I was pretty sure he was bullshitting me, but there wasn't much I could do about it. So I girded myself and bent over the table.

"Good boy."

My face burned with embarrassment as Adrian gloved up and prepared me, then inserted my tail while the other ponyboys watched or pretended not to. It was only a matter of time before they would suffer this indignity. I bit down hard on the ball gag and tried not to make a sound as the butt plug pushed in and filled me, and Adrian fluffed the horsehair and stood me up.

I avoided looking at the others as Adrian took off his glove and dropped it in the trash before making me turn so he could unbuckle and remove the gag.

"Adrian," I said, voice ragged and rough. "I don't know if I'm ready for this."

He placed a hand soothingly on my shoulder. "Kamal thinks you are, or he wouldn't have me do this."

I licked my lips, staring at the bridle. "But I've never been in front of an audience before."

For all the times I'd played with men in the clubs, we were always in a private room with one or two other men. I knew that appearing in a pony show at the BCR would be a major challenge for me, but I'd assumed I'd be dressed like all the other ponies.

"Hey, I get it. But Kamal will be with you the entire time. You'll be able to do it for him, right?"

His confidence in me was misplaced at best— completely inaccurate at worst.

"Sure," I said, willing myself to continue. "Probably."

"Let's get this bridle on you; then we can start making you pretty for the show."

I let Adrian put the bridle on me. With the bit settled between my teeth and the metal rings framing my face, I felt calmer. Maybe I'd be able to pull this off. For Kamal. The last thing I wanted to do was disappoint him.

Once I was fully tacked, Adrian put me with the others and the stable hands got to work adding fancy attachments to our outfits. Jake and Biskane got sparkly eye masks with feathers on each side.

Adrian showed me the mask that would snap right onto the forehead strap of my bridle. It was midnight black with a sparkly white lightning bolt down the middle, and two huge white feathers on each side.

"But first he wants me to braid your forelock with some pretty string."

I rolled the bit in my mouth in time to my eyes as Adrian divided the front part of my hair into pieces and braided it with blue, purple and yellow cord. I felt like I was getting ready for the biggest pride parade of my life. Except I wasn't at a pride festival. I would be the star attraction at the first summer pony show at the Braided Crop Ranch.

My heart beat pounded in my ears. I clasped and unclasped my fists as Adrian braided my hair and then tied it off and affixed the mask to my bridle. He buckled my arm bands behind my back.

"Want to see?" he asked.

I shook my head slowly from side to side. Not safewording—only letting him know that seeing myself in all this show gear was the last thing I wanted right now. Maybe for the next show, when everyone else was similarly attired, it would be different. But now? I just wanted to be done with the whole thing.

He shrugged. "Suit yourself. You look amazing though, Blaze," Adrian said, tweaking my nipple and grinning as my eyes widened at Kamal's nickname for me. "This mask Kamal dug up matches your pony name perfectly."

Fuck it, I'd forgotten I'd have a pony name for the show. Holy fuck. If Tamara could see me now, she'd be laughing her ass off.

I shook my head and the tiny braid bounced against the edge of the mask. It seemed weird not to have hair partially blocking my view. I didn't like it.

I glanced at the others. They preened with pride at their accoutrements. Biskane looked fucking amazing with his long hair braided with red ribbon and a sparkly red mask over his eyes. He caught my gaze and winked, looking me up and down like he wanted to mount me like a prize stud and ruin my pretty outfit.

That made me feel somewhat better. Although I wasn't particularly interested in Biskane now my mind was always filled with thoughts of Kamal, he was a very attractive man, and I would definitely not rule out another assignation in the showers.

"All right, you lot, off we go," Enzo said as Carrie grinned like we were the queen's stallions. "Tut, tut."

The three stable hands accompanied us to the arena, where our trainers waited. Kamal took one long look at me and nodded once. "Right. We're good to go."

I didn't feel quite so prepared. Luckily, Adrian had my back.

"He's a little unsure about all of it. Doesn't like the idea of standing out." He handed my reins to Kamal. "Good luck."

Kamal took my reins and narrowed his eyes. "You look fucking regal, Owen." He stepped close and fondled the metal rings of the bridle, tickling my cheeks and teasing the corner of my mouth. "You already outshine the others. What's the difference if I want to show you off?"

Show me off? Is that what was happening here? But I didn't care about looking pretty for everybody else. I only cared about looking pretty for Kamal.

I ducked my head and pushed my forehead into Kamal's shoulder, begging for mercy. Did he have to make me do this? His hand came around the back of my neck, cradling me against him.

"I know you'll be fantastic." He rubbed his fingers through the short hair at the nape of my neck, tickling me above the leather collar. "You simply have to walk beside me two times around the ring. Then pull the cart beside me. Piece of cake."

I puffed out a breath and rolled the bit. *Easy for him to say.*

"Are you going to be my brave little pony?" he asked, and I knew I had to try.

I rubbed my head against his shoulder and he chuckled. The sound rumbled in his chest and vibrated against me.

"Good pony," he crooned as I straightened and took a shuddering breath. I just had to commit to it and everything would be fine.

He had the decency to put me last in line. We waited, Kamal dressed in fancy slacks, riding boots, and a clean white cotton shirt, as Jake and Biskane were led out of the building.

At first sight of the bleachers full of kinky tourists, my steps faltered and I almost tripped. Kamal steadied me with a strong hand to my elbow. "Steady on, Blaze," he whispered. Even with Kamal's nearness, his musky male smell and his confident attention, my cock lay calm and small in its cage because I was genuinely terrified. But I forced myself to walk beside Kamal with my head up, my heart pounding erratically, and an out-of-body sensation coming over me.

Adam Marsland, whom I had yet to meet since he'd been so busy, began to speak into a microphone, introducing the ponies and their trainers. My ears started to ring as the other ponyboys were announced with their pony names. Biskane's pony nickname was Thunder and Jake's was Precious.

Listening to Marsland announce the nicknames of my friends as they pranced out into the arena made the sweat rise on my neck and face. I scuffed the ground with my boots and rolled the bit back and forth in my mouth.

Fuck, fuck, fuck.

"Kamal Salib, with his stunning ponyboy, Blaze!"

Kamal stepped forward and tugged on my reins, assuming I would go with him.

But my feet wouldn't move. My boots were glued to the ground, and I wasn't budging.

"Owen," he whispered harshly. "Let's go." He tugged the reins again and stared as I began to move my head rapidly back and forth, eyes wide with fear, body clenched and tight. I couldn't go out there. I couldn't.

Kamal stared at me as I shook my head and stamped my foot. At that moment I didn't care what he did to me, or how disappointed he would be. I couldn't do it and safewording was the only option.

"Fuck," Kamal said softly.

Adam looked over, and Kamal gave him a signal, shaking his head. Marsland seemed concerned but turned back to the crowd.

"It looks like our final ponyboy, Blaze, has balked. I'll have his trainer take him back inside, and see if we can't get him out here later. For the moment, take a look at Precious and Thunder in their fancy show gear!"

Kamal gathered my reins close to my chin and turned me back toward the arena. "Come on."

He sounded embarrassed and disappointed, but he'd told me if I safeworded by shaking my head back and forth we would stop or take a break, and I wouldn't be punished or demeaned. I was starting to wonder if that was true.

When we got inside the arena he led me to the table and immediately removed the mask and bridle, laying it down and placing his steadying hands on my shoulders.

"What's wrong, Owen?"

I licked my lips as relief flooded through me. Relief to be inside out of the heat and away from the stares of all those people.

"I can't—I won't—" The words wouldn't come.

"You can't do it right now."

I nodded, weak with relief that he understood, and I tried to speak again. "I can't do it right now. I just can't. Not with all the gear. It's too much."

He gazed at me, disappointment obvious in his expression. "I wanted to show you off. You've been doing so well."

I shrugged, my arms pulling on their bindings. "I know. I *want* to do it, but I can't. Not yet."

Kamal rubbed my shoulders. He didn't yell at me or force me to go through with the performance. I knew the BCR had standards of care, but you never really knew what might happen.

"Okay. Fair enough," Kamal said, looking me over and running a hand along my chest and over my belly, smoothing the soft hairs that gathered above the pelvic belt. "I am disappointed, but maybe I pushed you too far too fast."

"I'm sorry," I said because I had wanted to do this for him.

"Hey, it's okay. Adam's got two good-looking ponyboys out there right now, and we'll get you there eventually."

"But not today," I said firmly. I couldn't go through with it. I wasn't sure I could do it at all.

"Not today." He looked me over, sizing up my distress. "Do you want to stand at the fence with me and watch?"

I thought about it, but shook my head. "No, Sir."

Kamal pushed his lips out in a funny-looking pout. "Fine. We'll go back to the grooming barn, then."

"Thank you, Sir," I said in profound relief.

He led me to the grooming barn, and I wondered what he'd do about the fact that the stable hands were all out watching the pony show. But I needn't have worried.

Kamal unbuckled and removed my arm bands, then took off the thick collar and the body harness so I was naked except for the cock cage and tail. He placed the tack on the table for the stable hands to deal with and crossed his arms, regarding me thoughtfully.

"I'm really disappointed," he admitted.

"I'm sorry, Sir. I'm really sorry."

His eyes flashed and he shook his head. "Not with you, Owen, you silly man." He reached out and pulled me against him so smoothly it took me off guard, but I let myself be enveloped in those strong arms, against that broad chest, under that firm chin.

He felt like home. And at the same time, he felt better than any home I'd ever known.

"Fuck," Kamal cursed, holding me close, broad hands roaming my back, drifting down to cup my ass and squeeze, pressing me into him. His fingers dug into my crack and nudged the pony-tail plug in my ass, making me gasp. He stepped back, resting his hands gently on my waist. "I'm sorry. You safeworded. I assume you want everything off and to go back to the bunkhouse."

Did I? I didn't want to go anywhere else right now.

"No. I want to stay here with you."

"In the empty grooming barn?" he whispered.

I swallowed thickly. "Yes."

One of his hands drifted over my hips and down to my captured penis.

"You want this off, Owen?"

"Yes."

Kamal gazed at me, his forehead creasing. He knew we couldn't fuck. *I* knew we couldn't fuck. But that didn't mean everything physical was off the table, did it?

I stood, arms hanging at my sides, as he reached forward and fumbled with the clasp. When it released he tugged the cage off. This time the metal bars were bone dry because my cock had only recently become interested in what was going on.

The relief was immediate, and before I knew what I was doing, I reached forward and slid my fingers into Kamal's thick hair. When he started to stay something, I took the opportunity to capture his mouth with mine.

Where this boldness came from, I don't know. Maybe from all the time I'd spent frustrated in bondage while Kamal ordered me around. Now it was only the two of us, and I took that and ran with it, kissing him with all the ferocious energy I possessed.

His hands came up to clasp my face, holding me steady while the balance of power shifted. He returned my kiss and then some. For once the bit wasn't in the way as he delved into my mouth with his tongue, as if he wanted to devour me, lick me until I was nothing but a vessel for his passion.

I made an excited sound, opening as wide as I could for him, before sucking on his tongue and biting at his plump lips like they were the sweetest candy. My hands slid down to clutch his shoulders as my head twisted to keep up with his frantic motions.

"Oh, you fucking wreck of a ponyboy," he murmured between grabs at my mouth.

I moaned, kissing him back like a dam had broken, gasping between words. "I'm such a terrible ponyboy, Kamal. I don't know how to be one. I don't know what the fuck I'm doing..."

Kamal chuckled, his breath on my face as he kissed across my jaw and cheek. "You're a beautiful mess, Owen, and I wouldn't want you any other way."

His hand slid from my face down my side to cup my ass and squeeze, pressing me against him. I groaned as my cock rubbed against his hip.

"Holy shit," I panted, feeling like I would explode and take Kamal with me. His fingers slid into my crack and around the plug, jostling it as I groaned into his mouth.

I whimpered.

He chuckled and repeated the action.

"I'm going to come all over you," I said, rutting against him as he worked the plug back and forth.

But he stopped and clutched my arms, pushing me away as he grinned and raised his eyebrows. "I'd have a lot of explaining to do." He wiped his mouth with the back of his hand as I vibrated with energy.

"Hands behind your back."

I blinked, immediately brought back into the dynamic of Dom and sub. My hands went behind me. I tossed the hair out of my eyes and licked my lips.

"Fuck. I want to turn you around and fuck the shit out of you right now," Kamal said.

"I have a pony tail in my ass, Sir."

He laughed. "I'm not losing my job because of you."

I lifted my head.

Kamal grinned. He grabbed me by the chin and stared at my mouth. I thought he was going to kiss me again. But he only smiled and let go, then sank to his knees, wrapping his hand around my cock.

Kamal on his knees in front of me almost made my heart stop.

I inhaled deeply, eyes wide open as Kamal took my cock in his mouth and sucked. My head tipped back and my eyes closed as I lost myself in the warmth and wetness. Those lips that had gone at me with crazed eagerness only moments ago now went at my dick the same way. His mouth was so hot, his throat so tight, so strong. He swallowed me down and then twisted and swallowed again.

I opened my eyes to see his brown irises flash to mine as he worked me so intensely, so skillfully, that after a few seconds I warned him I was close.

His hand squeezed the base of my dick hard, and he slid his mouth off me, watching me twitch in the cool air as he held back my orgasm.

I whimpered with distress. "No, please, I want to come."

"I want you to come too. But you need to turn around so you don't make a mess on me."

"Okay. Okay." I was beyond the use of proper terms. He led me to the table and bent me over it as if he were going to fuck me.

"Oh, Jesus," I moaned.

Kamal pressed his pelvis against the tail in my ass, shoving it deeper. The side of my face lay against the table as Kamal fumbled for a nearby tube of lube. He squirted some onto his hand and reached beneath me.

"We're going to play a game, Owen," Kamal said, thrusting against me so the plug moved inside me.

"Yes, Sir." I gasped.

"You're going to pretend this plug is my dick, and I'm going to jerk you off while I pretend to fuck you."

"Oh, God."

"You ready?" he said, wrapping his lubed fingers around my dick.

"Fuck, yes."

Kamal gasped and moved against me. The plug shifted as if it was his cock plunging back and forth, not as far as I would like, but enough to make me whimper with pleasure.

"Oh my God." I unclasped my hands and stretched my arms against the table.

"Hands behind your back, Owen." Kamal grunted.

I whimpered but obeyed as he began a steady rhythm of thrusting against the plug and jerking my cock.

I blubbered nonsense about being his good ponyboy and doing whatever he told me to do as I got closer and closer, my balls tingling. When I came, I shouted into the empty grooming barn and shot streams of semen onto the floor.

"Good—" *thrust* "—boy" *thrust,* he said, pounding me through my orgasm until I whimpered in surrender.

The warmth of his body disappeared as his fingers slipped from me, and he appeared beside the table. Mouth open, breaths wild, eyes wide, he yanked his zipper down and pulled his dick out of his underwear.

The skin was darker than the rest of him. His pubic hair had been trimmed but still curled around the base of his thick penis, the circumcised head of which swelled rosy purple like a ripe plumb.

He held my gaze as he jerked himself once, twice, and came on the third stroke, shooting onto my face and neck as I smiled with exhausted pleasure.

"Oh, fuck," he gasped. "Oh, fuck you, Owen Lipke," he groaned, milking the last of his come and painting me with it.

Chapter Fourteen

"The show must be almost over," Kamal said.

He'd cleaned us both, then pulled me from my reclined position to standing. We gazed at each other shyly, as if what had happened had taken both of us by surprise.

"They'll be coming back," I said.

He smiled. "If you trust me, I've got an idea for something we can work on next week. It might help put the merits of pony play in some perspective."

"Sounds interesting," I said, still dazed from my orgasm.

He grinned. "Oh, it will be. But right now, I'm going to hose you down and send you back to the bunkhouse."

I smiled. "Yes, Sir."

He started to move away but I grabbed the front of his shirt and pulled him in for a scorching kiss. After, he bent me over the table again and gently removed the butt-plug tail, then fastened my wrists to the ceiling and hosed me down, as gently and thoroughly as any stable hand. By the time he toweled me dry, we heard footsteps and the clomping of heavy boots.

He kissed me again, quickly. "Take it easy tomorrow. Rest and relax. I'll see you on Monday. Don't forget, you're on afternoons next week."

"Kamal," I said, so many emotions brimming. "Thanks for...understanding."

"Hey. You say that safeword and I stop what we're doing. I will never be angry at you for being honest. Never."

He sent me around the partition a moment before the others came in.

"Hey, Kamal. Sorry you had to miss the show. How is Owen?"

"He'll be okay. A bit of stage fright; that's all. I shouldn't have put him in full tack."

"He looked freaking amazing though."

"Yeah, he did. Anyway, I'll get out of your way. You've got your hands full cleaning up these two."

Carrie laughed. "Sure do. But they were awesome! And I'm sure Owen will be good to go at the next one."

God, I sure hope so. For my sake and Kamal's.

I got dressed quickly, feeling loose-limbed and exhausted, and walked back to the bunkhouse in the heat of the afternoon.

*

Sunday dawned dark and stormy, so we stayed inside, lounging on our bunks or playing board games in the loft. No one had claimed the upper area for sleeping so it became a games room of sorts, although I'm pretty sure I had heard Sam and Miles playing a different kind of game late last night, what with all the grunts and sighs.

Well, good for them.

I did some more sketching, which always relaxed me. I tried to draw Kamal's hands—those capable, strong fingers—knuckles covered with a touch of dark hair—flat, even nails. They turned out all right. Then I drew a sketch of the pretty mask from the pony show. I had to admit, it did suit me.

I had been so tired from the emotional stress and physical release of my afternoon, I'd drifted off to sleep to the sounds of Sam and Miles getting busy. I was jealous, because I wanted Kamal to take me somewhere and fuck me, but I knew he wasn't allowed, and that made me frustrated.

Of course, after all these years of trying to find the perfect man, now I'd found him, and we couldn't carry our interest in each other to the next level. Well, I'd have to be patient. He wouldn't be my trainer forever.

But what would happen then? What would happen when my time was up after six weeks at the Braided Crop Ranch? Could I stay one extra night for the sole purpose of finally fucking Kamal to see where that might lead? I doubted it, because we had to make room for the next batch of ponyboys and Kamal would have to get ready to train someone else.

Fuck my life.

I groaned and rolled over, mashing my erection into the mattress. The thought of him brought back sensory memories of what happened between us in the grooming barn. I'd half expected him to be furious with me for backing out of the show, but I should have known better. Kamal was a professional. He knew the basic rules of BDSM that encouraged trust between two players. No one ever got mad at someone for saying their safeword because it was there to protect both parties.

I had no doubt that if I'd been able to force myself into that show ring, I would have been so traumatized and damaged by the experience I might have decided to leave this place and return home to my boring suburban life in Ottawa. And that would have been fucking tragic.

"Hey, Owen. You okay?" Biskane asked from his bunk.

I grunted and pressed my dick into the mattress again. "Sure."

A blond head appeared beside my bunk and blue eyes blinked at me. "Well, he looks like he's trying to have an intimate relationship with his mattress, so I'd say he's lying."

It was Sam. I gave him the finger and rolled to the side, which was a mistake.

"Oh, holy shit," Sam whispered, seeing my erection in my boxer briefs.

I tried to cover it with my hand.

"Yeah, one hand's not gonna do it, scaredy cat. That's a huge boner you've got there."

Then Biskane was beside him.

"Fuck off, will you?" I groaned, too conflicted to deal with this right now. "Just leave me alone."

"Or..." Biskane said, glancing at Sam and then at me. "I mean, I'm pretty sure I could brace the shower door with a chair or something. If you guys want a little... distraction?"

I realized they weren't there to make fun of me, but to help me deal with my problem. I raised my eyebrows and pursed my lips. "You mean...both of you...and me?"

Sam eyed Biskane up and down, then looked at me and quirked his pretty pink lips. "Sure. I need to take the measure of Kamal's other ponyboy. The one he seems to have already chosen as his favourite."

I opened my mouth to protest, except that his words reassured me there wasn't a similar connection between the two of them, and I couldn't deny it.

He raised his hand. "It's fine. Everyone can see the way you two are when you're together. Doesn't bother me. He's a great trainer, though, and I count myself lucky to have been placed with him. But I also want to find out what makes you so special, Owen."

"Fuck. I'm not special," I said. I wasn't special. The only thing that was special was what happened between me and Kamal when we were together.

"Let's see, shall we?" Sam said, gesturing for me to descend from my bunk, which I did.

"Jesus," Biskane hissed. "That ass is so fucking amazing. I almost came when I saw it with the pony tail sticking out of it yesterday."

"I know, right? I can't wait to try it myself. What's it feel like, Owen?"

"Feels like a regular butt plug but the horsehairs tickle," I said. "I'm sure you'll find out soon."

Sam glanced at the bathroom door, then looked to make sure none of the others were watching—not that they'd care.

"I'll go first. Then Owen. Then you." He pointed at Biskane. "I'm so fucking horny I could fuck a horse." He opened his mouth in a silent laugh as he turned and strode to the showers.

*

We braced a chair against the door, and I watched Biskane fuck Sam in one of the changing stalls while I stood in the open doorway and stroked my cock, urging them on. Biskane came in Sam's hand while Sam plowed him from behind. I didn't have the greatest view, but the sounds were hot as hell.

"Shit, that was awesome," I murmured as they recovered and turned toward me with purpose in their eyes. "Oh, shit."

They took turns sucking me; then Sam went behind me and fucked me with his fingers while Biskane finished me off. It was quite something to be stuck in the middle of a Sam and Biskane sandwich, but it didn't hold a candle to my experience with Kamal in the grooming barn or the paddock.

After lunch, the weather cleared, and the six of us headed to the lake to swim and relax on towels on the sand. I watched lazily as the other ponyboys did cannonballs off the dock and swam in the cool water. My head was filled with thoughts of Kamal that my assignation in the showers hadn't done anything to diminish. That had been a bit of fun, but I was chomping at the bit to see Kamal on Monday afternoon and find out what he had planned for me.

*

I woke early the next day to the sounds of the guys on the morning shift getting ready. Even though I had the option to sleep in, my body was used to rising before eight, and I was excited about seeing Kamal again. Plus, I was starving. I got up and grabbed a protein bar and some leftover coffee as the morning crew were leaving for the grooming barn. Sam blew me a kiss and winked at Biskane as he stepped out the door and closed it behind him.

"That man is so hot!" Biskane sighed, collapsing on his bunk and rolling over, maybe to see if he could go back to sleep.

"I guess. If you like muscles."

"Who doesn't like muscles?"

I shrugged. Sure, a perfectly sculpted body looked amazing in some respects. But often the attitude that came with it was a turn-off. Give me a less-than-perfect man with personality and stature any day. Kamal had muscles, but he wasn't physically perfect in a way that would win any bodybuilding awards. Instead, he had a shitload of charisma and a massive presence that made people shudder from a single look of his deep-brown eyes.

Sam was cool and funny, but I didn't feel anything more than a passing attraction to the guy. Biskane was physically more my type, but even his beauty was eclipsed by Kamal's rugged and stoic physiognomy.

Adrian strode out of the washroom, replacing his walkie-talkie on his belt. "Shit, I'm late," he said, grabbing a piece of toast off a plate and rushing past us. "Owen, you're wanted at the main house."

I barely realized he was speaking to me until a few seconds later when Adrian turned back to me.

"Adam wants to see you at the main house. In his office. Like, now," he said, rushing out the door and shutting it loudly behind him.

I glanced at Biskane as if he might know what was going on. He tilted his head on the pillow and opened sleepy eyes. "Are you in trouble?"

"I don't know," I said.

I dressed in my nicest pair of jeans and a short-sleeved button-up shirt to look presentable, brushed my hair and teeth, shaved quickly in case I didn't have time later, and headed across the grass, wondering why I was being summoned. I hadn't met Adam Marsland formally, and I didn't know what to expect. He'd seemed professional and reasonable from the emails we'd exchanged.

What if Kamal had told him what had happened in the grooming barn? I didn't think we'd violated any of the Ranch rules, but what did I know? Kamal didn't seem the type to break rules, especially at a place he'd been working for so long and obviously loved.

Or maybe Kamal had told Adam how we felt about each other, and Adam had decided he should switch me to a different trainer. If that was the case, I'd be leaving. But then I wouldn't be able to see Kamal at all.

By the time I got to the main house and walked up to where Connor was staring with frustration at his computer, I was a wreck of nerves. I still couldn't help but notice Connor was having an issue.

"Hi, Connor. Adam said he wanted to see me?"

"Yeah, he's not in his office yet. But he'll be down shortly. You can wait out here or in there, whichever." Usually polite and friendly, Connor seemed out of sorts.

"What's wrong? Do you think he's pissed at me?" I said quietly, figuring if he was I might as well find out now.

Connor's head jerked up and his eyes scanned me quickly. "What? No, I don't think so."

I shoved my hands in my pockets, not comforted.

"Sorry, I'm having issues with our software. It's been a fucking nightmare recently."

My ears perked up. Or would have, if I were actually a horse.

"Can I take a look?"

Connor eyed me carefully. "You know computers?"

"I know software. I'm a software engineer."

Connor smiled quickly. "Oh! Then, hell yeah. See if you can figure this bastard out."

I came around the desk and had a look at the program he was working with. I recognized it right away. "I know this one. I've got you. Can I sit down?"

Connor got out of his chair and let me sit. After a few minutes I figured out what was causing his problem and fixed it with a click.

"There you go," I said. "All better."

He gaped at me. "Seriously? I've been struggling for *two days.*"

I shrugged and gave him his chair back as Adam Marsland came down the stairs.

"Sorry, Owen. I didn't mean to waste your time." Adam gave Connor a wink and extended his hand to me. "Sorry I haven't introduced myself to you yet. I'm usually not so busy at the start of a session. Anyway, I'm Adam."

Adam Marsland in person looked like some famous actor from a film noir with his salt-and-pepper hair and his buttoned-up style. I took his hand and shook it. "No worries. Nice to finally meet you."

"Has Connor been keeping you entertained?" he said with a smile. Then he turned to Connor. "Did you offer Owen some coffee?"

Connor looked embarrassed. He stood from his desk. "Shit, no I didn't. I was too busy swearing at this stupid system. But Owen fixed it for me. Like, in two seconds."

Adam looked me over. "You know computers?"

"Software. I'm a software developer. Engineer. What have you." I was starting to calm down now that Adam seemed friendly and normal. It didn't seem I'd been summoned for a disciplinary meeting.

"Oh? Well, that's handy while you're here." He grinned. "Come sit in my office, Owen. I need to talk to you about something. It won't take long."

"Yes, sir," I said, following him as he asked Connor if he'd mind bringing the pot of coffee in.

"Not at all, Adam. One second."

"I've got mugs in my office."

"Sure. Be there in a sec."

I followed Adam into his small office and he closed the door behind me, gesturing to a chair.

"Have a seat, Owen," he said, opening a cabinet in the large mahogany wall unit behind his desk and pulling out two mugs.

He glanced at them and then put one in front of me with a smirk.

I looked down at the words: *Save a horse. Ride a cowboy.*

"I like to give that one to Jensen when he's in the office," Adam said.

I laughed. "Seems fair."

He showed me his mug, which said *Head Master* on it. "No double meaning there, I promise."

"Sure."

"Anyway, I asked you to come see me this morning because Kamal and I had an interesting discussion yesterday."

Oh shit. Here we go.

"You did?" Always best to fake confusion in a situation like this.

Adam nodded. "We did. It was about you."

"Me?"

Suddenly, his eyes narrowed, like he knew he was being played. "Yes, you." He folded his hands on the desk and leaned forward. "Kamal is my best trainer, Owen."

I felt my breath leave my body. "Yes, sir."

Adam might not have Kamal's dominating presence but he had his own undeniable charisma and the ability to cut right to the chase.

"We're also very good friends, and we don't keep secrets."

"Oh shit," I said, not knowing where this was leading, but aware that Adam probably knew everything. Or figured he did.

He leaned back, eyeing me thoughtfully. "You haven't done anything wrong."

The breath whooshed out of me with relief.

"Except to capture the heart of one of the most important men on my ranch. In the space of two weeks."

Capture the heart of—? I'd only come here for some fetish play.

"I'm sorry," I said quickly. "I didn't mean to. I wasn't looking for...that."

He regarded me quizzically. "Do you have feelings for him, or is this all one-sided? He didn't think so, but then, Kamal's not used to feeling this way about anyone."

"I...I mean, I think so? I mean, it's hard to talk about it. But, yeah. I have feelings. Strong feelings, I guess." This was fucking embarrassing, and I couldn't help downplaying it.

"You guess?" But Adam wasn't having that. He gazed at me sternly. He sure had that whole Daddy vibe going on. I gave up trying to keep anything from him.

"Yes. I have strong feelings for Kamal. I probably shouldn't, but I do. They...came out of nowhere."

Adam relaxed his expression. "Yes, that's what Kamal said. I was surprised. He's never felt like this for anyone."

"Even Luke?" I asked, staring at the desk in front of me as I heard a knock and Connor came in with the coffee pot. Adam waited while Connor put it on the trivet and took his leave after Adam thanked him.

Adam grinned and raised his eyebrows, pouring some black brew in both cups. "He told you about Luke."

"Yeah. And, actually, Luke was waiting for me at the bunkhouse on Thursday."

Adam blinked. "That little shit. He's not supposed to just wander the property like he owns it. And I don't recall being asked."

"Well, he was there, and he introduced himself. He said he wanted to see the place again."

"I'll bet. He had quite a summer last year."

"I heard. He wanted to make sure I could give Kamal what he needed," I said carefully.

Adam stared at me silently for a long moment. "And can you?"

I licked my lips, nodding. "I think so. Yeah."

"Well, that leaves me in a strange predicament," Adam said, rubbing his forehead. "Kamal is a trainer here, and I can't break the rules for him or for you."

"No, sir."

"And I'd really hate to lose him, Owen."

What the hell did he mean?

"When your session is over, if you and Kamal want to explore something together, I'd rather you did it here."

Oh.

Shit.

Was I ready to give up my other life for the possibility of something meaningful with Kamal?

"I could probably find a way to keep you on here. Not as a ponyboy, obviously." He nodded toward the door. "Maybe as an IT troubleshooter or something."

I tried to process what Adam was saying.

"The pay wouldn't be as good as you're probably getting back home, but you'd be able to stay. Anyway, I'm getting way ahead of myself now. I actually need to talk to you about something Kamal has in mind for today."

My brain was already spinning from this conversation, and now there was something else?

"Sure," I said when I was anything but.

"He's asked me to get your permission to do some pup-play with you today. And he'd like to keep you for the night if you're okay with it." He narrowed his eyes. "Not for anything against the rules. He merely thinks you'd benefit from a lesson in true submission and extreme role-play. Not extreme in terms of activities. He wants to take you to a place you might not have been to before. In your own head."

I stared at Adam and rubbed the edge of the table with my fingertip. I hadn't tasted my coffee, but the aromatic smell of it was grounding.

I'd never engaged in any kind of animal role-play before my experience at the ranch. I wasn't sure about pup play, but then my experience with pony play had been relatively positive so far. And I *did* trust Kamal. And, hello, *true submission. What the fuck did that mean?* I was dying to find out. "Okay."

"That's not good enough."

"What? I mean, pardon?"

Adam smiled. "I need your explicit consent, Owen. This is not something we normally do at the BCR, and I need to ensure you're okay with the idea. And that you know you can safeword at any time if it's too much or you change your mind."

"Okay." That made sense.

He leaned forward. "Are you okay with engaging in some pup play with Kamal in his rooms and possibly staying the night there? I trust him implicitly, but that doesn't mean you have to go through with it. And Kamal won't be upset if you say no. I promise."

"I want to try it. I do consent to it." I said quickly. *How's that for explicit consent, Adam?*

Adam grinned and sat back, trying to hold in his laughter. "Well, in that case, he's waiting for you upstairs."

"Like, right now?" I said.

He inclined his head. "Jensen's working with Sam on his own while Kamal prepares things for you. But I'm sure he'd wait if you needed some time."

I shook my head. "No, it's not that. I haven't showered this morning. Yet."

Adam laughed. "Well, Kamal has a pretty nice en suite in his room. I'm sure he won't mind making sure you're all clean and polished for his games."

My mouth dropped open.

Chapter Fifteen

Kamal's room was number five on the second floor. I tried to walk slowly up the stairs of the main house once Adam dismissed me, but my steps quickened as I got nearer to my fate. The wood floor creaked as I walked down the hall and rapped sharply on his door, my heart rate speeding up like I was about to jump off a cliff.

It opened quickly to a Kamal in grey sweatpants, a faded black T-shirt, and bare feet. I blinked at this unexpected apparition, my fist still in the air. I'd only seen him in proper clothes. I shoved my hands in my pockets and gazed at him through the fall of black hair on my forehead.

"Owen. I'm so glad you agreed to this."

I gave him a small smile in response. "Yeah, I'm nervous. But I trust you."

He beckoned me in. His room could have been in an expensive hotel. There was a sitting area on one side and a Queen bed on the other. A door, presumably to the bathroom, was to the left of the bed. I hoped Kamal wouldn't be mad that I hadn't showered.

"I didn't shower before coming here this morning. I told Adam and he said you could let me shower here? If you want? If you don't mind?" God, I sounded like a nervous twelve-year-old in his presence sometimes.

He looked me up and down and shook his head, clicking his tongue as he walked toward the bathroom. "Dirty, dirty boy."

Those words made my dick spring to attention, especially when he pushed open the bathroom door and beckoned me through. "I don't mind in the least."

As I walked past him he laid a gentle hand on my bicep, stopping me in my tracks. "Do you need me to wash you?" He was breathing hard and I stared up into his intense brown eyes and was about to say, "Yeah, okay," when he stopped me.

"No, don't answer that. Probably not a good idea. I promised Adam I'd be good and obey his rules. Our rules. The BCR's rules. The rules I had no problem not breaking until you got here. Jesus Christ."

He ran a hand through his hair as I felt equally the cause of all his troubles and the solution.

"I'm sorry."

"I'm not," he said softly. "I'm not sorry at all. Go have your shower and dry off. Don't put your clothes back on. As long as I keep mine on, we'll be okay."

I gave a little pout at the thought that I wouldn't get to see Kamal naked over the next twenty-four hours. But it was probably for the best.

Anyway, he laughed. "Get on with ya."

I went into the en suite, again impressed by the finishes and the style of the space. Kamal closed the door behind me and I tried to forget he was out there waiting. I needed to take some time and space to relax and get into the right headspace.

I took off my clothes and piled them neatly on the chair, wondering what the other ponyboys would think if

I didn't return to the bunkhouse before dark—probably that I'd left or been kicked out.

He'd left a douching kit on the counter, so I used it, flushing anything that might have gotten in the way of our play, and then stepped into the shower.

Cleaning myself under the hot spray, I got that nervous and excited feeling in my gut about what was going to happen. Kamal seemed less intimidating in sweatpants and a T than he did in his regular outfit. But he'd told Adam he wanted to show me the meaning of true submission and puppy play. I figured he would have to channel some big Dom energy for that. I kind of adored his big Dom energy.

"Don't jerk off," Kamal's voice came from the other room just as I slid my hand down to my cock in unconscious reaction to my thoughts. I jerked it away and smiled wryly. *Talk about big Dom energy.*

"Yes, Sir," I said loudly. "Almost done."

I finished and dried off. Standing quietly in front of the closed door, I took deep, calming breaths before pulling it open and stepping into the carpeted room.

I stopped dead. Kamal had been busy.

While I'd been in the bathroom for approximately thirty minutes, he'd produced a padded spanking bench from somewhere and set it up near the sofa in a space between the living area and the bed. It didn't escape my notice that he'd placed a clear plastic mat beneath it— something easier to clean than carpet if any wet spots...happened.

On the bed were an assortment of items my eyes scanned apprehensively while Kamal looked up from his spot on the arm of the small sofa.

"Don't worry, Owen," he said.

I forced myself to walk into the room and over to Kamal where I sank to my knees, gazing up at him with innocent eyes. "I'm not worried."

I was lying.

Even though I hadn't spent much time looking at the items on Kamal's bed, I'd definitely seen a dog collar and leash, two dog bowls, some plush toys, a rubber ball, and what looked like a butt plug rubber dog tail, as well as a riding crop and some paddles.

"Good boy," Kamal said, ruffling my hair and winking at me. "I expect you know what that is?" he said, pointing at the bench.

"Yes, Sir."

He raised his eyebrows.

"A spanking bench."

"Have you ever been restrained on a spanking bench?"

"Yes, Sir."

"Have you been teased over a spanking bench?"

"Yes, Sir."

"Crops? Paddles?"

"Yes, Sir."

"Okay. Well, that's all we're going to do here so there's nothing to worry about. Same rule applies. If you need to stop or need a break, use your safeword, which is..." he waited for me to say it.

"Pineapple."

"Very good. I won't be gagging you for any of this, so you'll always be able to say it."

"Thank you, Sir."

He knelt down so we were at eye level and cupped my chin in his hand. "What exactly did Adam tell you I wanted to do with you?"

I swallowed, my cock becoming rock hard in an instant. "He said you wanted to do some pup play, and you wanted to show me what *true submission* felt like."

"Wow, okay. Well, he was right about the pup play. And I do want to see if I can show you how it feels to be lowest on the totem pole. But true submission? I mean, that could be different for everybody."

"Yes, Sir."

"Stay there. You look beautiful on your knees." He stood and walked over to sit on the edge of the bed. He picked up the leather collar and examined it while he spoke. "When you think about dogs, Owen, what comes to mind?"

I couldn't help laughing, because it *wasn't this.* But I knew he wanted me to answer honestly, so I did. "Uh, friendship, loyalty, joy. Looking after something."

"Looking after *someone*," Kamal said.

"Looking after someone."

"That's all this is. You are going to be my pet, and I am going to look after you. Not in the ways I'd look after a real dog in some respects. But you aren't a real dog. You're a man. And your needs are different than a dog's needs, at least in relation to what I can give you."

My skin flushed as I thought about how it would feel to be taken care of by Kamal for the rest of the day and maybe overnight. Would I enjoy it? Or would I get bored and restless and ruin this experiment for both of us? There was only one way to find out.

"Yes, Sir."

"Still on board?"

"Yes, Sir."

"All right then. Crawl over here so I can put this collar on you."

I looked at him.

"Yes. On your hands and knees, Owen," he stated. "Like a dog. Because that's what you're gonna be for me today. Mostly."

My skin flushed and my ears tingled at the outright humiliation of it, but I forced myself to crawl to Kamal where he stood beside the bed. I stopped and stared at his broad bare feet. I'd never really looked closely at a guy's bare feet before, but I liked Kamal's. They were smooth and strong, a dusting of hair over the toes. They smelled clean and looked like the most vulnerable part of him.

Instead of putting the collar around my neck, Kamal said, "Lick my feet, Owen."

I felt a deep shame in my belly, but my cock throbbed. Maybe it wouldn't be so bad. I bent my face to his instep and licked a long line from the ball of his foot to his ankle.

"Good boy," he murmured, affection and pleasure in his voice.

I bent and did the same to the other foot, closing my eyes and enjoying the curve of bone and muscle beneath his clean skin.

"That's enough," he said, a tremor in his voice. I wondered if this turned him on. But of course it fucking did. I was down here naked on my hands and knees with my ass in the air, worshipping his feet.

I crouched there, waiting, as he picked up something from the bed and leaned down. He stretched the soft leather collar around my neck and buckled it so it was comfortable. It didn't seem all that different from my pony collar except it was narrower and softer, and made me feel smaller.

I wasn't a pony, now. I was a pup. And the difference seemed extraordinary.

As a pony I had some dignity. I was able to walk upright with my chin and my chest out. Down here on all fours I felt lowly and insignificant.

It wasn't without its charm, and I hoped through the course of the day more of that would become evident.

I heard a soft jingling as Kamal bent and clipped the leash to my collar.

"Heel," he said, as he stepped to the side and jerked the leash gently. I needed to check in so I flicked my gaze to his, seeing in those brown eyes a look so dark and aroused it scared me. Then the jolt in my cock answered it, and the fear disappeared.

I knew Kamal would take care of me. I knew I was safe.

He walked a slow circle around the room with me at his heel, then stopped by the spanking bench.

"Up."

When I glanced at him he motioned to the bench. I climbed onto it as he helped me get in position, my wrists buckled to the tops of the forward legs, my collar attached to a ring and my cock jutting underneath the end of the bench with my belly supported. This meant my knees were bent in a sort of crouch as he fastened my ankles to the bench legs. It was a humiliating position but if Kamal wanted me like this I couldn't protest.

He cleared his throat and hummed softly to himself as he prepared the items he planned to use on me. Would it be the crop or the paddle first? I had no idea. The anticipation made me sweat with excitement and fear. But it was good fear—the kind I liked.

I flashed back to the hidden rooms at the Stocks where I'd been trussed up in similar positions and Dominated by weird, power-hungry men who barely knew how to treat a sub properly. Either that or they simply didn't care to. There had been some close calls before I'd safeworded and gotten the hell out of there. Then there were the sessions that bored me to tears, where I kept waiting for something genuinely exciting and terrifying at the same time but had never felt it.

Here I was bent over a bench in Kamal's room at the BCR and he hadn't even touched me yet, but I was quivering with emotion.

Yes, yes, yes, my body screamed as my brain spun in joyous circles. I heard the soft footfalls as Kamal walked over to me. The palm of his hand landed sharply on my ass as I yelped in surprise and then whimpered and rubbed my cheek against the padded leather of the bench.

"Good boy. Another?"

I nodded, sighing. *Yes, please.*

It was nothing. A fucking bare hand spanking my ass, but it was the best thing I'd felt in a long, long time. Because it was Kamal's hand, and he had me displayed and bound for only him. A bare hand was more intimate than a tool.

His hand came down again and I moaned.

"Fuck," I whispered.

"You like that?"

"Yes, Sir." My voice was shaky already, my dick stiff and surging.

My belly warmed to the sound of his laughter. "You look fucking hot like this. I might just keep you like this all afternoon. I'll put that dog tail in you and sit back on my bed and look at you. You'll probably die waiting for me to do something."

I groaned in agony at the thought—probably the wrong message to send someone who was looking for a good way to torture me.

"That's a special dog tail, you know. Just for you."

I whimpered.

"It vibrates."

I stiffened all over. *Oh fuck. Oh fucking hell. A vibrating dog tail?*

He laughed. I turned my head, pressing my other cheek against the leather so I could gape at him silently.

Kamal sat on the bed, holding the dog tail and stroking the butt plug, staring at me with dark, dark eyes. He lifted it slowly and pressed it to his lips, closing his eyes as he kissed and licked the thing he was about to stick in my ass and torture me with for the next, well, who knew how long?

I think I almost passed out. I jerked against my restraints, making the bench creak and Kamal smile, lowering the toy. He wiped his mouth with the back of his hand as the plug shone with his saliva.

"Oh, you won't be going anywhere. You're going to stay right there, Owen, tied down and helpless, with this beautiful tail in your ass. And it's going to tease you for hours while I watch and maybe jerk off a few times."

He was in charge, and I was nothing—a human toy for him to play with. He could pretend I was a dog if he wanted, but the things he was doing to me, and wanted to do to me, were human things and I wasn't fooled. Was that what Adam had meant by true submission? Being tied down and teased until I embarrassed myself or went fucking crazy with lust in the process? All for the amusement of my Master?

I moaned and licked my lips, eager for him to begin. Because I wanted this. I wanted this *so badly*. No matter how utterly humiliating it would be, it would be for him. And he would be watching it all.

He reached for the bottle of lube and squirted some onto the plug, using his broad fingers to rub it all over. It was as fascinating and erotic as if he was stroking his cock, knowing that plug was going in my ass when he was done.

When he stood and walked over, I struggled as if I wanted to get away, when in reality I couldn't wait for that goddamned tail.

He chuckled and stroked my ass, sliding his fingers between my cheeks and rubbing lube onto and into me. No glove, only his bare fingers, so slippery and agile, preparing me for the medium-sized plug.

I felt the broad tip as he pressed it against my hole. I was used to the pony tail by now, and this was a similar size. It didn't take long for my ass to open of its own accord as Kamal inserted the plug slowly.

The pleasure of it was incredible. Kamal was gentle and slow, not like he was with the pony tail in the arena. In the arena Kamal was efficient and dispassionate. In his room he was kind. He undid me with pleasure as he pushed the plug all the way inside.

He wiggled it to make sure it was seated then stood and wiped his hand on a towel. "How does that feel, Owen?"

"Debased." My voice was so quiet even I barely heard it. My eyes were shut tight.

He chuckled. "Good."

I tried to laugh but it came out a moan. Fuck it, I was doomed to embarrass myself many times over today.

Kamal came close again. He snapped something tight around the base of my cock, and something else around the top of my balls. "A little assistance so you don't come too quickly. Want to keep you in that sweet spot between spilling over and going crazy."

Oh fuck me. I was so doomed.

"Sir?" I murmured.

"Yes, Owen?"

"Are you...are you really going to sit there and watch?"

"Yes, Owen. Even though this isn't a punishment for safewording yesterday, I feel like you owe me some entertainment value, since I didn't get to see you parade around that show ring with all your fancy gear on," he said, massaging my buttock as I got used to the feel of the plug. "It's only you and me today. Nobody else watching. Just us."

"Yes, Sir."

He slapped the rubber tail with his hand so it wobbled violently back and forth, jiggling the plug and causing me to pull at my wrist restraints. I felt objectified and displayed with my legs bent awkwardly, my ass in the air, and my cock jutting into the air below the bench.

Kamal stood and walked back to the bed. I still faced that direction and figured I'd at least be able to watch Kamal. He picked up the dog bowls and put them on the floor beside the bed.

"For later on," he said. "You'll eat your lunch, and maybe your supper if you make it that long down there."

I sighed at the thought, at the debasement of it, as he opened a drawer in his dresser and brought out a soft black cloth.

"I'm going to blindfold you, because I want you to focus on the pleasure and the struggle and the utter humiliation of your position, and not on what I'm doing."

Bastard. I wouldn't even get to see him while he was torturing me. I would only know he was watching everything.

He placed the fabric over my eyes and tied it behind my head while I licked my lips and tried to keep my breathing steady. It was fine. I was going to be fine. I'd probably come at least once with that vibrating plug teasing me, but so what? Wasn't that what he wanted? Wasn't that exactly what he wanted to see?

Or did he want to see the way I suffered with the agony of getting close but not being able to come because of the ring on my cock? Because that would last some time before I finally went over the edge and got some relief.

I knew how cock rings worked. And I knew how it felt to have something vibrating in your ass against your prostate. So, I knew exactly how fucked I was and that I was destined to be teased out of my mind for as long as Kamal wanted.

I stretched my back out, arching like a cat in preparation.

Chapter Sixteen

"Good boy," Kamal said, "Are you ready?"

I puffed out a breath. "No, Sir."

"Do I care?"

"Probably not, Sir."

He laughed, a full hearty laugh, and sighed. "You got it. A plus. You look a sight, Owen. And I can't wait until you're writhing and begging for mercy." He walked over and slapped my ass. "What's your safeword, Owen?"

"Pineapple," I grunted, the sting from his spank spreading across my skin.

"Use it if you want. But everything stops if you do, and I send you to the bunkhouse. If you get to a point where that's what you want, use it. Otherwise, I'll assume you're still on board."

"Yes, Sir." Going back to the bunkhouse was the last thing I wanted.

"All right then. I'm going to make myself comfortable over here on the bed," he said.

I heard the squeak of the mattress and the rustle of bedclothes as Kamal arranged himself against the pillows, settling in for a morning's entertainment. I didn't know what time it was, but it had been eight o'clock when I'd presented myself in Adam's office. It was probably about nine thirty—if that—and we had a long way to go until lunch. A lunch I would have to eat out of bowls on the floor.

The plug began to vibrate slightly. It was so low I barely felt it but it was there. I was surprised he didn't start it at full strength to scare me. It potentially could give a much more violent vibration than he'd set it for at the moment. Maybe that was scarier—knowing it could go a lot harder but not having any idea how much.

At the moment, it was a gentle, peaceful hum of sensation deep inside me where I liked it. In my current position, the tip of the expertly made plug grazed against my prostate, and the low vibration was soothing.

I relaxed and settled against the bench as the soft vibrations massaged me from the inside out. The cock ring kept me hard although I was nowhere near ready to come. My dick ached and throbbed while the plug teased me gently. I felt pretty good about how things were beginning.

Kamal shifted on the bed. I heard him pick something up as the pages of a book rustled.

Was that fucker going to read a book while I was tied here? As if he wasn't even interested in watching me?

My mouth opened and I licked my lips, rubbing my cheek against the bench in confusion and frustration.

"Relax, Owen. We've got all morning," he said, and I realized I was nothing more than a distraction. He'd read his book and think of other things while I crouched here in this awkward position, becoming more and more aroused until he was forced to attend to me. *Maybe?*

I let out a pitiful moan at the diabolical frustration of it. My utter objectification and his bored dismissal of it roiled in my veins like heroin to a junkie.

The vibrations kicked up a notch.

I moaned again as my dick jerked and sweat began to bead on the back of my neck. More from fear of the unknown than how I felt right now. At the moment I was still able to deal with things, but as the vibrations increased I began to doubt myself. The soothing waves of stimulation became torturous, teasing ebbs and flows of rising pleasure. Restrained as I was, I couldn't control anything about it. The more I struggled the more I realized how helpless I was.

I whimpered to see if that helped. It didn't. The vibrating plug became my enemy as its sensations went from enjoyable to exquisite, sending waves of pleasure through me that I couldn't figure out what to do with. I groaned and grunted out of desperation, and shifting my position as much as I could to try to find some relief.

I thought I heard a soft moan from the bed but then Kamal spoke, so I must have imagined it. His voice sounded steady and unaffected.

"Relax, Owen. The more you fight it the worse it will be." He flipped another page in his book.

Fucker.

He knew what this was doing to me and all he could do was sit there and read? He wasn't even jerking off or doing anything remotely interesting while I crouched here with the devil's tail in my ass. The rubber tail wagged as I struggled, adding insult to injury and making me feel ridiculous and small. I felt the cool ambient air of the room on the head of my dick. It had nudged out of its protective hood and now leaked pre-ejaculate in quantities that felt like Niagara Falls but were probably dribbles. I thrust instinctively into the empty space under the bench while a low chuckle came from the bed.

"It's no use, Owen. You're not going to be able to come for a while." Now his voice sounded breathy and rough, and I realized he was only pretending to read. He was flipping pages deliberately to distract me when he was actually watching me and it was doing things to him. Very good things, I hoped.

That thought made my distress a little bit sweeter. At least Kamal was enjoying the show. I heard a definite gasp as the mattress springs creaked.

What was he doing? Had he taken his dick out? Was he starting to jerk off while he watched me?

"Oh, fuck, Owen. You should see what you're doing to me."

I made a pitiful, desperate sound—an impatient whine from deep in my chest. But Kamal only laughed.

"Oh, Sir... Oh, *please!*" The words tumbled from my mouth but I didn't know what I was asking for. Except I wanted to see him. I wanted to see him holding his cock and stroking it while he watched me. I wanted to see it *so badly.* But I also wanted his hand around my dick so I could fuck it and come hard to end this continuous build-up of ecstasy that had strung me out along a very thin line.

He clicked his tongue. That sound alone made me feel I wasn't fulfilling his expectations. I tried to stay still to be the stoic sub he wanted. Which lasted a mere second as the vibrations increased drastically.

I yelped and thrust into the empty air as my dick jerked. The pleasure rolled in waves from my prostate to my dick and back again. More fluid oozed out, and my balls tried to draw up as the hint of a climax seemed within reach.

"Oh, fuck, oh fuck, oh fuck," I muttered as my body left my conscious control. I writhed and wriggled like a piece of bait on a fish hook to try to mitigate the rising pleasure that became everything in that moment. My cock felt gigantic and impossibly swollen as my balls tightened in their cruel containment.

But it was happening. It was happening now. I was going to come. And I was going to come with absolutely no control over my body's reaction to the violent culmination of this torture.

I squeezed my eyes shut beneath the cloth and wailed as my body jerked and spasmed against the bench, the orgasm barreling through me like a bull through a farm gate. I felt the semen squirt out of me onto the mat, actually making noise it hit so hard. The vibrations continued, prolonging my orgasm until I slumped, defeated, against the bench and my breathing began to calm, even as my head spun with confusion and relief.

I didn't realize Kamal had approached until I processed the sound of skin against skin and heavy breathing and the warm splash of his come against my ass.

He cursed and gasped as he came, then let out a tiny hiss of a moan that slayed me with its vulnerability. I sagged there feeling owned and debased and utterly undone by Kamal's mastery.

When he finally spoke, it was to say, "Well, that didn't take as long as I thought it would."

He reached under me and wrapped his hand around my dick, stroking it a few times while I wriggled and protested.

Where was that hand a minute ago? Now he wants to touch me?

"No," I moaned. "No, stop," I hissed as his touch hurt the so-sensitive skin of my slowly shrinking penis.

"Are you safewording, Owen? You need to say your word."

"No," I whined. Goddammit, I wouldn't give him the satisfaction. "Oh, fuck," I swore as he released me and chuckled.

He disappeared for a moment and returned, holding something near my face. "Have some water."

"Why?"

He laughed. "This isn't pee torture. If you need to piss you can piss. But you're going to need to re-hydrate if all your orgasms are as productive as that one."

"All my—" *What the hell was he saying?*

"We're not done here, Owen. This vibrating tail is staying in you for at least an hour or two. I wonder how many times you're going to come?"

"*What?*" I said, mind spinning.

"Here. Drink." He tipped the water bottle against my lips. I opened them and swallowed some of the cool liquid while I contemplated my predicament.

"I wonder how long it'll take for that tail to get you revved up again. I'm going to get myself cleaned up."

I groaned in frustration as I felt the low hum of energy deep inside. It wouldn't work. I'd had a massive orgasm and I was sensitive and spent and exhausted. There was no way the vibrating tail would be able to get me off again.

But it did. Three more times before lunch.

It took slightly longer to achieve the last one. By then, I'd given up and simply lay there and let it happen, moaning and crying while it rung me out again. The pleasure surged and subsided, and Kamal came over and knelt by my sweat-streaked face. He pushed the blindfold off, and I blinked in the sudden light.

"Well done. Fuck, that was..." He shook his head. "I don't have the words. Are you okay?"

Was I?

I felt wrecked, but the muscle memory of those powerful orgasms shuddered through me with hints of the heights I'd reached and, yeah, I was fine. I was more than fine.

"Yeah," I said barely above a whisper. "You bastard."

And he laughed. The skin beside his eyes crinkled as his face lit up and I couldn't help giving him a defeated smile myself.

"You must be hungry. And you need to get cleaned up. I may have come on you a few times."

"*May have?*" My voice sounded like I'd been screaming for days when it had only been a couple of hours and not the whole time.

"Three times, Owen," he said with his eyebrows raised as he held up three fingers.

"Uh-huh. I still win."

"Oh, I think I'm the winner here." He pushed the damp hair off my forehead and kissed the sweaty skin, his lips so soft and gentle it took me by surprise.

He undid my restraints and took out the tail, throwing it on a towel on the bed. "It's going back in, in a minute, once I clean you up."

I must have looked terrified because he quickly said, "I won't turn it on. But I like the look of it curving over your back."

"Fine," I said, relieved. But I might need a fucking nap after lunch. Or before lunch.

Kamal helped me up. My legs felt like jelly and my abdominal muscles were sore from convulsing.

"Look," he said, pointing to the plastic sheet.

I blinked. "Fuck. That's a lot."

"Yeah. I should have given you a bucket."

I was surprised I had the energy to huff out a short laugh.

"Next time," he said.

"Fuck you, Kamal."

"Not yet, pup."

Chapter Seventeen

He helped me to the bathroom where he told me to sit on a chair as he started the bathtub filling. He knelt beside me and cupped my chin in his hand. "Seriously, are you okay? That was pretty intense."

"I'm fine. A bit sore and, uh, sticky."

Kamal grinned. "Your struggling was beautiful. A religious experience."

"What the fuck religion are you talking about?"

"The only one I practice." He shrugged. "Anyway, that's all the endurance training for the day."

"Oh, thank God," I said, looking forward to not orgasming any time soon. Which was quite something for a guy like me. "And I can't believe I'm saying this except that apparently I am a true masochist, but I'd love to do that again sometime."

Kamal's mouth opened like he wanted to say something but thought better of it.

"*Once I've fully recovered,*" I said, enunciating every word.

I reached out and touched a finger to his lips. He opened his mouth as I pushed it inside and stroked his tongue as he closed his lips and sucked. And goddammit if I didn't feel a tiny spark light in my belly. I pulled my finger back, narrowing my eyes at Kamal. "No, you don't, you sexy monster. I'll be having my bath now. Then some lunch. And maybe a nap."

He raised his eyebrows.

I back-pedaled. "I mean, please may I have my bath and then something to eat, Sir?"

*

After I'd had a soak, Kamal filled one dog bowl with mini-wheats and some milk. He sat on the bed and watched me lap it up with the dog tail arching over my back and wagging from my movements.

I didn't feel so sore anymore, but I did feel *owned*. I would do anything he wanted for the rest of the day if he'd consider dominating me like that again sometime. Because it had blown my fucking mind.

I'd never before trusted another man to do something like that. As intense as it had been, I hadn't been tempted to safeword. Because I knew Kamal was watching and he would know if it was too much. Maybe that was putting too much trust in him, but I knew he could tell when I was truly distressed and when I was just distressed enough to make things interesting.

Eating my lunch from a dog bowl on the carpet was a new experience. Kamal watched from his perch on the bed, the handle of my leash in his hand, and told me what a good boy I was as I made a mess of myself. I might need another bath.

He brought me a cloth when I'd finished and wiped my face, then brought me up to his bed for a cuddle, of which I took thorough advantage.

I was supposed to be his pup, so I acted like one. I climbed over top of him and rubbed my face against his shoulder, licked his chin, turned around to wiggle in his lap and wished I could have farted in his face. Instead, I wagged my rubber tail against his cheek while he laughed and told me I was a bad, bad dog and would soon be punished.

But it was only a short burst of exuberance before I promptly fell asleep on his leg.

When I woke up, Kamal was reading. Probably the book he'd pretended to read while I was being tortured by the plug that lay dormant in my ass. Probably why I was sacked out on my stomach on the mattress with the rubber tail waving above me.

"Morning, sunshine," he said, gazing down at me fondly.

I stretched and gazed up from beneath the fall of my hair. "Pretty sure it's afternoon."

Kamal checked his watch. "Oh, so it is."

I yawned, rubbing at my mouth and taking measure of the rest of my body. I felt amazing. Loose and relaxed and completely de-stressed.

"How's your book?" I said.

"It's good."

"I, uh, heard you turning pages this morning while I was otherwise engaged."

"Well, you know how it is. When you're reading a good book, absolutely nothing distracts you."

I grinned. "Suuure."

And he was on me. It was unexpected, the way he tossed the book aside and rolled on top of me, careful not to squish my tail.

"You are a little upstart, Owen Lipke. But I like your smart mouth."

"Oomph. You're heavy, Kamal."

"Let this be a lesson. I can subdue you with my muscular body."

I squirmed under him and laughed. "Fuck, you can subdue me with your muscular body anytime you want."

"Mmm." Kamal rubbed against me, cock hard under the cotton of his sweatpants. "See, that tail in your ass serves two purposes," he whispered in my ear, sending electric shocks to my dick—apparently, it lived.

"Oh yeah?" I breathed, licking my top lip.

"Yeah. It looks fucking perverted, and it keeps your ass safe from *me*. And keeps my job at the BCR safe from *you*."

I huffed. "Kamal, I would never let you lose your job. I believe in rules, too, y'know."

He pushed his dick against my hip again. "I'm glad to hear it. I hope you don't mind bending those rules. I'm probably not supposed to do this either," he said, rolling me to my side and pressing his lips to mine.

I welcomed his tongue, groaning with pleasure as he kissed me with barely restrained passion. He rutted against my hip while my cock filled and lengthened.

"God," I moaned, shoving my tongue into his mouth and down his throat. "Fuck, Kamal."

He gave a little high-pitched gasp that completely undid me as his hand cupped the back of my head. He held me still as he fucked my mouth with his tongue, slowly and softly, savouring every little thing.

"Make me suck you," I gasped.

"What?"

I pulled back from his mouth. "Make me suck your cock, Kamal. I want to do it, but I want you to *make* me do it." I was babbling and filled with desire to do this one thing.

He stared at me, his expression serious. "Suck my cock, Owen Lipke."

I whimpered, moving down his body, my arms on each side of his hips as I kissed down his chest. I slid my fingers under the waistband of his sweatpants and boxer briefs and eased them down as he lifted to help me out.

He sighed as he settled his bare ass on the bed and his erection bobbed free and hit my cheek.

"Ow," I muttered.

Kamal reached out to cup my cheek in his palm. "Owen."

"Yeah?"

"I've been fantasizing about this for days."

"Oh yeah?"

"Yeah. Having you all to myself, watching you suck me..."

I closed my eyes and swallowed. "God. Yes," I said, bending to take his cock in my eager mouth.

Kamal groaned, dropping his hand to the sheets. "Ah, fuck."

I made rude noises in my throat and slurped as much as I could, knowing he'd like it. Most men liked messy blow jobs—the messier the better so everything slid and slipped along nicely. Noises were a bonus.

Kamal groaned as I licked and sucked him, twining his fingers in my hair. He held me steady and fucked up into my mouth, making the most erotic facial expressions as I drooled and choked mildly.

I loved it. I loved that he did what he wanted and used me, knowing he would be careful, that he was experienced and kind, but enjoyed things rough and real, like I did.

I opened my mouth wide and let him fuck my throat until with a soft cry he came, fluid gushing from his cock, making me cough and sputter as I tried to swallow.

"Sorry, I should have warned you," Kamal panted, trying to pull away, but I lurched forward and swallowed his cock again, wanting all of it, not wanting to let him go.

"Fuck!" he swore, as I finished cleaning him off and finally backed off to sit smugly on my haunches.

"Mmm." I said.

He stared at me for a long moment, then laughed sharply, throwing his head back and beckoning me close. "C'mere, puppy."

I snuggled happily into his side, my cock hard, but I really didn't care about that. I'd come enough times today to satisfy me for a while.

"So, you said in your religion every boy gets circumcised."

He glanced over at me with a puzzled expression. "That's a weird segué."

"I mean, I'm curious. I'm assuming you're referring to Islam?"

He inclined his head, still looking confused. "Yes."

"Do you... Are you still a practicing Muslim?"

He stared at me. "Oh yes. I pray five times a day. There's a special room in the arena where I keep my prayer mat."

My eyes widened. "Really?"

"No."

I blinked. He was making fun of me. I kneed him in the thigh. "Don't be an asshole."

"Well, what do you think? You think I go to the mosque on Fridays?"

"No. But you could still be practicing your religion in your own way."

He smiled. "Well, when you put it like that, I guess I do." He leaned toward me, pushing me onto my back and pressing his hand to my throat, angling my chin up so I had to stare at the wall. I struggled for a second and then let him hold me, his broad hand pressing onto my throat so I gasped a little. He licked a line up from my nipple to his hand.

"This is my religion, Owen."

"Sex?" I said, garbled and gasping.

"And dominance." He opened his mouth and pressed his teeth against my throat—a veiled threat.

I groaned, my cock twitching like a live wire, and then gasped. "Fuuuuck."

He let me go and moved back to his earlier position. I lay there a moment, my breathing ramped up, my cock so hard I'd come if I moved. Then I turned my head to regard him.

"I'd worship *you*, Kamal."

He smile. "You already do. Every time you look at me like that."

*

When I woke the following morning, I didn't know where I was.

Although, as my vision cleared, the sight of Kamal in his dark jeans, boots, and a black T-shirt—his regular training gear—standing by the door to the bathroom and talking on his cell became focused.

"No, that's great! I can't wait to see you." He caught my eye, giving me a little wink. "Come to the main house. I'll tell Adam and Connor to expect you. Friday? Okay, sounds good. See you soon."

He lowered his phone and thumbed it, then put it on the dresser, and walked over.

"How did you sleep, Owen?"

I yawned, stretching out on my back. Kamal hadn't made me sleep with the plug in, but he had made me put on my boxer briefs. And he'd resisted pulling them down and climbing on top of me, even though we'd stayed pressed close together all night. He was a strong, strong man.

There had been more pup play after supper, basic stuff, and I'd enjoyed it. But I couldn't wait to be a pony again. There was something dignified about being a pony. Even with a butt plug horse tail in your ass. A majestic fall of black hair was a lot more dignified than a curvy, wavy rubber thing.

I'd told Kamal as much.

"So, puppy play isn't for you?"

"Well, I wouldn't say that. I've had a lot of fun."

"You did have a lot of fun. And about six orgasms."

"Really? I lost count."

"I'm not surprised."

"Who was on the phone? Sounded like it was someone important." I played with the bedspread and peeked at him through my forelock. "I mean, you don't have to tell me..." *but I hope you will.*

He shrugged. "An old friend of mine. From out West."

"He's coming here?"

"Yes. On Friday. For the weekend."

I cleared my throat, face flushing. "Will he be staying here? In this room? With you?"

He stared at me, his forehead crinkling. "Owen," he said softly.

"What? I'm jealous, okay? I'm just feeling my way here."

"He's an old friend."

"Old lover?"

Kamal shook his head lightly, once. "Old...friend with benefits."

My eyebrows shot up. "So, you *have* fucked him."

"It's not really any of your business, Owen."

I sighed, resigned to my predicament. "No, it's not. Except I really want to fuck you, and I *can't*. I feel like I'm playing this game with one arm tied behind my back. Ironically."

Kamal came over and sat on the bed beside me. He pushed the fall of dark hair off my forehead and gazed into my eyes. "Owen, you don't have to worry about anything. I can tell you right now I'm only capable of paying this close attention to one beautiful man at a time. At least in my private time."

I blushed and smiled. "Me?"

Kamal laughed and kissed me. "Yeah, *you*. Nitwit." He ruffled my hair and sighed.

"Hey. That would make a good pup name." I winked.

He rolled his eyes. "For you? Yeah, it would."

Kamal left for the arena, and I took my time showering and getting dressed. I found an empty notebook and a pen and sketched a quick portrait of Kamal with my name and the words "You are my religion" and left it on his dresser.

Connor seemed much happier at his computer today.

"Hi, Connor. How's the software working?"

"Great! Thanks, man. You saved my life. Well, my sanity."

"No problem. Listen, can I have my cell phone, please? I need to make a call before I head back to the bunkhouse."

"Of course." He grabbed the key for the safe from his pocket and opened it. As he handed me my iPhone 12, he bit his bottom lip and grinned. "So, how was it?"

I shook my head, avoiding his eyes. "Pretty fucking awesome, actually. You can pass that on to Adam if you want."

"I'll let him know. Bring the phone back before you leave, okay?"

"Sure. Just need to call my bestie." I waggled the phone back and forth. It felt strange and heavy in my hand.

"You can go into the front room if you want. Nobody's in there."

"Thanks," I said, walking down the hall and into the large room at the front of the main house. Or the back, depending on your perspective. Anyway, the side that overlooked the fields and outbuildings. It was a lounge of sorts, with a couple of armchairs and a coffee table, large windows letting in the early morning sun.

I closed the glass-panelled door for some privacy and sat down in one of the chairs. My body felt well used and loose. The soreness from my fall and from being restrained had completely disappeared. I called Tamara, hoping it wasn't too early.

I wasn't prepared for the shrieked greeting.

"Oweeeeen!!! Finally!"

"Hiya, Tam."

"Oh my God, I've been dying to hear about your visit to the kinky ranch! How is it going? Are you being a good pony?"

I laughed. "Well, I'm trying. It's all, uh, pretty fucking weird. And pretty fucking awesome."

"I knew it! I knew you'd love it!"

I heard her moving around. "Are you getting ready for work?"

"Yes, but do go on. I've got some time," she said. "I'm sitting down now. Brushing my hair. Tell me, tell me, tell me."

"Tell you what?"

"I don't know. Do you have to wear a bridle? And a saddle? Do they, like, ride on you somehow?"

Holy shit. That would be really weird. "Uh, no to the saddle. Yes, to the bridle. And, no, there is no riding going on."

"Oh." She sounded disappointed. "Then what do you have to do?"

I shrugged. "I'm learning to trot. And to pull a little cart."

"Fuck off."

"Yeah, it's true. It's kind of...interesting. And fun."

"Do you have a hot trainer?"

I sighed. "Tam, I have *the hottest trainer*. His name's Kamal. And, uh, you remember the cowboy?"

"What the fuck do you think? Of course, I remember the cowboy. Why? Are you fucking him? I'm going to murder you if you're fucking him."

"We're not allowed to fuck the trainers. Or the trainers-in-training. But Kamal is helping him learn how to train ponyboys. So, they both train me sometimes."

"Lucky dog! I mean, pony."

I couldn't help laughing. "Well, uh, actually..."

"What? Why is that funny?"

"Oh, Tam, you wouldn't believe it if I told you what I spent all of yesterday doing. It wasn't pony play, because Kamal needed to teach me something different."

"Why? Did you do something wrong? Owen, you have to be a *good pony*. You can't be all "I didn't sign up for this" because you actually did."

"Fuck off, Tamara. I'm being a good pony, okay? Well, mostly. Anyway, you know that stuff we looked at online when we were researching pony play?"

"Oh yeah. With the leather pups."

"Yeah. Well, Kamal made me his pup for almost twenty-four hours, and it was fucking glorious."

"Shut. Up." She whistled through her teeth. "Man, I would have given my balls to see that. Except I don't have any. But I thought you were a *pony*?"

I sighed. "I *am* a pony. He wanted me to see what it was like to be something less noble than a pony, so being a pony wouldn't seem so bad, I guess. Not that it's bad. It's not bad. It's just...well, I... I safeworded on Saturday. Because I didn't want to perform."

"Perform?"

"In the pony show."

"You didn't do it?"

"I couldn't. Not yet."

"Oh. How did that go over? Was Kamal mad?"

"No, it was fine. I mean, he was disappointed but, uh, he let me know it was okay." I remembered our little tryst in the grooming barn. "Fuck, Tam, he's amazing. I think..."

"You think what, Owen?"

I couldn't help the big smile that took over my face. "I think I might be falling for Kamal. I mean, I think that ship has actually sailed. It's still sailing. And I've got the mast to prove it." I rubbed at my cock which had hardened from all this kinky talk and the memories.

She shrieked again. "What? You found true love on a pony-play ranch?"

I laughed, the blood rushing into my face, and looked around to make sure nobody had snuck into the room.

"Shh. I don't know if it's actually *love*...but it might be heading in that direction."

"Is the trainer in love with you? Or is this unrequited?"

I played with a loose bit of wood on the window frame. "Well, neither of us has actually *defined our terms*. But, whatever it is, we both feel it."

"Wow. This sounds like a fucking romance novel."

"Fuck off, Tam."

She giggled. "A very kinky one. *Lost boy finds love on a BDSM pony-play ranch*. Wonders never cease."

"I wasn't lost."

"Yeah, you were. You were looking for something you couldn't find here in the city. Looks like you might have found it in the Muskokas."

I sighed. "Yeah. Hopefully. Anyway, I've got to go. And you have to get to work."

"Hey, I'm so glad you called. We are gonna need to get together for a major hangout when you get home. Because I'm going to need to hear about everything. In detail. Every. Kinky. Detail."

"Sure, Tam. Bye."

I sat there for a few seconds after disconnecting, trying to figure out if I missed my old life in Ottawa. I missed my apartment. I missed Tamara and a couple of other friends. I didn't miss my job. I'd worked hard the past few years and I was enjoying the break, to be honest. I wasn't ready to go back. Luckily, I had a few more weeks under Kamal's strong hand. Would that be long enough to figure shit out?

It would have to be.

Chapter Eighteen

Kamal was all business on Tuesday.

As if he hadn't strapped me over a bench and milked the come out of me four times and then led me around his room on a fucking leash. But every now and then, when Jensen wasn't looking, Kamal would wink or give me the hint of a smile, and I knew the man I'd shared a bed with was in there. The man who remembered curling up beside me and holding me against him like a cherished pet—or a man he may be developing feelings for.

As for me, I tried hard to learn the necessary skills to avoid embarrassing myself when I finally made it into the show ring. I was more motivated than ever to please him, and it turned out being a pony wasn't the same as being a pup. Perhaps it was more demanding physically. But as a pony I was able to maintain some dignity and recognize that although I was pretending to be an animal, a well-cared for pony could be proud, even in a leather harness pulling a cart.

So that was what I strove for, and I must have succeeded according to the pleased looks and praise I received from Kamal and Jensen.

That Friday, before he sent me back to the grooming barn with Adrian, Kamal squeezed my ass and tweaked my tail, while giving me a quick kiss on the cheek. "You did amazing work this week, Owen."

"Thank you, Sir," I said, his words of praise doing crazy things to me.

"Do you think you'll be okay tomorrow? The others will be in the same gear this time. You won't stand out. Well, I think you will, but only because you're cute as fuck and your form is perfect." He flicked the black hair that fell over my face. "And this thing? I'm not going to have them braid it, because with it falling over your mask and you tossing it back? They're gonna love it."

"You'll be beside me the whole time?"

"I'll be beside you, Owen."

"Then I'll be good."

I meant that in so many more ways than one.

*

After getting my hose-down and putting my clothes back on, I waited for the others. We stepped out into afternoon heat together and started for the bunkhouse.

A familiar laugh and loud booming voice made me look to the main house.

Kamal was approaching the porch and a tall man with wavy black hair and a beard who stood there holding his arms out. Kamal climbed the steps and grabbed the man in a close embrace, while something in my belly squirmed and shifted.

"Who the fuck is that guy?" Jake asked, lifting his hand to shade his eyes.

"Kamal's friend," I said. *With benefits*. I'd forgot to ask Kamal if he still had access to those benefits. I'd never been jealous before, and I didn't like the feeling. I didn't know what to do with it except bury it and pretend I was fine. "He's here for the weekend."

"Woot, woot, Kamal. Getting some weekend action. Probably helps him control himself around naked ponyboys six days a week."

"Probably," I muttered, hoping that all the action Kamal would be getting this weekend was outside of his bedroom.

"You okay, Owen?" Biskane asked.

"Yep. Nervous about the show tomorrow."

He smiled and put a long arm around my shoulder. "You'll be fine. Once you get out there and they start clapping and cheering for you? It's an amazing feeling. I'll never be on stage or anything like that. So, this is as close as I'll probably get to satisfying an audience."

"True." I was pretty sure I'd never be on a stage either. It wasn't something I'd ever aspired to.

But, suddenly, being one of three admired ponyboys in the show ring tomorrow didn't seem so bad. It was all acting anyway. And Kamal said I was damn good at acting like a pony, so I just had to keep that thought in my head the whole time.

Piece of cake.

I tried not to think about the man with the wavy hair and beard.

*

Saturday morning dawned fresh and clear, the perfect day for a pony show.

In the grooming barn, tacking up like the others didn't seem so bad. Now we all wore bridles, tails, and fancy masks with feathers in them.

When Kamal saw me, he smiled, as if I were the answer to all his dreams of how ponyboys should look.

He whistled. "Yeah, you'll do. That goddamn forelock is gonna kill me."

I gave my head a toss, and he closed his eyes and put a hand to his heart. When he opened them they blazed with heat.

I wanted to ask him how he was enjoying his friend's visit but I knew better than to talk with my bit in. So, I rolled the metal over my tongue and waited for Kamal to tell me what to do. This was the one advantage I had over that black-haired friend of his and I was determined to ace the pony show.

"We're at the end of the line again today. You going to be able to go out there?" Kamal asked.

Adrian appeared beside Kamal with something in his hand which he passed off to Kamal. "There you are, Kamal."

"Thank you, Adrian," he said, holding up the two square leather pieces for me to see. "These are blinders. They snap onto your bridle and block your peripheral vision so it's easier to focus. I don't think they'll call any extra attention to you, and they might help."

I trusted Kamal. I bobbed my head up and down. I'd take any assistance I could get.

He attached the blinders to the side straps of my head piece, and I immediately felt calmer. I could only see straight ahead of me now.

"I'll be beside you the whole time. If you need to escape, signal me again, okay? I won't be upset, and I'll get you right out of there."

I nodded again. He leaned close and kissed the side of my head.

We waited in line while the other ponyboys and their trainers were announced.

Finally, it was our turn. If I was telling myself I wouldn't stand out in that show ring, I'd be lying. Not because of how I looked, but because I'd be trotting beside the hottest goddamn trainer on the BCR.

Kamal looked at me with raised eyebrows, his hand on my reins as we listened to Adam announce us. I breathed out slowly and inclined my head, winking to show him I was okay.

"Good boy," he whispered, and smiled. And that made all the difference.

I walked carefully beside Kamal to stand in the centre of the show ring. As I lowered one knee to the ground and dipped my head, my black forelock falling over my mask, the crowd whooped and cheered. I honestly didn't care. I was doing this for Kamal—only for him.

The show passed by in a blur. I trotted and cantered and went over some jumps.

When it was time for Kamal to hitch me to the pony cart, he checked in with me again.

"You okay, Blaze? Holding up?"

I nodded and pressed my forehead against his shoulder. He wrapped his hand around my neck and held me to him, kissing the top of my head. "Good boy. You're being such a good, good pony for me, Owen."

I wanted to stay like that, but I had a cart to pull and a trainer to please. So, I straightened up and jingled the bit in my mouth, tossing my head like an excited animal.

Kamal jogged at my side as I pulled the little cart, following Biskane and Hiro in front of me and Jake and Lorraine in front of them.

After several turns of the large paddock, we were allowed to file out the gate and gather in the field where our trainers unhitched us and led us into the ring again for a final tour, as Adam announced that photos of each ponyboy could be purchased at the front desk or a personal photo could be taken with the ponyboy of their choice.

Our trainers led us to a small tent where we could stand while we waited for photo requests. Kamal ruffled my hair. "Good job, Owen. You were fantastic! I knew you would be."

I tried to tell him with my eyes how pleased I was that I'd been able to pull it off and how happy I was to make him proud.

A familiar-looking man approached.

"I want a photo with this stunning specimen," said Kamal's supposed friend, handing him a fifty and saluting me. "Hello, Blaze. I don't know if you realize how amazing you looked out there."

"It's his first show, Craig. He did wonderfully," Kamal said as I tried to stand tall and not let my insecurities get the better of me. Now that I saw Craig up close I was even more intimidated. He was really good-looking, in a way that I wasn't and could never be. He was older, for one thing, with a beard and big muscles. The kind of guy with a stature like Kamal's. The fact I found him hot made my jealousy flare higher. But I couldn't let it show.

By now, a line of people had begun to form. Adam had told the audience members they were forbidden to touch any of the ponyboys but could stand beside us for a photo. Hot Craig obeyed the rules and stood between me and Kamal for a photo.

"See you tonight," he said to Kamal as he moved aside for another audience member to take his place.

"See you at five. Are we taking your car?"

"Might as well."

I stared at Kamal, surprised. He was going off-site with Hot Craig? The friend with benefits? Did they have a hotel room booked?

I shuffled my feet and rolled the bit back and forth with my tongue, wishing I could speak properly.

Chapter Nineteen

Kamal wasn't anywhere to be seen at supper.

I'd thought, since it was my first show today, we might celebrate by sitting together. It seemed stupid now. I felt like a high school kid whose crush had abandoned him for another, cuter, guy. This feeling was the worst.

I had absolutely no claims on Kamal. He was my trainer. We'd spent an astonishing day and night together in his room. But, other than some small, unspecific declarations we'd made, we hadn't promised to be exclusive.

I wasn't used to this feeling. I was used to guys wanting me more than I wanted them, not the other way around.

So, I chatted with the guys at supper and pretended nothing was wrong. When we went back to the bunkhouse later I wondered what Kamal was doing with Hot Craig. Had they only gone to dinner? Or had they gone for dinner and a hotel for a nostalgic fuck-a-thon?

Goddammit. My feelings didn't even make sense. We were adults. We weren't *together*. Kamal could do what he wanted and so could I.

I dug out my sketchbook and drew furiously—a picture of Hot Craig with his sexy black beard and wavy hair with devil horns. I made it so realistic he could have been the actual devil. Which he probably was. Then I threw my pencil down and peeked over the edge of my bunk.

Biskane was reading in a pair of soft cotton shorts and no shirt, his bare feet crossed at the ankles. As much as I wanted to punish Kamal by getting sexy with Biskane, I hesitated. I didn't want to use the handsome ponyboy to my own ends even though he probably wouldn't complain.

I climbed down the ladder and walked over. "Hey. You want to go for a walk?"

He glanced up and his face flushed. He looked at my groin and grinned.

I rolled my eyes. "Not for anything like that. I just need to clear my head. I guess I need a friend."

Biskane smiled wide and put down his book. "Sure. I'm totally your friend. Before any of that," he said, gesturing toward the showers. "I'm your friend."

I held my hand out and he clasped it as he stood.

"Thanks, man," I said.

"Let me put a shirt on."

We decided to walk along the path to the beach even though we didn't plan to swim.

"So, what's up?" he asked. "Why are you so jumpy?"

"I can't stop thinking about fucking Kamal."

He stared at me. "You can't fuck Kamal. You know that. He'll lose his job."

I blinked, confused. "No, not me *fucking* Kamal. I can't stop thinking about goddamn Kamal, is what I meant. I know I can't fuck him. And that makes it worse."

"Oh, man. You've got it bad, don't you? That sucks."

"It does suck, Biskane. I don't know what's happening," I said, picking up a pebble and tossing it at a tree. I missed. "Why do I feel like this?"

"Because love is hell, Owen. Haven't you figured that out by now?" Biskane looked at me sadly. He wasn't even joking. Seemed like he might have had some experience in this area.

"It's not love, for fuck's sake," I scoffed, even though it might be. Or, at least, heading in that direction.

Biskane raised an eyebrow. "I've seen the way he looks at you, Owen."

My heart rate sped up. "How does he look at me?"

Biskane smiled. "Oh, man. Like he's never seen anything so beautiful as you. No matter how you're dressed or what you're doing. But especially when you're his pony. Seems like he doesn't have eyes for anything else but you."

"Yeah, right," I snorted. I hoped Kamal looked at me like that, but I couldn't quite believe it.

"It's true. And I've seen the way you look at Kamal too, y'know. Those looks don't lie, Owen."

*

That couldn't be true. It *wasn't* true. Biskane had an overactive imagination. He was a romantic, and I was not. Which is why it made no sense later that night when I put on my shoes and headed to the main house.

I wasn't sure I'd be able to get in. It was after eight thirty so they'd probably locked up. I'd be stuck prowling the porch and staring up at what I thought was Kamal's room.

The string lights that wrapped around the porch railings were lit, and as I got closer, I saw two people sitting on the broad steps. One was smoking a cigarette, the glow of which lit up his face.

I put my hands in my pockets, slowing my steps, wondering what I was doing. But it already helped to see Kamal sitting beside Hot Craig, dressed in nice clothes and *not* in town fucking Hot Craig's smoking ass. Smoking, in both senses.

"Owen. What on earth are you doing here?" Kamal said, reaching out for my hand in a gesture that saved me from total embarrassment. Hot Craig looked up at me, his eyes roaming over by body as he lifted the cigarette to his mouth. "Owen," he said, with a friendly smile. "Kamal's been telling me all about you."

I took Kamal's hand, and he pulled me toward him, making room for me on the wide step. "You are a sight for sore eyes," he said.

I grunted as I sat. "How can your eyes be sore? Not from looking at *him*." I gestured to Hot Craig, who laughed softly.

Kamal clicked his tongue. "Owen. I told you not to be jealous of Craig."

"Yeah? Well maybe I can't do everything you tell me to do." It was a weird and stupid thing to say, and I was surprised Kamal didn't get mad. But he didn't. He stared at me, and I stared at him.

"I guess that's fair," he said finally. "You're only supposed to obey me in the stables."

"Anyway, Owen, Kamal and I are good friends with a bit of a history. That's all," Hot Craig assured me, leaning back and taking another drag.

"Adam won't let you smoke in the house?" I asked.

"Fuck, no. He barely lets me smoke out here." Hot Craig said. "Is he watching from the window?"

Kamal laughed. I smiled. I felt a lot better and was glad I'd come. I didn't even crave a hit off Hot Craig's cigarette.

"Is the bunkhouse noisy, Owen? Is that why you came?" Kamal asked.

I shook my head but didn't say anything.

Hot Craig pointed at Kamal with his cigarette. "He came to check on you. He thought you were fucking me instead of going on and on about how great he is."

I blinked. "What?"

Hot Craig nodded. "You're all he's been talking about, Owen. And I can see why. I mean, I can see now, and I saw it in the show ring."

I felt heat in my cheeks as I gazed at Hot Craig and he gazed at me. There was something there besides a mutual respect. Maybe a friendship ready to blossom if I'd let it. And interest—he was attracted to me.

"Craig, you're revealing all my secrets," Kamal muttered.

"That's what friends are for."

Kamal laughed, and I was starting to really, really like Hot Craig. For making him laugh like that.

"What's your story, Owen?"

"Hmm?"

"Why are you at a pony-play ranch in the middle of nowhere?"

I shrugged, feeling put on the spot. "I don't know."

"Sure, you do. Nobody comes to a place like this on a whim." He butted out his cigarette in an empty coke can, dropped it in and leaned back, gazing up at me. I was glad he'd told me he and Kamal weren't a thing anymore because he was even hotter than I'd remembered.

"Well, actually..." I put my hand to my face, pushing the hair off my forehead.

Kamal laughed softly. "Owen filled in for a cancellation we had. He'd only known we existed for about a week when he sent in the form."

Hot Craig clicked his tongue. "What? No way." He sat up, staring at me intently. "I'd love to know what was going on in your head."

"Honestly? I was bored as fuck with the kink scene back home. Couldn't find a Dom worth a dollar. Some guy who picked me up at a club told me about this place. I looked it up online the next day and my mind was kind of blown."

Kamal watched me closely. I kept meeting his eyes, which were dark and glowing in the soft light from the porch.

Hot Craig whistled. "So you were bored and looking for adventure?"

I nodded. Because that was about right.

"Did you find it?" he asked with a knowing smirk.

"Yeah," I said, glancing at Kamal.

"And a Dom worth a dollar?" He winked.

"Worth a thousand," I said, not brave enough to meet Kamal's gaze.

Kamal took my hand and pulled me against him, pushing my black bangs aside and kissing my forehead. We were silent as we looked out at the warm night.

"You still looking for adventure?" Hot Craig said quietly.

I glanced at him and then at Kamal, who regarded Hot Craig warily.

"What are you getting at?" he said.

Hot Craig shrugged. He looked at me, looked at Kamal, grinned. "Well, you've got an awfully nice room upstairs, Kamal. Shame to let it go to waste."

I blinked, my cock hard in an instant. "I thought you and Kamal weren't..."

He didn't look at me. "We're not. But he might remember I have a hell of a voyeuristic streak."

"Craig," Kamal said softly.

"Hey, it's up to you guys. But if you don't mind showing off a little, I'd be into it."

"Okay," I said quickly. It was a no-brainer. I'd get to have fun with Kamal, and Hot Craig could watch and get off on it. I had absolutely no issue with that. At all.

Kamal laughed again. "Jesus, Owen."

"What? He's incredibly attractive. Are you surprised I was jealous?" I stood, ready to go.

"A little, yeah. But in a good way."

Hot Craig stood and looked me up and down again. "Shit, kid. You look like a pony even when you're all dressed."

Kamal stood and offered me his hand. "It's the hair. And the sleek muscles. And the sweetness."

"It's everything," Hot Craig said, picking up the coke can and heading inside.

Kamal paused and regarded me as Hot Craig went ahead. "Are you sure? I don't want you doing anything you're not comfortable with."

"Are you kidding? He can even touch me if he wants. But I don't want him touching you."

Kamal rolled his eyes. "Oh, that seems fair."

I grinned. "What? You don't want him touching me?"

Kamal's eyes burned with heat. He squeezed my hand as we moved forward. "I didn't say that. As long as I'm in control, maybe it would be okay."

And, just like that, my evening was looking way, way up.

*

Before we went upstairs, Kamal touched my shoulder and beckoned me down the hall.

"Excuse us for a second," he said to Hot Craig, who inclined his head and leaned against the stair rail patiently.

I caught up to Kamal as he peeked into the front room.

"Aha," he said, knocking and entering. He pulled me inside the cozy space, now lit with several lamps. Adam Marsland, sitting in an armchair in the corner reading on his Kindle, looked up.

"Kamal," he said. "Owen."

"Hi, Adam," I said, unsure what this was all about.

"How was dinner with Craig?" Adam asked Kamal.

"Great. It was nice to catch up." Kamal cleared his throat. "He's, uh, waiting for us."

Adam didn't say anything for a second. Then he put his e-reader down and took off his glasses. "For both of you?"

Kamal grinned. "Well, yes. I wanted you to know so Owen doesn't get into trouble. There won't be any rule breaking, I can assure you."

Adam raised his eyebrows. "I certainly hope not." He turned to me. "Owen, you've agreed to...whatever this is?" He waved his hand at Kamal.

I grinned. "Yes, Sir."

Adam narrowed his eyes. "What is it?"

I glanced at Kamal and then back at Adam. "I mean...um...it's...well...y'know..."

"If you can't tell me what you're going upstairs to do, Owen, then you're not capable of consenting to it. Do you know what you're going upstairs to do?"

My face burned with embarrassment but Kamal seemed...amused? He wouldn't look at me.

"Yes, Sir."

"Then tell me."

Jesus, Adam was merciless. Then again, I was his responsibility, and he wanted to make sure I knew what I was getting into.

I cleared my throat. "Hot Craig wants to watch. Me and him." I gestured to Kamal. "Do stuff."

They looked at me funny.

"Oh, shit," I muttered, staring hard at the floor.

"*Hot Craig*?" Kamal said.

I shrugged.

"Do what, exactly?" Adam asked.

I rolled my eyes. "Everything but fuck, presumably?" My teeth were pressed together, and my words came out garbled.

"Pardon?" Adam said. In the corner of my vision Kamal tried not to double over with hilarity. I wanted to punch him.

"Adam," I whined. "Come *on*."

"I want to hear you say it."

"Fuck. Fine. Kamal and I are going up to his room to do everything but fuck, and Hot Craig is going to watch." I cocked my head to the side, licking my lips and meeting Adam's calm gaze. "You wanna come too?"

And Kamal couldn't hold it in anymore. He broke into loud laughter as Adam smiled and said, "As tempting as that offer is, Owen, I'm in the middle of a good book here. Go on. But *don't break the rules*." He eyed both of us.

"But...how would you know?"

Adam narrowed his eyes. "Pardon?"

"How would you know if we did fuck? Me and Kamal? Is there some kind of examination I have to submit to before I leave?" Oh, I was getting punchy now. Must be the relief of finding out Kamal was still with me and only me and the excitement of sharing that knowledge with another sexy man.

"I'll pretend I didn't hear that," Adam said icily, and his whole proper Daddy vibe was starting to intrigue me. "And I'd know because Kamal would tell me if he screwed up by fucking his ponyboy. Which hasn't happened in five years and isn't going to happen now. Because he's too valuable of a trainer for the BCR to lose over something like this."

"Over me?"

"Yes, Owen, over you. I can tell there's something between the two of you. But if it's worth anything, waiting until you're not a client here to fuck Kamal isn't going to kill you. Or him." He waved cheerily at Kamal. "Off you go then. Enjoy your evening."

I grinned. "You sure you don't want to join us?"

Kamal groaned. "Owen, come on. Hot Craig is waiting. And so am I."

"Yes, Sir," I said, throwing a big smile and a salute Adam's way. "See ya."

He laughed and waved me off. "Good night."

"It sure fucking will be," I said as Kamal dragged me into the hallway and ushered me up the stairs behind Hot Craig.

Chapter Twenty

As soon as we got inside Kamal's room he took control.

"Owen, on your knees."

It was an offhand order, as if he'd told me to grab his phone off the dresser. I dropped obediently to my knees on the carpet and laced my fingers behind my neck, keeping my eyes down. We'd never discussed proper positions, but I'd been in the kink scene some time, and Kamal knew that.

"I want to show you something," Kamal said to Hot Craig.

"Sure."

I heard the rustle of a piece of paper.

"Owen drew this picture of me the other day."

My cheeks flushed at the embarrassment of Craig seeing my quick sketch of Kamal, but also in pleasure that Kamal thought enough of my work to show him.

"Wow. That's very good."

"I know. He's talented as well as cute," he said, putting the picture back.

"Do you mind if I use your washroom?" Hot Craig asked.

"Not at all," Kamal said, "We'll be waiting."

While Hot Craig was using the facilities, Kamal walked over and crouched down to speak in my ear. "I'll keep things light. No serious kink tonight, just a little domination and submission. That work for you, Owen?"

"Yes, Sir." That worked perfectly for me.

"Listen, drop the Sir for right now. We're having a conversation."

"Okay."

"Craig will let me order him around if you want me to use him as part of our games. But that's up to you."

"I'd like that."

"What are your limits?"

"You know my limits," I said, confused. They were on a form in Kamal's desk and in a file downstairs.

"I mean your limits in terms of Craig, excuse me, *Hot* Craig, and myself. What would make you uncomfortable? You said something downstairs about not minding if Craig touches you but not wanting him to touch me."

"Yes. I'm fine with him touching me anywhere. I don't want him to touch you. Or kiss you. Or anything like that."

"That's fine. Craig and I haven't been intimate in many, many years."

"Okay." That made me feel so much better.

"What do you want him to do to you? I'm not letting him fuck you, just so you know. Or kiss you on the lips."

I smiled, glad Kamal had some limits concerning me. "Good."

"But I need to know what you're okay with in terms of Craig's involvement."

I began to suspect Hot Craig had gone to the bathroom on purpose so Kamal and I could have this discussion.

"I mean, I'll do anything with you, and he can watch."

"Yes, I figured that. But what can he do to you? What do you want to do to him?"

"I want to blow him," I said right away. Because the thought of Kamal watching me do that to another guy was the hottest thing I could think of.

Kamal chuckled softly. "I'm sure that would be fine."

"And I want him to blow me." *Because obviously.* "But not at the same time."

"Certainly. I'll take that into consideration."

I smiled, looking at the carpet. The grey carpet where I'd crawled like a dog for Kamal only a few days ago.

"Can he play with your ass?" Kamal asked. "Or do you want me to do that?"

Holy. Fuck. This was getting incendiary all of a sudden.

"Both," I whispered.

"Pardon?"

"I want both of you to play with my ass."

He hissed and ran a hand through my hair. "Holy shit, Owen. You are a dream come true."

I snorted. "That's a very romantic thing to say to someone kneeling on your carpet getting ready for some serious ass play."

I heard a loud laugh and looked to the source. Hot Craig stood against the door frame of the en suite, watching us.

"Well, shit," Kamal said. "Let's get busy."

"I feel the same way," Hot Craig said, unbuttoning his shirt. "Your boy is fucking sexy on his knees like that, Kamal."

"You'd better fucking believe it," Kamal said and I glowed inside at this praise.

"Even with all his clothes on. But maybe we can take them off him?"

"That's a wonderful idea."

Kamal had me stand and together, he and Hot Craig divested me of my shirt.

"What is your safeword, Owen?" Kamal asked.

"Pineapple," I said clearly.

"May I touch him, Kamal?" Hot Craig asked Kamal.

"You may."

Jesus, I felt like a gourmet entrée at a fancy restaurant. It gave me a heady feeling. The sensation of Hot Craig's soft fingers on my nipple, rubbing it and trailing down my chest and over my abdomen, made me dizzy.

"Jesus, Kamal," Hot Craig breathed, voice rough.

"I know. Believe me, I know."

"But you see so many gorgeous guys here," Hot Craig commented. "I can't deny that Owen is a particularly delectable specimen," he said, gliding his hand over the bulge in my shorts while Kamal bent to kiss my neck. "What makes him stand out?"

Kamal kissed a line down across my chest and up over my throat. "Everything," he said, a quaver in his voice. "Every fucking thing."

I whimpered as Hot Craig unfastened my shorts and pulled them down, leaving me in my rainbow boxer briefs.

"Those are so pretty," Hot Craig said.

Kamal helped me step out of the shorts and removed my shoes and socks. It was pretty wonderful having two sexy men undressing me, worshipping me, getting hard for me. Pretty fucking wonderful.

I hissed as fingers slid beneath the waistband of my boxers, and I had to look to see whose they were. They were Kamal's. They slipped around my cock as Hot Craig pushed my boxer briefs down. Then Kamal cupped my chin in his other hand and pressed a fierce kiss against my lips.

I opened my mouth to take him in and wrapped my arms around his neck, not sure if I was allowed but sure I'd find out. He didn't make me stop, so I held onto him, pushing my cock into his firm grip and moaning against his devouring mouth.

"Jesus, I'm gonna need the fire hose," Hot Craig murmured, his hand running down my back as his fingers pushed gently into the crack of my ass.

"Mmph" I grunted as my legs spread of their own accord and Hot Craig found my hole and pressed it, cursing.

"So sweet," he whispered. "So soft."

Kamal wrenched himself away from my mouth and turned me around to face Hot Craig whose fingers slid from my ass as he watched me with dark eyes.

"He wants you to suck him," Kamal said, his voice gravelly. I felt the bulge in his black slacks pressing against my back.

God, I was going to combust.

"Put your hands around my neck," Kamal instructed as I watched Hot Craig go to his knees and glance up at me with a grin.

"Don't hold back," he said. "Come if you want."

"Not until I say you can," Kamal warned, nuzzling the side of my face. His hands slid down along my sides. One splayed on my belly right above my arching cock, the other took my erection and offered it to Hot Craig.

My lips formed a silent O as Hot Craig placed his hands on my thighs and bent to take my dick in his mouth. I stared down at his dark head and the pale skin of his back as he got to work with his mouth and tongue while

Kamal held me firmly against him and watched over my shoulder.

Even through the bliss, I felt Hot Craig's fingers tremble as he sucked me, and I realized he was as caught up as Kamal and me. He pulled off and rubbed his short carefully groomed beard up and down my length, making me gasp at the rough texture.

"Be still," Kamal said, splaying his hand wider and holding me steady as Hot Craig swallowed me down.

It wasn't going to take long for me to come, watching Kamal's handsome friend eat my dick and feeling Kamal's throbbing, trapped erection behind me. It wouldn't take long at all.

"I'm coming. I'm coming," I panted, pleased not to hear Kamal forbid it as I spilled into Hot Craig's willing throat. He closed his eyes and swallowed, only a tiny dribble of come leaking out as he kept up his mouth action until I quieted and sagged against Kamal.

He released me and sat back, staring at the two of us with intense blue fire. "Delicious," he said, licking his lips, brushing at his mouth with his hand and sliding his gaze from mine to Kamal's and back.

"Fuck," Kamal said, rubbing his erection against me from behind. "Jesus, that was hot, Owen"

"Hey, I did all the work. He only stood there looking cute and making wonderful noises," Hot Craig said, smiling.

"Yes, you did well too," Kamal told him.

I was still blissed out and floating as Kamal pulled me over to the bed and lay me down. "He's in no condition to suck you yet, so now might be a good time for the ass play."

Hot Craig groaned. "Oh, holy fuck. I should visit you more often, Kamal."

I watched as he unzipped and pulled his sizeable, circumcised dick from his boxer briefs. He wrapped his hand around it and pointed it at me, winking. "You get this later, okay? In your mouth?"

I grinned. "Can't wait."

"You can, and you will," Kamal said, flipping me over onto my belly and spreading my legs wide. "I'm going to get some restraints."

I shuddered and hugged the mattress while Hot Craig watched and seemed to be stroking himself—if his little gasps and grunts were evidence. I arched my back and stuck my ass in the air, hearing a moan in response.

When Kamal came back, he threw some items on the bed, then fastened my wrists to the front corners of his bed with leather cuffs and hidden eye hooks. He'd gotten rid of his shirt and shoes and socks, but still had his jeans on. I wondered how painful his cock felt inside that tight denim. I twisted my head around to peer over my shoulder and saw him pick up a spreader bar with two cuffs.

"Oh shit," I murmured, pulling at my wrist restraints. "I thought you said we weren't going to do anything kinky."

"A spreader bar and some wrist cuffs?" Hot Craig said, taking his hand off his dick and laughing. "Obviously, you don't know Kamal well. That's vanilla for him."

"Bring it on."

Kamal eyed me as he clicked the spreader bar into its final length. "You sure, Owen? I didn't think you'd mind, but I can get rid of this." He waved it in the air.

"Don't you fucking dare. Now you've got me all excited again."

He laughed. "Good." He buckled the cuffs around my ankles so I couldn't pull my legs together. I was displayed for them with my chest on the bed, arms pulled taut in front, and ass in the air, with a bar holding my legs apart for anything they wanted to do to me.

It fucking rocked.

All the times I'd gone to the Stocks in Ottawa and wanted to hook up with a practiced Dom, this was what I'd wanted—someone to take charge in a way that gave me the confidence to fully enjoy my submission. But nobody had ever done that before Kamal, and having his trusted longtime friend, Hot Craig, here only added fuel to the fire.

I might never leave this ranch.

I felt a soft tickle on my ass and realized it was someone's lips against the skin of my buttock. A gentle finger drew a circle around my hole. But I didn't know whose finger it was or whose lips they were, and that was fucking amazing because I didn't even care.

"Oh," I said, closing my eyes. Instinctively, my thighs tried to pulled together but were hindered from doing so by the steel bar between my ankles. The feeling of being forcefully displayed for two men was intoxicating and I shuddered as my cock throbbed and jerked. "Fuuuuck."

"What a gorgeous young man Owen is, Kamal. Especially from this angle," Hot Craig murmured.

"He is that, and much more," Kamal said, as the finger tracing my hole disappeared. It was back in a moment with slippery lube, getting me ready for...something. I trusted Kamal that neither he nor Hot Craig would mount me. It would be fingers and some kind of dildo or the pup tail or something. I shuddered with anticipation.

"If I can't fuck you with my cock, I'll do it with this," Kamal said, pressing something hard and domed against me. "Open, Owen."

I went down further on my front and arched my back, bearing down and opening myself for the invasion.

"Oh, Jesus," Hot Craig said as the dildo pushed into me.

"That's it. Beautiful," Kamal breathed, twisting it gently and letting me get used to its size. The girth was perfect—the same as the largest part of the tail plugs. I wondered how it compared to Kamal's dick and the thought made me moan loudly.

"I think he likes it," Craig chuckled.

"I think you're right," Kamal murmured, pulling it out and pushing it back in.

This time I gave a long guttural groan and fisted the bedspread.

"Oh, he definitely likes it." Hot Craig confirmed.

I forced myself to make words while my eyes rolled back in my head. "Do...do you like it?"

Hot Craig whimpered. "Oh fuck, Owen. I love it. Thank you for letting me watch."

"You're...welcome...*Hot Craig*."

Kamal stopped and snorted a laugh.

"What did you call me?" Hot Craig's astonished voice.

My face flushed with embarrassment.

"He called you *Hot Craig*," Kamal replied. "And I have to concur, although that ship sailed a long time ago. For the record, I still think you're hot."

"Well, damn," Hot Craig, said. I felt the mattress dip and then he was within my range of vision, moving up beside me and sliding his fingers into my hair. "That's the nicest thing anyone has ever called me."

I grunted as Kamal resumed his motions with the dildo, but gazed into Craig's kind eyes and smiled. "It's true. Kamal is so perfectly my type. But you're definitely hot."

"I'm very glad you think so." He licked his lips. "And for the record, Owen? If Kamal hadn't already claimed you for his own, I'd be courting you like a bastard right now. Alas, I'll have to settle for this."

"I'll try to make it good, then," I murmured, pushing back against the penetration and lighting all my nerve ends on fire.

"You already have, Owen," Hot Craig said, kissing me on the shoulder and retreating back to where he had a good view of what Kamal was doing. "I'm going to go back home with some great memories."

The dildo slid home and Kamal's knuckles brushed my taint. I groaned as my dick surged and dripped.

"Oh, fuck *me*, Kamal. *Harder.*"

Kamal cursed and whispered, "God, Owen, you're killing me. One day you're gonna say that and mean it."

"I'd mean it today if it wasn't against Adam's stupid rules," I said.

"They're not stupid. Be a good boy, now."

"For you, Kamal, I'll be the fucking *best* boy," I said, pressing my forehead into the mattress and groaning as he fucked the dildo in and out of me.

Slippery fingers circled my cock and jerked me slowly, making me groan louder and thrust into the firm grip.

"Oh fuck, oh fuck," I moaned, voice high-pitched and needy. I didn't know whose hand it was but I didn't care. As Kamal fucked me harder with the dildo and someone milked my cock, I shuddered and writhed like a desperate animal. It didn't take long. They were experienced men.

"I'm gonna come, Kamal. I can't... I can't...hold back," I grunted.

"Don't hold back, Owen. Show us what you've got," he said in a husky voice. "Show Hot Craig what you can do."

I squeezed my eyes shut and went to pieces as my dick shot streams of come onto the bedspread, and Kamal continued to fuck the dildo into me, the hand on my cock moving until I collapsed onto it.

The mattress dipped again, and I felt the heat of a large body beside mine. A soft kiss on my cheek and the hand around my dick squeezed gently, making me wiggle.

"You're in the wet spot." Hot Craig's voice.

I forced my eyes open. Hot Craig smiled and winked.

"Believe me, I know," I said.

Hot Craig smiled. "We'll clean you up. And then you can suck my cock. Because, holy hell, Owen I almost came watching you."

I yawned and blinked. "Cool."

Kamal had withdrawn the dildo and thrown it on the bed beside me. He undid the spreader cuffs and released the wrist restraints as he gazed at me with warmth and desire.

"Beautiful boy. You did great."

I grinned. "I know."

Kamal laughed and that sound filled me with light. "I'll have to work on that proud streak you've got going. Makes you a bit of a smart ass."

I yawned again. "I'm sure you can spank it out of me, Sir."

"I'm sure I can," Kamal said, "But right now Hot Craig needs a blow job, since he was promised one. Let's get you cleaned up.

Chapter Twenty-One

They led me to the bathroom and together wiped me clean with a soft cloth. It was hot to watch them concentrate on their task, thoroughly wiping every part of me that needed it and a few places that didn't.

"Okay, guys. I think I'm shinier than when I came here. But, thank you."

"Our pleasure," Hot Craig said. His erection hadn't flagged. It jutted out of a thatch of black curls in a wild, caveman way.

"I've changed the bedspread. I want you to get up on the bed on all fours for a second." Kamal said.

I raised my eyebrows, curiosity making my dick twitch. It was coming back to life from all the attention. I was glad to be young and able to rebound so quickly. I'd sleep like a log tonight, but I was eager to get my mouth on Hot Craig's dick. "May I ask why, Sir?"

"You may. I want that vibrating dog tail in your ass while you're sucking him. What do you think?"

"Oh fuck," I said.

"Jesus, Kamal. Are you trying to kill me? Nice way to treat an old friend," Hot Craig muttered. He gripped his dick and pumped it, regarding me hungrily.

"Thought you might like that idea. Owen makes a damn cute puppy."

"I bet he fucking does," Hot Craig said, licking his lips.

I whimpered and crawled up onto the bed. "Oh God. Remember what that thing did to me the last time?"

"I remember. I'm sure you do as well."

"What are you two on about?" Hot Craig asked, climbing on the bed and lying beside me with his elbow crooked, his head on his hand, while he watched Kamal.

Kamal cleared his throat. "I strapped him down and milked him four times, using different vibrations on that thing. Not a hand on his dick or anything. It was *exquisite*."

Hot Craig gasped. "Four times? Four separate orgasms? Jesus Christ, Kamal, you are one sick fuck. And very talented."

Kamal laughed. "The tail did most of it. And Owen's natural responsiveness. He was amazing. It was a sight to see, I'll tell you."

Craig grunted, arm moving as he stroked his cock and watched Kamal insert the tail plug into my freshly lubed ass. "You will tell me, Kamal. In great detail. Tomorrow. I wish I didn't have to leave so soon."

Kamal nodded. "I wish you could stay longer. But I will tell you all about it if Owen doesn't mind."

"Don't mind," I gasped, accommodating to the plug and wagging the rubber tail exaggeratedly. "It's all good."

"What a happy puppy," Hot Craig commented, stroking my hip.

I wasn't prepared for Kamal to slap my ass so hard. I yelped and glanced back at him.

"We have some things to discuss."

"Yes, Sir." I stopped the tail wagging and waited.

Kamal glanced at Craig, then returned his gaze to me. "Craig had a negative test screen about five months ago. But that's not recent enough to make him entirely safe for you, Owen. He's had sexual contact with other men since then."

"Only a few, and I used condoms with the ones I didn't know well. But I agree with Kamal we need to take precautions."

I frowned. "You want him to wear a condom for a blow job?"

Hot Craig held up his hand. "Let's not get crazy. It's up to you, Owen, but I'd rather not."

"No," Kamal said quickly. "But Craig won't come in your mouth. He'll warn you when he's close and you'll stop." He grinned and winked at Craig. "He'll come on your face."

"Oh, fuck yeah," I said. That was almost hotter.

"How does that sound? I'm sure *Hot Craig* would wear a condom if you preferred."

"Jesus, Kamal, stop calling him that." I was embarrassed about the nickname I'd given Kamal's friend.

"Hey. I will henceforth be widely known as Hot Craig, thank you very much. And, yes, I will wear a condom for my blow job if you prefer, Owen."

I shook my head. "No, it's fine. I'm good with a semen facial. Maybe Kamal can come on me too? I haven't been bukkaked in a while.

"Oh, holy fuck, you little tease," Hot Craig groaned while Kamal laughed.

I jumped up. "Come on. Let's get started. Where are we doing this?" I looked at Kamal.

He pointed to the floor in front of his dresser. "Craig— Excuse me, *Hot* Craig— You stand there with your back to the dresser, and, Owen, you kneel in front of him. That way, I can sit on the bed and watch."

"I'm sure you'll only be watching," I said sarcastically.

"Owen, you have no idea how restrained I've been not to have whipped my dick out and come all over you and Hot Craig this evening."

"Good point. God, you're such a romantic."

"Uh-huh. Now, look, Hot Craig is waiting. Go get him." Kamal said, as he took my place on the bed and stretched out on his side, propping his head with his hand.

I knelt in front of Hot Craig and eyed his large penis. "Hello, Hot Craig's dick. We are about to become intimately acquainted."

Hot Craig puffed out the breath he was holding. "Oh, God. I'd laugh if I wasn't so turned on." He stroked his dick a few times, aiming it at my cheeky grin. "Also, that rubber tail coming out of your ass is killing me. In a good way."

I waggled it and he cursed.

"Owen, stop being a tease and give the poor man what you promised."

I glanced up and pushed his hand away from his cock, then wrapped my fingers around the base and slid my mouth over the tip.

"Jesus," Hot Craig gasped as I went to work, sucking and licking and using my hand to stroke his length. He was rock hard and probably wouldn't last long after everything he'd seen tonight. But I could do this forever. Knowing Kamal was watching everything, feeling the thick plug in my ass, and enjoying the plump heft of Hot Craig's cock between my lips was the trip of a lifetime.

A jolt of unexpected energy deep inside made me twitch and groan. I almost choked on Craig's dick as I pulled off and glanced at Kamal. He held the remote and watched me with heavy-lidded eyes, a hand on his dick, stroking firmly. Probably wouldn't take him long either.

I whimpered as the vibrations circled outward from one spot into my whole body and made my dick swell and thicken. Hot Craig's thick cock became my opus now, because I had to get him off before this vibrating plug made me come again.

I listened to the sounds both he and Kamal made as I worked him with all the skills in my substantial arsenal. I knew all that practice would pay off someday. Because getting Hot Craig off while Kamal watched would be the highlight of my week.

After slobbering up and down his dick and swallowing it to the root, my nose in his silky pubes, Hot Craig told me he was close. I pulled off and sat back on my heels like a very good boy with my lips tight as he jerked his dick a couple of times, made a staccato series of cries, and spurted all over my forehead, nose, and one cheek.

He groaned and finished with a couple more dribbles and wiped the head of his cock against my chin and cursed. "Oh fuck. Jesus." He panted, backing up as Kamal rose from the bed.

"How's that tail feel, Owen?" he said, stroking his cock which was now purple at the tip and ready to blow as he aimed it at my face and Hot Craig made room.

"Like it's gonna milk me four more times," I grunted, wiggling my ass where I sat.

Kamal's mouth opened and his eyelids drooped as he came, jizz coating my neck and shoulder as I preened like a barn kitten. Hot Craig cursed again and shook his head as Kamal groaned and finished, my face a Pollock exhibition of mingled juices.

Once they'd caught their breath, they had me lean over the end of the bed and took turns jerking my dick while the plug throbbed against my prostrate and the rubber tail wagged crazily. I came with a yell and a whimper on Kamal's bedspread as Craig stroked my dick and Kamal spanked my ass.

An evening out of my dirtiest dreams had come true.

*

"Thank you for one hell of an evening. I will always think of myself as 'Hot Craig' now."

Kamal rolled his eyes. "Wonderful."

"Well, good. Cause you are hot. Craig." I winked and licked my lips exaggeratedly.

"Stop it, you instigator. Don't start something you're too tired to finish. I'm trying to leave," he said, smiling and winking back.

"Oh, I'll finish you. I'm not too tired," I said, taking a step forward but Kamal jerked me back and held me tight.

"Oh, no you don't. You're mine for the rest of the night. And only mine."

I waggled my eyebrows at Hot Craig and shrugged. "Sorry. What can I say? I guess I'm taken."

"I guess you are," Hot Craig said, smiling at Kamal. "See you tomorrow? Come for brunch at the resort café, and we'll reminisce."

"About old times?" Kamal ginned.

"What?" Hot Craig scoffed. "No, about everything that happened here. This is an evening I will relive many, many times, my friends. Thank you."

When he'd gone I sat on the edge of the bed and gazed at Kamal. "Hot Craig is awesome."

He looked at me and folded his arms over his chest. "Yes, I think so."

"Well, I think so too."

"Good."

"Good."

We started talking at the same time.

Kamal held up his hand. "If I may?"

"You may, Sir."

"At the risk of giving you a big head, you were spectacular, Owen."

I opened my mouth and crinkled my eyes in silent laughter. "You said *giving me a big head*."

"Good Lord. You've regressed to the maturity level of a sixteen-year-old."

I stuck out my tongue.

Kamal raised his eyebrows. "Careful. I know lots of things to do with an overactive tongue."

"Oh, goody." How had I become such a gigantic man slut in the space of three hours? The BCR was doing a number on my libido.

"Owen, you can stay here if you want, but we're going to sleep."

"Fine."

"Is that a yes? You'll sleep here tonight?"

"It's a yes. I'd love to."

Kamal smiled and walked over, taking my chin in his hand. I pressed my cheek against his palm. "Let's go to bed, ponyboy."

*

I must have looked starry-eyed when I walked into the bunkhouse the next morning, after kissing Kamal goodbye and whispering in his ear that I planned to be a very good ponyboy for him this week, because both Biskane and Jake gave me funny looks.

"What?"

"Where the hell were you?"

I blushed and tried to hide my smile. I made a popping sound with my lips before saying, "Nowhere."

Biskane sat up. "Right."

Jake said, "Seriously. Where were you?"

I laughed. "In the middle of a Kamal and Hot Craig sandwich."

"What?" Jake whispered.

"Who the hell is *Hot Craig*?" Biskane asked.

I peeled off my T-shirt and tossed it on my bunk. "He's a friend of Kamal's. A very hot friend of Kamal's. I mean, if you like older, dark-haired dudes. Which I do."

"Goddammit." He sounded jealous. "This is the second night you've spent in Kamal's room. I thought trainers weren't supposed to fraternize with ponyboys."

I put my hands on my hips. "Well, it's not officially banned. The only thing that's banned is actual anal intercourse between a ponyboy and his trainer. Other types of...penetration are fine," I added.

Biskane swore. "You little slut."

I grinned.

"Well, fuck," Jake said, throwing himself onto his back on the lower bunk. "We were hoping you wanted to go swimming this afternoon. But you're probably too tired after all your sex adventures."

I laughed. "I'm twenty-seven. That kind of shit energizes me. I'd love to go to the lake."

*

We spent the afternoon like a bunch of ten-year-olds at summer camp—me, Biskane, Jake, Sam, and Miles. Andrei couldn't swim and didn't like the heat.

We swam, did cannonballs off the dock, and dunked and pantsed each other. After a few hours of such wholesome entertainment, I felt refreshed and invigorated when I got dressed to go to the main house for supper.

Hot Craig had left, but Kamal was there. I walked right up to him in front of all the other ponyboys and gave him a kiss on the cheek. I didn't give a whit about his dominance anymore since I knew whatever he decided to do to me would be wonderful.

But he seemed uncomfortable with the gesture, then smiled with a wary expression.

Which set off alarm bells inside my head.

"What's wrong?"

He shook his head. "Nothing." He ruffled my hair and left for the buffet table without another word.

I stood there, feeling uneasy. Something had happened. Something had happened since the previous evening when we'd all been at ease together.

Had he actually slept with Hot Craig and decided he preferred him to me? Did he regret Saturday? I had to know.

I looked at my shoes for a second to regroup, then looked up to see Kamal talking to Lorraine. He shrugged and glanced my way, but didn't smile before he turned back to her and kept talking.

Shit. Something was up, and I needed to know what before my entire world came crumbling down. I'd thought we had something. I'd thought Kamal might actually have feelings for me. Or was it all a fucking game?

I girded my loins and strode across the lawn to the buffet table and clutched Kamal's elbow. "I need to talk to you."

He gazed at me with surprise, but he turned to Lorraine and said, "Excuse me," as he let me guide him toward the porch, away from the crowded lawn.

"What's wrong, Owen?" he asked as we stepped up onto the broad, empty porch.

I blinked. "Me? You're the one acting all distant and weird."

He stared at me for a second and then put a hand to his forehead and stared out at the crowd of ponyboys, trainers, and staff.

A split second before my heart sank and I decided my life was over, because if this thing with Kamal wasn't real I didn't know if I would ever be okay, he turned and took my chin, cupping it in his hand like he always did. He rubbed my cheek with his thumb and smiled.

"I'm sorry. I don't mean to be that way."

I narrowed my eyes, not quite ready to relax. "What's wrong? And don't say nothing's wrong because I can tell something is."

"Here, come sit down." He sat on the step, looking out at the gathered ponyboys, trainers and staff, giving Adam a little wave while I settled in beside him.

"Is it me?" I asked breathlessly, not wanting to consider it but needing to know. "Did I do something wrong?"

"No, Owen. It's not you," he said, and I felt some relief. "At least, not the way you might think."

What did that mean?

"Kamal, you have to tell me, because I feel like you're going to pull the rug out from under me, and I'm going to hate you," I rushed. "I really don't want to hate you." My face burned from more than the summer heat, and my heart ran like a freight train.

"Craig wants me to help him run a fetish club in Vancouver."

I stared at him, trying to process what he'd said. Vancouver? That was so far away from the BCR, from Ottawa, from me. But he was obviously considering it.

"You...you want to?"

Kamal stared at me for a long moment, then shrugged. "I'm thinking about it."

Well, shit. That wasn't good. I'd assumed Kamal was a fixture here. I hadn't considered he might up and leave for the other side of the country. And now I was furious at Hot Craig. I'd been right all along. He *had* come here to steal Kamal but not in the way I'd imagined. And I'd given him the night of his life before he'd betrayed me!

I stood up and stepped down to the lawn, then turned back and sat on the bottom step. I couldn't believe it.

"Fuck Hot Craig. I thought I liked him, and now I fucking hate him," I said, my hands clenching into fists. "I wasted a fucking awesome blow job on that guy."

I glanced up to see Kamal laughing quietly.

I continued. "Shut up. I *knew* he came here to take you away from me. Right when we were starting to..."

His eyes widened. "To what, Owen? What were we starting to do?"

I narrowed my eyes at him. "You know."

"I want to hear you say it. I need to know how you feel before I make a decision about this."

"Why? You'd stay here for me?" I said.

"Or ask you to come with."

Whoa. Now I was really off balance. But I hadn't answered his question. It seemed he was invested in whatever we had, so maybe I could tell him.

I scuffed my shoe into the dirt, prevaricating. "I don't know how I feel about you."

"Yes, you do. You looked like you wanted to murder Hot Craig a second ago."

I shrugged. I looked at Kamal. Our gazes held. "What? What do you want me to say? I'm not gonna tell you I love you. We've only known each other three weeks!"

Kamal laughed again. "I don't want you to tell me you love me."

I narrowed my eyes. What kind of game was this man playing?

"Well, I might not love you, but I love the way you talk to me," I said. "I love the way you look at me. I love the way you touch me. And I love the way you make me want to be the best ponyboy in the world for you."

He watched while I all but drowned in the vulnerability of this admission. But when I'd finished he smiled. "You know what I love about you, Owen?"

I shook my head, not trusting myself to speak. All the noise of people talking and the movement of the crowd on the lawn in front of us faded into the background.

"I love that you have the courage to explore something new, the audacity to challenge me."

I opened my mouth to say something, but he held up a finger.

"And the soul of a child in the body of a full-grown man. That comment might be controversial, but I don't give a fuck." He cupped my chin again. "You are a sweet, sweet man, Owen. Full of curiosity and cheek and a quiet, sometimes saucy, intelligence. And I would miss you terribly if we couldn't be together."

He released my chin and clasped both hands together. "That being said, I need to seriously consider Craig's offer."

I got that. I was still processing everything Kamal had said, but I understood he needed to think about it. Kind of.

"But you love it here, don't you? I love it here."

"The BCR is an incredible place, Owen, I'll give you that. And Adam and I are close friends. He'll be upset if I decide to leave."

I nodded, remembering what Adam had told me earlier. "He basically offered me a job if I'd stay. So you wouldn't leave."

"He did?"

"Yeah. As the IT guy or something like that. I'd consider it, you know."

"Hmm."

"What does that mean?"

"That means that you've given me something else to think about. But I need to ask you something important." He picked a daisy from the garden beside the steps and played with it in his hands.

"Okay."

"Let's say I did agree to move to Vancouver and start a fetish club with Craig. Would you even think about coming with me? We can give you a job there too."

I laughed because it seemed absurd. "As what? Official come-target?"

He rolled his eyes. "I'm sure you'd hold the *unofficial* title. But I assume we'd have some kind of complex computer system to keep track of clients."

This was an alternate universe, and I couldn't think straight. As much as I wanted to say "Sure, let me grab my bag," there was a lot to consider.

"I don't know. That's pretty far from here."

"Yes, it is."

"I've got friends in Ottawa. And a good job."

"Of course."

"Lots of friends." I had four at most, so this was a bit of a lie.

"I'm sure."

"So, I'd have to really think about it, Kamal."

"Absolutely. I'd want you to be sure."

I silently mulled things over. "Would we live together? We're only just getting to know each other."

He shrugged. "It's up to you, really. That's something we'd have to figure out."

I nodded. "I mean, rent is pretty expensive there."

"True."

I stared thoughtfully at Kamal, not ready to give him an answer, but thrilled beyond words he'd ask me to go with him. "I can't give you an answer right now."

"That's okay. I'm still deciding if I want to go or not. But it's been a dream of mine to own my own fetish club. And co-owning with Craig would be ideal. He's a great guy."

"Yeah, I guess. But just so you know, I'm changing his nickname from "Hot Craig" to "Marcus Junius Brutus" because I feel like he stabbed me in the back."

Chapter Twenty-Two

The week passed quickly. Kamal was professional and stern in the paddock, and I relished every moment of learning new tricks and postures, submitting to his control, and enjoying his appreciative glances. It felt good knowing we were more than simply a ponyboy and his trainer, even if we ended up going our separate ways at the end of my six weeks.

"Owen, you need to pick up your feet. You're getting lazy."

I huffed a breath out my nose and tried to satisfy him by trotting more expertly around the paddock. He'd placed low-to-the-ground hurdles at intervals that I had to jump, and I accomplished this without great difficulty since he didn't bind my arms. The arm bands were apparently for showing off the posture of a ponyboy for prancing around the ring a few times or pulling a fancy cart for a short period. Any intense or long-lasting activity precluded the arms being bound in deference to safety and increased agility. We always wore the bands since they looked sexy and a ponyboy could be punished by being bound and relegated to standing or performing rounds of the paddock for his trainer's enjoyment.

I enjoyed the running and hurdles so I worked hard to pick up my feet and do what Kamal asked of me. And tried not to let the thought of my impending decision run around my head. I didn't know if Kamal was going to take Craig up on his offer. Until he decided, there wasn't anything to consider. Although I needed to decide if I was willing to accompany him if he did go.

A big part of me wanted to go with him—a romantic, idealistic, and bored part of me. A sensible, practical part of me thought it irresponsible to uproot my life for a man I'd only known a short time. It had been five weeks since I'd come to the BCR, and though my affection and respect for Kamal continued to grow, it didn't seem to be enough time to base a long-term relationship on or to follow him across the country for.

I knew Vancouver would be beautiful. It was also rainy, cool, and expensive. I enjoyed the heat of summer and the bright sunshine. I wasn't sure I could live without that. Then again, the lush vegetation on the West Coast appealed to me in its own way. And we'd be right on the ocean and near the mountains where we could hike and camp.

But I didn't even know if he was going.

*

I didn't tell the guys in the bunkhouse what was going on with Kamal, but they knew something was up. The way they tiptoed around me, I figured they thought he'd given me the brush-off which was the furthest thing from the truth. Our bond had become more intense with the knowledge that we might not be together after the following week.

But I was subdued and quiet in the evenings, drawing in my sketch book on my bunk. I sketched the pup tail, and I drew what I thought my cock looked like shooting on the plastic sheet in Kamal's room. And I did some landscape images—the grooming barn, the arena, and the bunkhouse, the beach, the main house.

All from memory.

*

The last Friday, at supper, when Kamal was busy getting things ready for the pony show the next day, Adam and I sat together on the porch steps.

"Has he decided yet?" Adam asked me.

I didn't know Kamal had even told Adam about the opportunity Craig had presented.

"I don't think so," I said.

Adam sighed and sipped his beer. "That man is my best trainer. Funny, I thought it would be you to take him from us. Never expected this."

"Yeah."

"That offer still stands, y'know. If Kamal stays and you want to stay too. Hell, even if he leaves. We could use a good IT guy."

"Thanks, Adam. I'll seriously consider it." I gazed at the green fields around us, and the red buildings, the paddocks. "I love it here."

"Yeah, me too." He sighed. "Kamal helped me get this place up and running."

"He did?"

"Yep. He was our first trainer. Then we brought Lorraine on board. Now we have the four of them, if you include Jensen who will be certified for our next session. Hiro was planning to take a leave but if Kamal jumps ship

I'll have to keep Hiro on or find someone else. I won't get anyone near as good as Kamal, though. Jensen comes close but it'll take him time to really get comfortable."

"So, Kamal has a personal attachment to this place."

"I should hope so. We built it together. We had a shared vision. But he didn't want to have any part in managing it. Just wanted to train ponyboys."

"Hmm."

"And now he might leave me for some new fetish club on the West Coast that doesn't even have a name yet."

I nodded. "Maybe he'll stay."

I was still hopeful that the pull of the BCR and the comfort of daily routines would be enough to keep Kamal here.

Adam nodded. "Maybe he'll stay."

*

It took Kamal another few days to make up his mind.

I was relaxing in the bunkhouse on my final Sunday at the BCR. The six of us had gone for a swim—we'd even convinced Andrei to join us—and now were lazing around in the air-conditioned comfort, reading, playing video games, and chatting. It sounded like Sam and Biskane were getting busy in the loft again. I think they were really starting to become a thing. But whether they'd carry it past the end of our six-week session was anyone's guess.

I was drawing, as usual, facing the loft while trying to catch a glimpse of a naked ass or a hard dick when the door creaked open and footsteps sounded on the rough wood floorboards. I knew it was Kamal even before I sensed a presence by my shoulder and he said, "What are you working on, Owen?"

He'd never visited me at the bunkhouse before, and I was equally thrilled and filled with a sense of foreboding.

"*The Sexual Adventures of a Twenty-Seven-Year-Old Manwhore*," I said, "*A Visual Journey.*"

I turned to see him grinning as he extended his hand, palm up, over the edge of the bunk. "May I?"

"Sure." I closed the sketchbook and handed it over.

He flipped the cover and gazed at the first drawing. It was the sketch of one of the ponyboys from the website. Kamal examined it as I waited on tenterhooks for his opinion. It was a pretty basic, quick sketch. But the image held hope and excitement.

"Owen, this is amazing. It's from the website, right? I recognize the picture."

"Yeah. I drew it right after I found out about the BCR."

Kamal nodded as he flipped the page.

He stared at this one for a long time. It was the sketch of his face I'd done after my first morning as a ponyboy.

"This is from memory?"

"Yeah."

"Jesus, Owen." He examined the sketch from another angle. "Do I really look so stern?"

I snorted. "Oh, fuck yeah."

He laughed. "Wow."

"I'll say."

He flipped to the next sketch—Biskane's statuesque profile.

"Owen, your eye is incredible. This is flawless."

I shook my head. "I see flaws." I pointed to Biskane's chin. "It's too broad here. And his dimple doesn't look right."

"Owen, it's almost perfect."

I raised my eyebrows. "See? Almost."

Kamal rolled his eyes, then flipped the page over. He stared at the image of Luke's eyes and hair for a moment then looked at me. "It's Luke."

"Yeah." I grinned, pleased he'd recognized the man from only half his face. Then again, Kamal knew Luke well.

He flipped again. To the quick sketches of the bridle and tail and cart. Then to the drawing of his hands.

"They're your hands. Don't you recognize them?"

"Owen, you are a tremendous artist."

I shook my head. "It's only a hobby. Wouldn't make me any money."

"That's debatable."

I remembered what was on the next page and held my hand out for the sketchbook. "That's pretty much it," I said, clearing my throat.

But Kamal paid me no attention and flipped to my drawing of Hot Craig with devil horns and evil eyes. He stared at it, then burst out laughing.

I tried to take the sketchbook from him but he wouldn't let me.

"Oh my God. You have got to show him this!"

"Fuck, no. Kamal, give it back."

"But he'd love it!"

"I drew that before he sucked my dick. Obviously."

"Obviously."

"I still think he's kind of evil."

"Oh, so do I."

I stared at the mattress as he flipped to the drawings of the pup tail and food bowls and then of my dick shooting come out the tip onto the plastic sheet.

"Holy fuck."

"I don't actually know if it looked like that."

"That's...astonishingly accurate."

I stared at Kamal as he licked his lips and adjusted himself.

"Are you hard?"

"Yes, I'm hard. Who wouldn't be after looking at that drawing?"

I chuckled, pleased.

He examined the landscapes, praising their accuracy and the shading. Then he closed the sketchbook and handed it back to me.

"Come take a walk with me," he said.

I felt my stomach churn as I hoisted myself over the edge of my bunk as a loud moan carried over the edge of the loft.

"Sounds like there's at least one manwhore up there," Kamal said, gesturing to the loft.

I laughed. "Two actually. Biskane and Sam. They're at it at least once a day."

"Good for them," Kamal said, opening the door for me.

"So, where are we going?"

Kamal shrugged. "I don't know. Maybe the lake?"

"Sure. But I just came from there."

"The dock, I know. But I'll show you a better spot."

"I bet that's what you tell all the boys." I said, trying not to let the strange sense of foreboding overtake me.

Kamal laughed hard this time and took my hand, pulling me along.

He took me through the brush to a secret little white pebble beach where wild grasses grew along the edge and minnows swam in the shallow water. We had to keep our shoes on because of the rocks, but it was pretty and secluded.

We found large boulders to sit on while we looked at the view.

I wasn't stupid. "So, you've made up your mind."

Kamal looked down at the pebbles in front of him. "It was the hardest decision I've ever had to make."

"So, you're leaving. You're going to Vancouver with Craig," I said.

"Yeah. I'm going to Vancouver with Craig."

My stomach churned, and I felt like I might throw up. The best thing I'd ever found and he'd be out of reach.

"Come with me, Owen."

I stood up because I couldn't sit still in the face of that request. "I'm supposed to follow you to Vancouver after getting to know you for five weeks?"

He stared at me straight on, not hiding, not pretending it wasn't the most ridiculous request in the world, but owning it. "Think about it. You did say you were bored and looking for adventure..."

"But I found it, Kamal! I found it here at the BCR!"

"So, have another adventure. Come with me to Vancouver. Craig thinks you're amazing. I know you like him."

"I fucking hate him."

"You don't hate him."

"I do hate him. For making you leave."

"Nobody makes me do anything I don't want to do, Owen. This is something I've considered before. I never planned to stay at the BCR forever."

"Adam said you started the ranch with him. That it was a vision you had together. And now you're going to abandon him to go west, chasing some other dream?"

Kamal stared at me for a long time without saying anything. He let me calm down a little, throw a few stones into the water, and sit down.

"The BCR was always Adam's baby. He had the initial idea. I supported it and agreed to work as a trainer here."

"But the ranch is amazing, Kamal! How can you leave this place?"

"It's just a place. And I've been here a long time. You're not the only one who gets bored, you know."

I raised my eyebrows. "How the fuck can you get bored working here, Kamal?"

He crossed his arms defensively. "I know it seems crazy, but believe me, you can."

"How can you leave me?"

Kamal uncrossed his arms and stood. "I don't want to fucking leave you, Owen. I want to take you with me!"

"To the other side of the country. Away from my friends, my job, my home."

"It's a lot to ask. I realize that."

We stared at each other because this discussion wasn't going anywhere. It seemed a desecration to the beauty of this secret beach to argue here, but we couldn't help it.

"Are you scared?" he said.

I looked down at my feet in my red chucks. *Of course, I'm fucking scared.*

"Look, I can't guarantee that everything will work out in Vancouver. But I can promise if things don't, I'll still be your friend. I'm not going to kick you to the curb after one argument or misunderstanding. We don't even have to move in together. You can rent a room in Craig's townhouse, and I'll get a place. Even though I don't really trust the two of you together. You seemed to get along *really well* the night we spent in my room."

"Yeah, well I don't think too much of him right now."

We sat silently together, wondering how to solve this problem.

"This sucks, Kamal."

He stared at me. "It doesn't have to."

Suddenly, I was furious at him for putting me in this difficult position. And annoyed with myself for letting my feelings get the better of me. "I can't go to Vancouver with you. You and Hot Craig will have to find another cute IT guy to suck your cocks on weekends."

It was a low blow, and a stupid thing to say, but I was angry and completely mixed up.

"Can you find your way back to the bunkhouse, Owen?" Kamal asked, his lips tight. "Because I don't think this conversation is going anywhere."

"Yes."

"Don't forget, you still have a week of training and a final show to put on. Are you going to be okay?"

"Yes."

"I'll see you in the arena, then."

He left me to contemplate the beauty of the scenery and the chaos of my mind.

*

The guys had left for supper when I got back to the bunkhouse. I ripped all my clothes off and got in the shower, jerking my cock aggressively to get rid of some tension. I had to get myself together before showing up at the grooming barn tomorrow because after investing so much energy into becoming Kamal's perfect little ponyboy, I was damned if I was going to ruin our last week together by being a pouty little bitch.

Maybe if I reminded him exactly how well we worked together, he'd change his mind and stay.

Chapter Twenty-Three

It was a long week.

Kamal was tense and regretful, but steadfast in his decision. I was not happy and had difficulty hiding it. That combination made for some strained moments.

We transformed them into sexy Dom/sub scenarios. The only way I could get through the week was to distract myself by acting up and having Kamal discipline me. At least, if we did go our separate ways after the pony show, we'd have this week and the ones before to remember.

"Owen, you're being a real bastard today. Are you *trying* to piss me off?"

I snorted and stared directly at him, rolling my bit and stomping my foot like a pissed-off stallion.

Come on, Kamal, give me what I need today. Distraction.

The wheels of his brain turned as I watched. How would he address this issue? How would he remind me I had to behave for him?

"Turn around, Owen," he said.

I lifted my chin defiantly. He raised his eyebrows.

"*Turn. Around,*" he repeated in a voice that sent chills up and down my spine and electric fire to my dick. "*Now.*"

I tossed my forelock but turned around, wondering what he would do. I already had my tail in and my bridle on.

"Cross your arms behind your back."

I hesitated for a second, then obeyed his order. He buckled my arms together, tight. Then he pushed me toward the wooden table and bent me over it, shoving me down harder than he needed to. I wasn't the only one suffering pent-up frustration.

"You know, a ponyboy can *lose* his tail as a punishment," Kamal said, twisting the tail plug in my ass and pulling it out slowly.

I groaned as it slid out, feeling bereft and empty.

He slapped my ass, twice. "Stay there. Don't move. You've been very naughty, Owen."

Yes, yes I have. All so I can have you like this. At least for a few more days.

The leather straps and steel pieces of the bridle bit into my face and twisted uncomfortably when I laid my cheek on the table, so I kept my head up, resting my chest against the hard wood instead, and waited for Kamal.

Caught up in my thoughts, I didn't realize he'd returned to me until I felt the cool flat of a wooden paddle against my ass.

Aha. He wanted to go old school on me.

I grunted, shifting my boots. Fine. I could take whatever he gave me.

"Hold up three fingers if you want me to stop at any time."

I grunted acquiescence.

Kamal started gently with the paddle. I might have laughed—which was the wrong reaction because Kamal began to use more force. Soon the cheeks of my ass became a burning, aching touchpoint between us.

I grit my teeth as Kamal continued longer than I'd anticipated, but I was determined not to break. Finally, he stopped, dropped the paddle to the floor and his cool hands splayed on my burning skin, soothing and rubbing.

I groaned and rocked under his attention, the pain and heat dispersing through my body and lighting me up. He pressed himself against me. He was rock hard under his jeans. I imagined Kamal pushing his jeans down and entering me, fucking me into submission like I wanted. As if he could read my mind, he gripped my hips and thrust his covered erection against me.

"Fuck it, Owen. You are killing me," he murmured, voice shaking. He stepped back and returned his hands to my burning, aching ass—petting and soothing as my breathing slowed.

"Stay still," he said and left me again.

When he returned, I felt his gloved fingers slide into my crack, rubbing lube onto and into me. I assumed this was to prepare me for the return of my tail, but it went on too long. I didn't complain.

I groaned, ignoring the discomfort of the bridle and rested my head on the table. I closed my eyes, focusing on the slide and fullness of Kamal's thick fingers as they brushed my prostate and caused fluid to leak out of my captured cock.

Was he milking my prostate? Is that what this was?

As he continued to thrust his fingers deep inside me, feathering them over that sweet, swollen gland, I knew that's what he was doing. He was going to make me ejaculate in the cage, as a way of punishing me for my behaviour.

What he didn't realize was how much I enjoyed a good prostate milking. I could even do it myself but it was always better to have some help.

I struggled, writhing against the table, feeling more fluid ooze from my glans as the rolling pleasure built and combined with the throb of pain from my paddled behind.

For some men, having their prostrate milked was the height of degradation and could work as a punishment, because it wasn't quite an orgasm and seemed like a waste of something precious. Maybe that was why I *liked* it so much. The objectification and reduction of my erotic response to something mechanical and functional, indifferent to whatever pleasure I derived from it, seemed both explicitly scientific and beautifully perverse.

I basked in my submission, writhing and whimpering on the wooden table as Kamal kept up the gentle pressure in a rhythmic massage. The soft waves of pleasure grew as my dick fought the confines of the cage and leaked more and more fluid, until with a low breathy groan from me and a satisfied sigh from Kamal, thicker ejaculate pushed out between the metal bars, dripping onto the floor.

I squeezed my eyes shut as the bliss of subjugation and humiliation turned my bones into jelly and made my soul Kamal's, as if there had been any doubt that he owned it.

*

The day of the final pony show dawned cool and rainy, and I wondered if we'd be able to have it outside like we usually did, or if we'd be relegated to the smaller space of the indoor arena. As it turned out, unless there was a risk of drenching rain or severe thunderstorms, the shows went on in the outdoors and maybe we got a little wet.

The grooming barn was crowded with members of the Pretty Pony Palace joining our final show. The stable hands got the girls ready first and then the boys.

While being scrubbed and tacked alongside the other ponyboys for my turn in the ring, I regretted this would be my last pony show at the BCR. This experience had been one I would never forget, and one I'd sorely needed to appease my existential ennui. My days here had lit a fire inside me that would continue to burn for months, perhaps years. There was always the option of putting my name on the waiting list and returning at some point in the future, for an injection of pure submission and sexual bliss when I needed it.

Except the BCR without Kamal wouldn't ever be the same. Was it more important that I had access to Kamal or access to the BCR in Kamal's absence? In other words, was it the kink itself, or my relationship with Kamal that was most important?

We waited with our trainers in the soft rain while the audience arranged themselves on the bleachers under a tent. I didn't have the blinders on—I didn't need them. When I glanced at Kamal beside me his lips were pressed in a firm line, and he didn't look at me. He must feel the same as I did about this being our final show together. I tossed my head to get his attention, and when he glanced at me, I quirked the side of my mouth as if to say, *Yeah, I know, but let's make the best of it, yeah?* He gave me a small smile back and stroked the reins between his fingers. I felt that small gesture like a kiss and rolled my bit, eager to get started.

This time, when he attached me to the cart, Kamal climbed up and sat in the seat, clicking his tongue and tapping my back with the reins. We'd practiced several times, but doing it now, in the ring, with the audience watching, gave me a feeling of joy. I was proud to pull my handsome trainer in the cart. I held my head high as we rounded the show ring to cheers and applause.

By the time the show wrapped up, we were all completely soaked. The rain had kept me cool, but it had been difficult to see out of my pretty mask, and I was covered with mud. Kamal's wet clothes clung to him deliciously as he led me back to the grooming barn with the others.

We waited outside while the others went in. The rain had stopped, and the sun was trying to break through now. Kamal unsnapped the pretty mask from my bridle and held it in one hand while he corded his fingers through his wet hair with the other, looking at me with a strange expression on his handsome face.

"You were incredible, Owen. Best ponyboy I've ever trained. I'm going to fucking miss you," he said, voice breaking. His face was so wet already I couldn't tell if it was rain or tears. He knew I couldn't reply without sounding like an idiot so that's why he was telling me this now. I'd have to stand here and listen, without rehashing our argument from the weekend. I didn't have the heart anyway.

I'd failed. He was still planning on leaving. Even my top-notch performance in the show ring hadn't made him waver in his decision. I felt helpless and sad and horrible—the only thing I could do was press my forehead against his shoulder and inhale the scent of his damp clothes and skin.

His hands came up behind my neck and pressed me to him as he kissed the top of my head with a fierceness that surprised me. Then they were on my shoulders and he urged me back. I lifted my head and gazed at him hopelessly, wondering what my future would mean if he wasn't going to be in it.

He smiled and pushed the wet lock of hair from my forehead. "Damn you are a beautiful pony, Owen Lipke.

And a beautiful man." He placed his hands on the sides of my face and kissed my lips, gently and sweetly, as my tongue stilled on the bit, a rotten feeling in my heart and gut and stomach.

Then he let me go and stepped back, opening the door to the grooming barn and calling Adrian to take me inside.

*

I walked back to the bunkhouse embroiled in frantic thoughts.

Was I going to go back to Ottawa, to my boring fucking life and my reliable but uninspiring day job, simply because that was what was expected of me, and I was scared to risk my heart and happiness on a man I'd so recently met?

My heart and happiness were destroyed right now because we had to say goodbye.

He'd already said goodbye to me. Did that mean he was leaving today? Would he leave without telling me he was going?

I picked up my pace to get to the bunkhouse and start packing my bag, so I could stop at the main house when I went to meet Tamara and make sure I saw Kamal one last time. She was supposed to be here at five to get me—it was four now. I'd miss the final goodbye barbecue Adam threw for the ponyboys on their last day, but I didn't have the heart to participate anyway.

I finished packing and bade a quick goodbye to the others. Biskane grabbed my arm and pulled me in for a hug. "Glad to know you, Owen. Good luck, eh?"

"Thanks, B. I've got your contact info. Keep in touch, all right? You too, Jake."

"Sure, Owen. Have a safe trip home."

I hoisted my duffel bag on my shoulder and left the bunkhouse, walking quickly on the path to the main house for the last time. I'd miss this fucking place. It was beautiful and sexy and mind-blowing and all the things I'd hoped for.

When I got to the house I happened to catch Adam talking to Connor in the hall. He saw me and flagged me down.

"Owen. Hold on a second."

"Is he still here?"

Adam nodded and my body flooded with relief. "He showed me this," Adam said, pulling a folded-up paper from his pocket. He straightened it out and held it in front of me—the drawing I'd given to Kamal. "He says you've got a sketchbook full of incredible artwork."

I shrugged, glancing at the stairs. I needed to see Kamal. "Sketches, yeah. It's a hobby."

"If you're interested, I think they'd sell well at our online store. You can make some money off your art." He shrugged. "Something to think about anyway."

"Sure. Yeah. That would be cool, Adam."

"I won't keep you. He's packing. Driving to Toronto for a few days, and then he's off to Vancouver. You better hurry."

"Fuck," I said, dropping my bag on the floor and hustling up the stairs to Kamal's room. I didn't even knock before I pushed it open.

He looked up, a pair of socks in his hand, and stiffened as if I were about to stab him in the heart. "Owen, I can't say goodbye to you again. I can't." He looked broken. I'd never seen him so sad.

"I want to go with you." It came out before I'd consciously made the decision.

He stared at me and swallowed thickly. "Owen, don't toy with me. If you're not sure and just think you might—"

"No, I'm sure," I said, with a confidence that felt right. I *was* sure. Everything now seemed straightforward and unavoidable.

"I want to go to Vancouver with you, Kamal." I swallowed and rubbed at my eyes, exhausted from fighting this very outcome. "I want to take the chance. Risk everything. Because if it works out—"

He dropped the socks into his suitcase and took four strides toward me, gathering me against him with a force that threatened to crush me.

"God, Owen, really? You'll really come with me?" he said, pulling back so he could look at my face. "All the way across the country?"

I smiled and shrugged. "Sure. What the hell, right?"

He grinned, laughing and shaking his head. "What the hell, right? That's all you can say? Not, *'I'm sorry for putting you through the hell of thinking we'd never see each other again, Kamal. I am begging for your forgiveness'*?"

I inclined my head, thinking it over. Then shrugged and knelt gracefully at his feet. "Please forgive me for putting you through hell, Kamal. Or punish me. I don't really care either way. Just don't fucking leave me."

He reached down and splayed one hand across my throat, cupping my chin with the other and gazing at me with a stern expression. "Don't you ever do that to me again, Owen Lipke. Because I will turn you over my knee and spank the shit out of you, come on your face, and make you clean up."

I gasped and waggled my eyebrows. "Oh Kamal. The things you say to me."

I turned my face into his hand and licked his palm as he came down to my level and kissed me hard, owning me, telling me silently that I was his, and I would be his for as long as we could make it work.

Which was good enough for me.

*

We agreed I'd go back to Ottawa with Tamara so I could pack properly for leaving for so long. Kamal said he'd as soon spend a few days with me in Ottawa than drive to Toronto and he had no problem leaving his car here for Adam to use or lend out to anyone who needed it for a short jaunt into town. He'd change his flight out of Toronto for one out of Ottawa with me.

Tamara was suitably taken aback at this change of plans.

"What the fuck, Owen?" she said, staring back and forth between the two of us. "You came here to play pony for kicks, and now you're in love and following your Dom across the fucking country?"

"Basically. I mean, we haven't said the L word yet..." I glanced at Kamal who rolled his eyes.

He laughed. "I'll say it then. Yeah, it's love with a capital L and a capital D and a small s."

Tamara twisted her features in confusion until she figured it out. "Oh, he's clever. You should keep him."

"I plan to."

"He's hot too."

Kamal laughed and pulled me to his side. "We promise not to get up to anything in the car on the way to Ottawa, as difficult as that might be for us."

"The deal's off, then," Tam said, exploding into sudden laughter. "Nah, I wouldn't be able to concentrate on driving with the two of you getting up to anything in the back seat. Once we get you home though…"

I sighed. "I think I've exhausted my exhibitionist streak for a while," I muttered, taking Kamal's hand.

"Do tell. In great detail, please, once we're back home." She turned to Adam and Jensen who were looking on. "Later, Adam. You promised me a pony show."

He laughed. "Anytime, Tamara. Just give me a heads-up."

She looked him up and down. "Uh-huh. Cool. Let's go. Before I make a rude remark about that cowboy."

"Yeah, we'd better," I said.

Kamal and Adam had already had a long talk about how Adam would address his absence at the ranch and they'd said their official goodbyes. But he stepped forward now and grabbed Kamal into an embrace.

"I always thought it would be a sexy ponyboy taking you away from me, not a charming old friend," he said, kissing Kamal on the cheek. "Figures it'd be both."

"Adam, I will miss this place. And sipping scotch with you on a Friday evening."

"Remember my idea for a Gymkhana? With returning staff and ponyboys for an exhibition of games and performances? It's happening. I don't know when, but get ready for my call."

"I will. Take care, guys," he said, waving and saluting to Jensen who nodded. "Keep up the good work, cowboy. Keep those ponyboys in line. We'll look up Noah and Luke in Ottawa."

"They'd be thrilled," Jensen said. "Bye, Kamal."

We left the house and tossed our stuff in the trunk of Tamara's car.

"I call shotgun," I said, sliding into the passenger seat.

Kamal chuckled and shook his head, opening the back door. He stood there for a moment, looking back at the main house and the outbuildings. Then he climbed into the car, and Tamara pulled away.

"No regrets, Owen?" she asked with a grin.

"No regrets, Tamara." I glanced behind me at Kamal's deep-brown eyes that watched me calmly. "Absolutely no regrets."

Epilogue

Our apartment in Vancouver was small, because it was all we could afford.

The club was called the Zoo and I had to give it to Hot Craig—he knew what he was doing. Within a few months, we had made a name for ourselves with members of the kink community in Vancouver. We specialized in offering space and accommodations for pet play but we had rooms for standard kinky activities too.

That complex computer system Kamal had mentioned? We needed it to keep up with our ever-changing clientele and the regulars who made appointments monthly. Maintaining that and running it efficiently, troubleshooting problems, and creating new applications kept me busy when I wasn't taking advantage of my status as co-founder to borrow one of the back rooms for an afternoon with Kamal.

Adam had let me keep the bridle and tail Kamal had dressed me in, and we put those items to good use whenever I wanted to be his very good ponyboy.

Or his very naughty ponyboy…

He still had all the pup gear, so we made use of that too.

Sometimes, we even let Hot Craig watch.

Vancouver began to feel like home. Because I was with Kamal, and Kamal would be home for me, wherever we were.

Acknowledgements

Thank you to my editor, who spends most of her time removing random capitalizations from my manuscript and making sure the terms and spellings remain consistent from book to book. She is a rock star.

About the Author

AE Lister/Elizabeth Lister is a Canadian non-binary author with a vivid imagination and a head full of unique and interesting characters. They have published ten books with MLR Press, one of which (*Beyond the Edge*) received an Honorable Mention from the National Leather Association–International for excellence in SM/Leather/Fetish writing.

Email
aelisterauthor@gmail.com

Facebook
www.facebook.com/aelister.elizabethlister

Twitter
@lizbethlister

Website
www.aelister.com

Other NineStar books by this author

Stable Hand

Also Available from NineStar Press

Connect with NineStar Press

www.ninestarpress.com

www.facebook.com/ninestarpress

www.facebook.com/groups/NineStarNiche

www.twitter.com/ninestarpress

www.ingramcontent.com/pod-product-compliance
Lightning Source LLC
Chambersburg PA
CBHW021506110726
47899CB00001BA/321